Books by Phyllis Reynolds Naylor

Shiloh Books
Shiloh
Shiloh Season
Saving Shiloh

The Alice Books
Starting with Alice
Alice in Blunderland
Lovingly Alice
The Agony of Alice
Alice in Rapture, Sort Of
Reluctantly Alice
All But Alice
Alice in April
Alice In-Between
Alice the Brave
Alice in Lace
Outrageously Alice
Achingly Alice
Alice on the Outside
The Grooming of Alice
Alice Alone
Simply Alice
Patiently Alice
Including Alice
Alice on Her Way
Alice in the Know
Dangerously Alice
Almost Alice

The Bernie Magruder Books
Bernie Magruder and the Case
   of the Big Stink
Bernie Magruder and the
   Disappearing Bodies
Bernie Magruder and the
   Haunted Hotel
Bernie Magruder and the Drive-
   thru Funeral Parlor

Bernie Magruder and the Bus
   Station Blowup
Bernie Magruder and the
   Pirate's Treasure
Bernie Magruder and the
   Parachute Peril
Bernie Magruder and the Bats
   in the Belfry

The Cat Pack Books
The Grand Escape
The Healing of Texas Jake
Carlotta's Kittens
Polo's Mother

The York Trilogy
Shadows on the Wall
Faces in the Water
Footprints at the Window

The Witch Books
Witch's Sister
Witch Water
The Witch Herself
The Witch's Eye
Witch Weed
The Witch Returns

Picture Books
King of the Playground
The Boy with the Helium Head
Old Sadie and the Christmas
   Bear
Keeping a Christmas Secret
Ducks Disappearing
I Can't Take You Anywhere
Sweet Strawberries
Please DO Feed the Bears

Books for Young Readers

Josie's Troubles
How Lazy Can You Get?
All Because I'm Older
Maudie in the Middle
One of the Third-Grade
　　Thonkers
Roxie and the Hooligans

Books for Middle Readers

Walking Through the Dark
How I Came to Be a Writer
Eddie, Incorporated
The Solomon System
The Keeper
Beetles, Lightly Toasted
The Fear Place
Being Danny's Dog
Danny's Desert Rats
Walker's Crossing

Books for Older Readers

A String of Chances
Night Cry
The Dark of the Tunnel
The Year of the Gopher
Send No Blessings
Ice
Sang Spell
Jade Green
Blizzard's Wake

Dangerously Alice

PHYLLIS REYNOLDS NAYLOR

Simon Pulse
NEW YORK · LONDON · TORONTO · SYDNEY

This book is a work of fiction. Any references to historical events, real people, or real locales are used fictitiously. Other names, characters, places, and incidents are the product of the author's imagination, and any resemblance to actual events or locales or persons, living or dead, is entirely coincidental.

W

SIMON PULSE
An imprint of Simon & Schuster Children's Publishing Division
1230 Avenue of the Americas, New York, NY 10020
Copyright © 2006 by Phyllis Reynolds Naylor
All rights reserved, including the right of reproduction
in whole or in part in any form.
SIMON PULSE and colophon are registered trademarks
of Simon & Schuster, Inc.
Also available in an Atheneum Books for Young Readers hardcover edition.
Designed by Ann Zeak
The text of this book was set in Berkley Old Style.
Manufactured in the United States of America
First Simon Pulse edition August 2008
2 4 6 8 10 9 7 5 3 1
The Library of Congress has cataloged the hardcover edition as follows:
Naylor, Phyllis Reynolds.
Dangerously Alice / Phyllis Reynolds Naylor
p. cm.
Summary: During fall semester of her junior year of high school,
Alice decides to change her good girl image, while major remodeling
begins at home and some important relationships begin to change.
ISBN-13: 978-0-689-87094-1 (hc)
ISBN-10: 0-689-87094-9 (hc)
[1. Self-perception—Fiction. 2. Conduct of life—Fiction. 3. High Schools—
Fiction. 4. Schools—Fiction. 5. Family Life—Maryland—Fiction.
6. Maryland—Fiction.] I. Title
PZ7.N24Dam 2007
[Fic]—dc22
2006024181
ISBN-13: 978-0-689-87095-8 (pbk)
ISBN-10: 0-689-87095-7 (pbk)

For Becca

Contents

Dangerously Alice

Labels

I had to hear it from Pamela. But then, the fact that she told me, and that she wasn't going back, sort of put a seal on our friendship. Ours was the real McCoy. So I couldn't figure out what was bothering me most: that Liz and I hadn't been invited or that our old gang was breaking up.

She told us about it on our ride to school that Monday. And to make things worse, we were riding the bus—one of the last places you want to be when you're a junior. Seniors would walk to school in snow up to their knees before they'd be seen on a bus. But Pam and Liz and I don't have cars of our own, and there was no one that morning to drive us. We sat close together on the back seat.

"This is the second time they've done it," Pamela went on as we listened uncomfortably. "Very hush-hush. The rule is that no one can speak. You can't move a deck chair or make any kind of noise, but you can do . . . well . . . almost anything else in or out of the water." She laughed.

"And everyone's naked?" Liz asked.

"In the pool, yes."

I couldn't help smiling a little—partly remembering the skinny-dipping we'd done at Camp Overlook two summers ago and partly thinking how Mark Stedmeister's parents were pretty strict about alcohol and drugs at their swimming pool, but completely oblivious to the fact that Mark and some of his friends were having midnight swims in the nude.

It was too painful to ask Pamela outright why Liz and I hadn't been invited, too scary to think that Pamela was being pulled away while we were being left behind. So I took the mature route and said, "Well, it sounds fun to me, Pam. Why do you say you're not going back?"

"For one thing, when you know you weren't invited the first time around, you can't help but feel that your invitation is borderline," she said. "But afterward—when we put on our clothes and drove to the soccer field so they could smoke and drink and talk—it was nothing but a big, malicious gossip fest. Boy, Jill and Karen . . . Brian, too . . . can rip into somebody faster than a tank of piranhas. Just mention a name—any name of anyone in the whole school—and in a matter of seconds, he's totaled. And you get the feeling everyone's expected to take a bite."

"I didn't think guys did that," said Liz. "I always knew that Jill and Karen were into it big-time— who's in, who's out—but I'm surprised that the guys are interested."

"Hey, they're interested in *Jill*—her body, any-way. And Karen, now that she's practically Jill's twin—hair, clothes, makeup, nails—parrots what-ever Jill says. Whatever turns girls on turns guys on, you know that," Pamela said.

"So how did you get invited?" Liz asked. "And what did they say about *us*?"

Pamela just shrugged it off as though it wasn't important, but we weren't letting her off that easily.

"I'd overheard Jill and Karen talking about the 'Silent Party,' or 'SP,' as they call it," Pamela explained. "I was nervy enough to ask what it was, so Karen described it for me—probably wanting to see if I was shocked. And when I wasn't, she asked if I wanted to come. I said 'Sure,' and asked if you guys were going to be there. She made this sort of face and looked at Jill, and Jill shook her head and said 'No.' And then she added, 'DD.' And they both laughed and walked off."

I tried to think what DD could possibly stand for. Dried dandruff? Dead as a doornail? Liz and I looked at each other, clueless.

"They speak in acronyms these days," Pamela went on. "When Jill and Justin and Mark and Brian and Keeno and Karen and some of Brian's other friends get together, they've got the whole student body divided up into groups, and each group has a label."

"Oh, every school does that," I said. "Walk in any high school, and they'll point out the Geeks, the Goths, the Nerds, the Brains, the Jocks, the—"

"That's not the kind I'm talking about," said Pamela. "Jill and Company divide the kids into the Studs, the Players, the Sluts, the Clueless Virgins, the Christian Virgins, the Freaks, and even *these* are broken down into UJ (Ugly Jock), TM (Typhoid Mary—don't touch), AG (Anything Goes) . . . you get the picture."

"And DD?" I asked.

Pamela dismissed it with a wave of her hand.

"*Tell* us!" Liz insisted.

"Dry as Dust," said Pamela. "But don't you believe it. I can only imagine what they'd been saying about me before I went and what they'll say now when I don't go back."

Dry as Dust. I felt my throat drying up just to hear it. This meant that somebody—some *bodies*—found me boring. Uninteresting. Unexciting.

Pamela grabbed my hand. "Who are *they* to decide who everyone else is?" she said. "And you know what Jill said they'd called *me*? Before I'd had the guts to come to their party?"

"What?" we asked.

"SS," said Pamela. "Serious Slut. I was mortified, but laughed it off. Yeah, right. Ha ha."

"They actually *told* you that?" Liz asked.

"Yeah. To see if I could take it, I guess. Boy, make *one* mistake, and you're labeled for life. After New York last spring, Hugh must have done a lot of talking."

We digested that for a moment or two, remembering what Pam had done in a hotel bathroom with a senior. Then Liz said, "It's hard to imagine Justin going along with all this. When I was going out with him, he seemed too nice to be so petty and malicious."

Pamela shrugged. "He's in love with Jill, and love is blind. Jill just laughs off all this gossip as a hobby of hers—labeling people, that is. And at some point in the evening, I asked the others what label they'd give Jill. This was at the soccer field later. They'd been drinking, and the guys were cutting up. Brian said BB for Beautiful Bitch. Justin suggested LM for Love Machine. It was sort of like Jill had never considered what others might think of her. I couldn't tell if she was flattered or annoyed, but I knew by the look on her face that she didn't appreciate the question.

Didn't appreciate *me*. I won't be invited back, you can bet, and if I am, I won't go."

I suddenly put my arm around Pamela. "*We* appreciate you!" I said.

"More than you know," said Liz.

This second week of my junior year, I sure didn't need any more hassles. Every minute of my day was filled with something, but I didn't know what I could give up. All juniors had to take the PSAT in October, ready or not, and I worked for Dad at the Melody Inn music store on Saturdays. I was the roving reporter for the junior class on our school newspaper, *The Edge*; I still belonged on stage crew in the Drama Club; I got up ridiculously early three mornings a week and ran a couple of miles to keep in shape; I visited Molly, my friend with leukemia, once a week; plus, homework was heavier and harder than it had been last year, and geometry was a killer.

"I feel like I'm going under for the third time," I told Sylvia, my stepmom, when I realized I hadn't called Molly all week. If anyone should be complaining about life, it's Molly.

"I know the feeling," said Sylvia. "I felt it every Friday for the first year I was teaching. But by Monday I'd usually recovered."

"So there's hope?" I asked. "The teachers are

merciless! It's like theirs is the only subject we've got. 'Make an outline.' 'Write a paper.' 'Research a topic.' When you multiply that by five . . . !"

"Well, teachers are hassled too," said Sylvia. "If their students don't do well, it's the teachers who get hassled by their principals. And if test scores are down for the school, the principals get hassled by the supervisors."

Sometimes—more than I like to admit—Sylvia gets on my nerves. It's like I tell her about a problem, and she's always got a bigger one. I wasn't interested right then in teachers' problems. I wanted to talk about *me*. *A little empathy here, please.*

"I'm not talking about test scores, I'm talking about assignments—about the timing of assignments," I told her. "When teachers get together in the faculty lounge, why don't they space their assignments so they're not all due at the same time?" I asked.

"Probably because we've got a zillion other things to think about," she said. "My guess is that after you get in the routine of a new semester, it will seem more bearable. If nothing else, you'll probably find at least *one* thing you can look forward to."

She was right about that. His name was Scott Lynch—a tall, lanky senior, our new editor in chief on the school newspaper. He was smart, like my *old* ex-boyfriend, Patrick, and knew his way around; he was thoughtful and caring, like my *new* ex-boyfriend, Sam, one of the photographers for our paper. When I walked in the journalism room after school for our meetings, Scott would give me this big, warm, welcoming smile that enveloped me like a hug. As though he'd been waiting just for me. But then, he did the same to the rest of the staff, including Jacki Severn, features editor.

Jacki's not a real blonde, like Pamela Jones, but her hair's gorgeous, and on this day she looked even better than usual. Great top, great jeans, great makeup.

"Idea!" she said when we'd pushed two tables together and sat down for our planning session. "If students have to read the stuff we write every two weeks, they should at least know what we look like. I think we should have a group picture taken for the front page."

Now I knew why Jacki was all spiffed up. I'd washed my hair that morning because I'd been running, but I hadn't taken time to blow-dry it.

"Not the front page," said Scott.

"Well, *any* page," said Jacki.

There were four guys on the newspaper staff: Scott; two photographers, Sam and Don; and Tony Osler, sports editor. Scott, Don, and Tony are seniors, and I seemed to have a thing about seniors this year. Of my two latest boyfriends, Patrick and Sam, Patrick has traveled all around the world with his parents—his dad is a diplomat—and sometimes he acts incredibly sophisticated. But he's a couple of months younger than I am, and he can also act incredibly juvenile. Sam's a junior too, like me, and sweet as honey, but sometimes I felt I was out with a little boy. I'd never dated a senior, and right now I was crushing on Scott.

None of the guys on the staff were remotely interested in having their pictures taken, and I voted with them. But all the roving reporters this year were girls, one for each class, and they voted with Jacki, along with the layout coordinator. So the vote was five to five. Miss Ames, our sponsor, broke the tie with a yes vote and went next door to get the chemistry teacher, who came over and took our picture. Jacki seated herself in the first row beside Scott, and the rest of us gathered around them.

"A little closer," the chemistry teacher said. "The guy on the end there—move in real tight next to the girl in green."

"With pleasure," said Tony, and put one arm around me, his hand on my ribs. I could feel his breath in my hair. Almost imperceptibly, one of his fingers moved a little under my arm, not quite stroking my breast. An electric shock traveled down my spine, but I didn't move away. And then—*flash*—the picture was taken and the group dissolved.

"Okay. Back to work," Scott said as we sat down at the tables again. "Here's what the classes have decided for Spirit Week."

A lot of high schools had been doing it for years, and though we'd always had a homecoming dance usually attended by the juniors and seniors, we'd never had Spirit Week—a time for students to bond and show loyalty to the school and its football team. Each day during Spirit Week, the students— and sometimes the teachers—came to school in crazy outfits, decided on in advance. So our school had assigned the freshman class to choose the costume for Monday; sophomores got Tuesday, juniors got Wednesday, seniors Thursday, and the faculty would choose the dress for Friday.

"Here are the votes," Scott read. "Monday, Pajama Day; Tuesday, Beach Day; Wednesday, Mismatched Day; Thursday, Wild Hair Day; and the teachers chose Victorian Day for Friday."

"Are you sure that's not Victoria's Secret Day?" asked Tony, and we laughed.

"Don't I wish," Scott said. "Nope. Victorian England."

The freshman and sophomore roving reporters were already chattering about what they would wear.

"Somehow I thought we'd be a little more original than that," said Jacki.

"Well, what we need are ideas for next year, and here's where you come in, Alice," Scott said, his blue eyes smiling at me. "Would you go around asking for suggestions so we can get people thinking about Spirit Week next year? Making it a tradition?"

"Sure," I said, lost in the blueness of those eyes. They were topaz blue, like the Caribbean Sea I'd seen on postcards. "I can do that." Scott could have asked me to climb up on the school roof and recite the Gettysburg Address and I would have said, *Sure! I can do that!*

Dad had let me use his car that day. He lets me have it sometimes when I've got something going on after school if Sylvia can drive him to work. I stopped by the CVS drugstore on the way home to buy a new steno pad and some eyeliner.

Jill and Karen were smoking at one of the little tables outside Starbucks next door. I hesitated for a second, and then—taking a chance to see if I was really as DD as they thought—I walked over to them and asked if they had any suggestions for Spirit

Week next year. When Jill saw me, she gave a sort of half smile and took another drag on her cigarette.

We've never been buddy-buddy, but ever since I stopped letting Jill and Karen use my employee discount when I worked at Hecht's last summer, I've felt they've cooled even more toward me. And after what Pamela told me, I was sure of it. Just the way they excluded me from their conversations some of the time. Once or twice I'd even had the feeling they'd turned away and whispered something to each other when they saw me. Their smiles seemed to have double meanings. The way they'd light up a cigarette, then glance my way. Just little things like that.

I know that a couple of times I've fanned their smoke when they lit up, and I've tried not to be so obvious about it, but I hate inhaling the stuff. This time, though, I tried to ignore it.

"Hi, Jill. Hi, Karen," I said. "I'm doing a short piece for *The Edge* with suggestions for next year's Spirit Week. Any ideas?"

"What kind of ideas?" asked Karen. She tilted her head back and blew the smoke straight up.

"How to dress. Hawaiian Day. Stuff like that," I told her, and added laughingly, "Tony Osler's already suggested Victoria's Secret Day."

They laughed too. "Hey, I'd go for that one," said Jill. "Bikini Day, maybe?"

"All right . . . ," I said.

"We could do Twins Day," said Karen, and she looked at Jill. "You and I could team up."

"That's a good one," I said, and wrote it on the back of my hand with my ballpoint. I really needed that steno pad.

"Or Preppie Day, and half the school would already come dressed for it," said Jill, who dresses more like she's going to work at Saks than going to school.

"That makes three," I said. "Thanks. I'm off to buy a steno pad."

"There she goes! Alice McKinley, Girl Reporter!" Karen sang out as I walked away.

I know that Karen and Jill look on my little job for the newspaper with amusement, but what else is new? This semester was already a grind. I'd missed a couple days of school that first full week when we went to Tennessee for my grandfather's funeral, and I still had a paper to write for one of those assignments. The only solution I could see was to stay up late at night till I got caught up. Bummer.

Still . . . the truth was, our old group wasn't the same. Until recently, we'd simply thought of ourselves as "the gang at Mark Stedmeister's pool." Now our differences seemed more important. I know that some of the kids think I take life too seriously, but . . . well, sometimes I do. That's me. Also, word had gotten around that I'd chickened out over the summer when Brian was going eighty in a forty-mile zone in the new car his dad had bought him and that I'd made Brian stop and let me out. I felt that some of the kids were still talking about it.

"So let them talk," I told myself aloud, and headed for the cosmetic counter. This was my junior year, and I had some decisions to make about my future. Jill had already confided that her number one objective was to marry the wealthy Justin, and as for Karen, she said she either wanted to marry rich or get into fashion design.

I'll admit that, other than going in to talk to the school counselor about a career, my immediate goal wasn't any more noble: I wanted to get Dad to relax his rule that I had to go six months without an accident before I could have any friends in the car with me. Finally, knowing how much I needed the car for after-school stuff, he'd said that he might—*might*—shorten it to five months instead of six, but I couldn't so much as get a traffic ticket during that time. This would mean I could have friends in the car with me by Thanksgiving, not Christmas. Just the thought of Gwen and Liz and Pamela in the car, with me at the wheel driving them somewhere, was number one on my "can't wait" list.

. . .

Lester came over on Sunday to rake leaves. The trees seemed to be shedding earlier this year, and he said it would make things easier if we did a first raking now.

I was glad to see Les back in our old routine. After he and Tracy broke up last month, I was afraid he might become a recluse or something. My twenty-four-year-old brother is getting his master's degree in philosophy next spring. I guess I always thought of philosophers as the hermit type, but that doesn't exactly fit Lester.

"It looks like you're going to make it, Les," I said as we raked, the bamboo tines of the rakes making *scritch scratch* sounds in the grass. "I mean, your degree and everything. I've still got all that ahead of me, and I haven't even taken the PSAT yet. I'm scared silly."

"Of what?" he asked.

"If I do poorly on the PSAT, I'll probably bomb on the SAT," I told him. "If I bomb on the SAT, I won't get into college, and if I don't go to college, I'll probably end up cleaning public restrooms on the night shift."

Les looked over at me. "Congratulations, Al. You just beat your all-time record. You went from a potential high to a major low in four seconds."

"But it's true, Lester. Life is just a series of hurdles, and no one ever tells you that. Right now everything's riding on that PSAT. You get over one roadblock, you've got another staring you in the face."

He laughed. "Well, *some* people *like* to have 'next steps' to look forward to. Some people *like* to have challenges. Ever think of that? Think how bored you'd be if everything came easy."

We raked in silence for a little while. Then I asked the question I'd been wanting to ask him for the past month. "When Tracy said no—when she broke it off—was that a roadblock or a challenge?"

"No getting around it, I was disappointed."

"You'd been dating since January, Les. Do you look at it as eight months wasted or what? I really want to know how you deal with it."

"Not wasted. I don't look at the time I've spent with *any* girl as wasted. I feel I learned something from each one, and . . ." He grinned. "I certainly had a good time."

I ignored the good time part and concentrated on the learning. "What did you learn?"

"About the kind of woman I'm looking for," said Lester.

"What kind is that? What did you learn from Loretta Jenkins?" I asked.

"She was never my girlfriend," Lester said. "But I was around her enough to know that I wanted a girl with her feet on the ground. Which was definitely not Loretta."

"Marilyn?"

"That I wanted a girl a little more . . . uh . . . physical. Like Crystal."

"Then what was wrong with Crystal?"

"I wanted a girl more sensitive . . . like Marilyn."

I wondered if I was naming these girlfriends in the proper order. "Lauren?" I asked, remembering one of Lester's instructors at the university.

"Too fickle."

"Eva?"

"Too sophisticated."

Should I go on? I asked myself, but I did. "Tracy?"

Les sighed. "With Tracy, I thought I'd found it all. But she broke up with me, remember. For Tracy, her family came first." And then he said, "Nobody's perfect, Al. I could fall in love with somebody tomorrow who's as different from me as night from day."

"That's scary, Lester," I said.

"That's life," he told me.

By staying up three nights in a row till twelve—two o'clock, one night—I finally finished the last assignment I'd missed when we went to Tennessee. I'd researched the Marshall Plan for World History and finished a list of suggestions for next year's Spirit Week for the newspaper:

- Victoria's Secret Day
- Towel Day
- Egyptian Day
- Twins Day
- Preppie Day
- Bikini Day
- Pimp 'n' Ho Day
- Garage Band Day
- Body Part Day
- Celebrity Day
- Crazy Hat Day

Scott was really pleased, and he gave my shoulder a squeeze when I turned in my list before homeroom the following morning. "Nice going!" he said. "We'll run it next time. Garage Band Day! I like that!"

That one shoulder squeeze was enough to make *my* day. I would have liked a Scott Lynch Day just to be able to tag along behind him for six periods.

I was beginning to feel, as Sylvia thought I would, that I was getting into the routine of things. That I was getting a grip. As I refreshed my lip gloss in the restroom after lunch, I came to the conclusion that I looked pretty good. Only a zit or two I couldn't cover with foundation, and if I was lucky, as the orthodontist said, I might get my braces off by spring.

I was putting a little blush on my cheeks when Jill and Karen came in the restroom.

"Alice!" Karen said, and looked genuinely glad to see me. "Did you do the essay question on *The Great Gatsby*? You know . . . that comparative thing?"

"Yes, and I was up until two in the morning finishing it," I said.

"I'm *drowning* in homework!" Karen said dramatically. "Absolutely *drowning*! I just couldn't get to it. Could I see yours? Just to get some ideas? I'll paraphrase it; I won't copy."

I had spent at least three hours struggling with that essay. I had come up with what I thought were original ideas for looking at F. Scott Fitzgerald's other works—finding trends, contradictions, repetitions. . . . There was nothing Karen could paraphrase that wouldn't take my original ideas and run with them.

"Oh, Karen, I can't," I said. "I worked really hard on that piece, and I want to keep the originality."

"Just this once?" she pleaded. "I'll be careful." I could see a crease deepening in her forehead.

I shrugged helplessly. "I can't. Sorry."

She turned to Jill as they left the restroom, and I heard her say, "Told you! MGT."

2

MGT

Liz, Pamela, Gwen, and I decided to make it Girls'
Night Out—to go to the Homecoming Dance
together. Jeans and sweaters. We'd argued about the
kind of shoes to wear, though. Pamela said she was
coming in the tightest pair of jeans she could find
and her silver stilettos with ankle straps. She also
wanted an escape clause: If any of us got asked to go
with a guy, that girl was free to back out. So much
for loyalty. But it didn't happen, so we entered Spirit
Week as a team. Monday through Friday were costume days; Friday night was the football game; and
Saturday night was Homecoming Dance in the gym.

The Friday before, at our lockers, Liz said,
"Mom's going to drive us to school on Monday,
seeing as how we'll be in pajamas." Her locker's
next to mine. They say you're lucky if your locker's
next to a gorgeous girl's because all the guys will
stop to talk to her and you can have the leftovers.

That was only partly true. Elizabeth was one of the most beautiful girls in school—long dark hair, thick black eyelashes—but she was also shy around people she didn't know, and that makes some kids think she's stuck-up, which couldn't be further from the truth. She's as brunette as Pamela is blond. I wear my hair shoulder length, Liz wears hers long and straight, Pamela still prefers the short layered look, and Gwen—who's African American—changes her hairstyle every couple of weeks. We never know what she'll try next.

"So what are we going to wear on Pajama Day?" I asked. "I'm just going in my T-shirt and flannels."

"Oh, but you've got to wear bunny slippers or *some*thing!" Liz said. "If we're not going to be out-landish, what's the point?"

The point, actually, as Scott told us, was to get the whole school doing something together to build school spirit and help the football team win one of its biggest games of the season. I couldn't see how bunny slippers contributed to that, but I told her I'd think of something.

"Listen," I said. "Do you know what MGT means?"

"Monosodium glutamate?" she guessed, stuffing some books in her bag. "Oh, that's MSG. I don't know. Where'd you see it?"

"I heard Karen say it to Jill when she was walking away from me the other afternoon."

"Just . . . MGT?"

"Yeah. And I don't think it was complimentary."

Liz shrugged. "Who knows? Who cares? It's just another stupid label. Did you ever hear either of them say anything *nice* about anyone?"

"Probably not," I said, and let it go.

It was a zoo at school on Monday. Mostly it was the cheerleaders, the class officers, the newspaper staff, the faculty, and maybe one fourth of the junior and senior classes who came to school in their pajamas. But at least a dozen showed up in animal slippers of one kind or another—big, fluffy bunny slippers like Liz's; cow slippers that mooed; pig slippers that oinked. Pamela had on a pair of duck slippers that quacked each time she took a step.

Jill came in tailored black satin pajamas with lace trim; Karen's were trimmed in fake fur. Penny, however, wore the same red flannels with the trapdoor seat that she'd worn the night of my coed slumber party two years ago—the night she and Patrick faked a kiss for the camera. That was probably the beginning of my breakup with Patrick. I felt that old familiar pang in the chest and was surprised that, after all this time, I wasn't over it yet.

The teachers were the funniest, though. Our principal came in his PJs with a pillow tied to his back like a backpack. The chemistry prof brought a teddy bear. One teacher even came in her pajamas with a pacifier on a string around her neck, and our English teacher had bedtime storybooks scattered around the room. It was a blast.

The one person who didn't quite get it was Amy Sheldon, or "Amy Clueless," as some of the girls call her. We've never decided what makes her tick, but Amy marches to a different drummer. On Pajama Day it appeared that she had simply got out of bed that morning, put on her shoes and socks, then her coat, and came to school—hair unbrushed, one thin, wrinkled pajama leg hiked up above her knee. She thought it was a "come-as-you-are" party or something.

"This is fun, isn't it, Alice?" she said, laughing, when I saw her in the hall. "My mom didn't believe we were supposed to come to school in our pajamas, but I showed her, didn't I? Didn't I, Alice?"

I thought of the teasing Amy had endured since she'd moved from special ed into the regular classrooms. She was undersized for her age, her features not quite symmetrical, and when she talked, her voice seemed too loud for such a small body.

"You sure did," I told her.

Probably because the cheerleaders got involved

and all the class officers, too, more kids took part in Beach Day on Tuesday. No one could wear bathing suits, but we could wear shorts. When we changed classes, the halls were filled with the squeakings and squishes of dozens of flip-flops. During P.E. the gym teacher gave us an exercise to do with beach balls, and almost every T-shirt had a slogan on it—the kind you'd see at the beach: EAT ME FOR DESSERT and LIFE IS A BITCH and GOD IS COMING, AND IS SHE PISSED!

I cut my lunch period short to put my name on the sign-up sheet outside the guidance counselor's door. I wanted to talk to her about majoring in counseling in college—what courses would be helpful now, what colleges have the best programs, stuff like that.

She wasn't in her office. There was a sign on her door that said GONE SWIMMING, but I took the clipboard off the hook and penciled in my name for the following noontime slot. As I was putting it back, Karen and Jill and another girl sauntered by the doorway in their cutoffs and halter tops.

Karen's sandals had sequins on them. Jill wore a huge pair of dangly earrings made of seashells.

"Oh, Alice!" Jill said, taking in the situation with the kind of condescending smile she's been giving me lately. "Having problems already?"

That's the first thing anyone thinks about when

you go to a counselor. What I should have said was, *Isn't everyone?* What I said was, "I just want some career information. I'm thinking about majoring in counseling in college."

"*Counseling!*" Jill said. "Spare me."

"Why?" I asked.

"With all the glamour jobs in the world, you'd pick *counseling*?" Karen exclaimed. "Gee, why not grow soybeans or something. Now, *there's* an idea!"

Jill laughed. "No, I've got it! She could design closets."

They were really getting under my skin. "I like the thought of working with people. I think it would be interesting," I said.

"Oh, absolutely!" said Jill.

"MGT!" Karen murmured as they turned in at the next doorway.

"What's that?" asked the girl who was with them.

And Jill answered, "Miss Goody Two-shoes."

I didn't react, just kept walking, but my cheeks felt hot. It was as though there were one gauge inside my body registering my discomfort level and another registering my self-esteem. The first one was rising; the second was bottoming out. Did I really care what Jill and Karen thought of my career plans? Evidently. I hated that they got to me so.

Forget it, I told myself.

You can say that, but how do you actually *do* it?

• • •

By Wednesday, Mismatched Day, at least half the students were in the swing of things. We came to school not only in different-colored socks for each foot, but in hideous combinations of colors and patterns. Pamela, all 105 pounds of her, came in a fur jacket on top, shorts on the bottom, a different earring in each ear. I made sure Sam took a picture of her for our paper.

It's interesting how well Sam and I get along now that we're not going out anymore. He seemed so hurt the day we broke up, and I felt so awful, so guilty, I wondered if he'd ever be the same again. But as soon as he got a new girlfriend, he was happy as a clam. Happier, maybe. Sam's probably one of those guys who's in love with love. As long as he has a girlfriend, life's good.

"I wish Spirit Week went on all year," Pamela said. "School would be more fun if we could dress in costumes all the time."

"Let's all go over to Molly's after school dressed like this," I said, showing off the lace-up boot and red knee stocking on one leg, the black net stocking and high-heeled pump on the other. Gwen had her brother's car for the day and said she'd drive.

When I went to see Mrs. Bailey at noon for my appointment, I found her wearing a baseball cap and a football sweatshirt. We laughed at each other's getup.

"Well, I'm not getting a whole lot of work done this week, but I'm having fun," she told me, and gave me a welcoming smile, then waited.

"I've pretty much decided that I want a career working with people," I began. "I used to think I wanted to be a psychologist, but I'm not sure I could get through a doctoral program. Statistics and everything. And the more I think about it, I want to go into counseling."

I expected her to get all enthusiastic, but she just nodded and smiled.

"Well, a degree is only one thing you need to consider," she said. "The other half is personality—your ability to empathize. How's your patience factor? Are you a good listener?"

"I probably do a better job of listening than I do of being patient," I told her. "But I can learn, can't I?"

"Definitely," she said. "You'll want to bone up on psychology and sociology, anthropology, literature . . . anything having to do with people. . . ."

We talked for ten minutes or more, and then I asked, "What's the best thing about being a counselor?"

"Good question," said Mrs. Bailey. She thought a moment before answering. "I think it's helping students connect with their real selves; helping them find out what they really, truly, down in their heart of hearts, want to do or be, not necessarily what their parents want them to be. And now you're going to ask what's the worst part, right?"

I nodded, and we laughed.

"Time," she said. "Not enough of it. I wish I could spend twice as much time with every student who walks in here. *Three* times as much. There are too many forms to fill out, reports to write. We're given too many tasks that aren't in our job description. But there's no perfect career, Alice. There are always going to be pluses and minuses."

So there, *Karen and Jill!* I thought as I left her office. *Your careers won't be so perfect either.*

At lunch Penny was showing us a fashion magazine article about how burlesque had influenced the fashion industry over the years. There was a photo of a 1930s fan dancer, supposedly nude except for a large Japanese-style fan covering part of her body; a 1940s-type bubble dancer who performed nude, half hidden by large bubbles blown from a fan behind the footlights; burlesque dancers who used large ostrich feathers to hide their bodies and tease the men. And then the magazine showed pictures of fashion designers' dresses with fantail pleats for the bodice; large round globes, like bubbles, decorating a neckline; dresses made of beads and feathers. . . .

We were laughing at the hairstyles in those old photos. The heavily mascara-lined eyes, the heavily rouged cheeks, the pouty lips. That same afternoon as I headed for my locker, I was approached by the roving freshman reporter for our newspaper, a shy girl who looked relieved to find an upperclassman—*any* upperclassman—she knew.

"Scott wants me to do a poll on what people plan to do after college," she said.

"To do?" I asked. "Like . . . travel?"

"Be," she said. "What do you want to *be* after college?"

"Bubble dancer," I joked.

And she actually wrote it down and put my name after it. I laughed out loud as I opened my locker and put on my jacket. *Chew on* that *for a while, Jill and Karen!* I thought. Miss Goody Two-shoes indeed!

Molly was definitely thinner and feeling pretty sick when we saw her. She smiled at our mismatched clothes, but it was a smile that looked as though it were holding back nausea.

"You guys are great to come by, but I'm the 'Puke-Up Kid' right now," she said.

We didn't stay long. We did the talking

mostly—Pamela told her about the first three days of Spirit Week and how we were all going to come to school the next day with the weirdest hairdo we could think of. Then Pamela's voice fell flat when we realized that Molly didn't have any hair at all under her bandana. In fact, she'd lost her eyebrows and eyelashes. You think of a head being bald, but not a face.

"We'll come back another time when you're feeling better," I said, signaling the others that I didn't think she was enjoying our company much.

"Yeah? When will that be? I wonder," Molly said plaintively.

"You're going to beat this, Molly," Gwen said. "Be strong, girl."

"You don't still work at the lab, do you?" Molly asked her.

"No, that was a summer internship," Gwen said.

"Then you don't really know if I'm getting better or not, do you?" asked Molly.

"No," Gwen said truthfully. "I don't. But I'm going to picture you well and strong and gorgeous."

"Good," Molly said. "I want to be a redhead next time, with hair down to my waist."

"You got it," said Gwen, and Molly closed her eyes.

Downstairs her mom said, "It's been a trying week. She can't seem to keep anything down, and she's behind in her schoolwork. She's discouraged and scared, and so are we, frankly, though the doctor says this is all to be expected."

"I'm praying for her," said Elizabeth.

"Thank you. I really appreciate it," said Mrs. Brennan. "One of her sisters is in town visiting now, and that should help too."

Outside, Pamela said, "Maybe we ought to start a fund drive and collect money for her."

"For what?" asked Gwen.

"I don't know. For whatever you need if you have cancer," said Pamela.

"We're not doctors, Pam. We don't know what she needs," Gwen said, and didn't say much more as she drove us home.

I think that most of the school came on Thursday with their hair a mess, literally. All colors of the rainbow. Spiked, frosted, peaked, molded, zigzagged, cornrowed, teased, and even shaved.

On Friday the wild hair was replaced with top hats and high stiff collars, only to be discarded that night at the football game, where we wore wool jackets and fleece-lined boots and cheered our lungs out, even though we lost by three points to the rival team. To be frank, I never really understood football. I cheer when everyone else is cheering and sit down when everyone else sits.

We were getting some good stories and photos for the next issue of *The Edge,* and during the second half of the game—for the third quarter, anyway—Scott Lynch and a couple more seniors sat with us, Scott next to me, thigh to thigh. I figured my junior year couldn't get much better than this and that I would remember this night, this moment, this warmth against me for the rest of my natural life.

On Saturday night Gwen got her brother's car again for the Homecoming Dance, and I went to Liz's house in my best tight-fitting jeans and a low-cut sweater. Liz did my makeup, and I did her hair, and we both looked eighteen when we left her house and climbed in Gwen's car, Pam in the front seat. Liz's little brother waved to us from the house.

"Tonight we are going to *howl!*" Pamela announced over her shoulder.

"Ow-ooooo!" I yipped, and we laughed.

The gym was decorated with streamers in fall colors, and a DJ played the music, taking requests and playing our favorite songs. He'd also recorded our school song and had a local band tape different variations of it.

There were a few slow numbers, the lights

dimming. The four of us danced together on the fast numbers, drifted away during the slow ones, but as I was leaving the floor near the end of the evening, someone swung me round and pulled me toward him. Tony Osler.

"Dance?" he said as he began moving with the beat.

"Do I have a choice?" I teased, smiling back, glad to have at least one serious dance of the evening—and with a *senior,* at that!

"All right, *may* I have this dance?" he said, grinning at me.

"You may," I said.

Tony's about my height—brown hair and eyes, nice-looking but nothing spectacular. Husky. We were cheek to cheek for a while, and sometimes I felt he was pressed just a little too close. But I'll admit I didn't object.

"So," he said into my ear, "I've been meaning to ask you a question."

"Yeah?" I said.

"How many of those answers were true?" he said.

"What answers?" I asked, pulling away a little to look at him.

"You know—on that 'Predict Your Future Love Life' questionnaire that Brian Brewster sent out."

I should have known he was still thinking about

that terrible trick Brian had played on me, when I'd answered some extremely personal questions online without knowing that all the answers had gone to Brian.

"That silly thing?" I said. "It's old as Methuselah. It must be the way Brian gets his kicks. I just wanted to stir him up a little."

Tony held me close again and whispered in my ear, "Stirred *me* up a little."

"You're easily stirred," I said.

"Well, all I can say is that you look good tonight," said Tony. "Good enough to eat."

And this was exciting to a girl without a boyfriend. A girl with braces. A girl of average intelligence, average everything, who hadn't been kissed since last spring.

3

Annabelle

Everyone says to get a good night's sleep before you take the PSAT. They say to eat a high-carb breakfast, don't have a quarrel with your parents, and if you can't answer a question on the test, go on to the next one and come back to it later. But you can do all these things and still be terrified.

Sylvia had invited Lester over for dinner and made an extra pumpkin pie for him to take back home and share with his roommates.

"Give me some sample questions, Les," I said.

"Al, it's been so long since I was in high school, I don't even remember taking a PSAT," he said.

"I don't care," I told him. "Make up something, and see if I can think clearly. Anything at all."

He took another helping of peas and onions. "If 'X' equals the number of women seeking eligible men, and 'Y' equals the number of men seeking eligible women, and 'Z' equals the number of men and women with cell phones, how many couples will hook up?" he said.

"Be serious," I told him.

"Alice, I think the best thing you can do at this point is put the test completely out of your mind and watch a movie or something," Sylvia said. "That test isn't going to define you for the rest of your life."

Dad grinned at me. "No matter how you do, you can always work at the Melody Inn."

"Yeah, right," I said.

After dinner I called to see what everyone else was doing. Gwen was reading a novel, Pamela was doing her nails, and Liz was planning to take a half-hour soak in the tub. I decided to go for a long walk in the fall air, then come back and watch a video.

I was thinking how much I liked our neighborhood—how much I liked Elizabeth living across the street and Pamela only a few blocks away. We'd been friends forever, and at least that much hadn't changed. But Lester had moved out, Sylvia had moved in, and what I had thought would be the perfect life with the teacher of my dreams for a stepmom turned out to be not quite so perfect after all. She just had her own way of doing things, and sometimes she seemed too much the teacher here at home. But Dad loved her, and I was glad they married. Besides, I only had two more years to live here full-time before I left for college, and that gave me a funny feeling in my stomach.

I was about four blocks from home when I heard someone call, "Hey, Alice!"

It was Keeno, Brian's friend, the guy from St. John's. His last name was Keene, but everyone called him Keeno.

I grinned and walked over to where he'd pulled up at the curb, then rested my arms on the open window. "Hey!" I said. "When did you get the wheels?"

"Dad finally caved and bought me a car. It's a second-hand, fourth-owner, with a hundred thousand miles on it, but it moves. What are you doing out by yourself? Running away?" he asked.

I laughed. "PSAT tomorrow. I'm trying to calm my nerves."

"I took mine last year," he said. "Not so bad."

"I hate tests," I told him. "I think I'd actually enjoy school if we never had to take tests. I get stomachaches and headaches, and my hands perspire. . . ."

"Want to go for a ride and relax a little?" he asked. "I'll drive slow and play soft music and let the wind blow through your hair."

I smiled. "No, thanks. I need the walk, but it doesn't stop the worrying."

"Then I could drive seventy miles an hour, and at least you could worry about something else," he said.

"Not that." I laughed.

"Starbucks? A caramel latte? Ice cream?"

"Naw. I'm just out clearing my head. Thanks. So where are *you* going?"

"Oh, just cruising around looking for pickups. Drugs. A little robbery, maybe. Nothing big."

I laughed again and backed away from the car. "Don't get caught," I said. He waved and pulled away.

When I got home, I watched an hour of *Gone with the Wind*, then fell asleep.

The next morning I wasn't nearly as worried as I had been the day before. Now that the day was here and there was nothing more I could do about it, I read the comics at breakfast like I always do. And as it turned out, I think I did okay on the test. I was sure of maybe 60 percent. A lot of kids finished before me, including Gwen, but I calmed down and tried to see it as an adventure. An experiment. We wouldn't get the results till December.

I decided that one thing I could do to make myself more interesting was to actually learn football. I don't know how I grew up to be so sports-challenged, but I did. When the gang gets together, the other girls seem to know about fifty yard lines and halfbacks and fullbacks, while I sit hunkered down in a corner chair wishing I were watching almost anything other than football. But no one is going to invite a girl over to watch football if she cheers for the wrong team and doesn't know it. No girl like that would be the life of the party. There was only one person to call.

"Lester," I said on Sunday, "will you be home this afternoon? I really, really need a lesson in football, and I was wondering if you were going to watch the game."

"Yeah, we're watching it here," Les said, meaning he and his roommates. "Come on over if you want."

I arrived with a bag of chili-flavored corn chips and some brownies. I was a little embarrassed that Paul Sorenson and George Palamas were there too, but I tried to ask only about things that really confused me. Les and I were on the couch, Paul was in an easy chair on one side, George in the contour chair on the other.

"Okay, you know who the Redskins are, right?" asked Lester.

"Yes, I'm not a total idiot. The guys in red and orange," I answered. "And the Cowboys are silver and blue."

"So far so good," said Les. "Now, at each end of

the field, you see two goalposts. Those are in the end zones. One end of the field is Washington's end zone. The other is Dallas's. A team scores if they can get the ball in the other team's end zone. If they do, it's a touchdown, worth six points. They get an additional point if their kicker can kick the ball between the other team's goalposts. Questions?"

"No, I think I understand that much," I said. "It's all the stuff between the two end zones that I don't understand."

"We'll get to those one by one," said Les. "But you can't think straight unless you have a beer in your hand. In your case, a can of Gatorade."

I watched for a while in silence. Les glanced over now and then to see if I had any questions.

Finally I said, "See, Lester? *See?* This is why I like basketball better than football. In basketball you can't take your eyes off the ball even for a second or somebody might score. It's easy to understand. If the ball goes through the basket, you score. What's to understand? But all these guys do in football is huddle and *talk* about it first. 'Just *do* it,' I want to say. Just get out there and *do* it! And even when they do move, it's only for a few seconds and you can't even see the ball."

Suddenly, however, as Dallas was moving down the field, there must have been a fumble because a Redskins player had the ball. He whirled around and ran . . . and ran . . . and ran for Dallas's end zone. One Cowboy after another tried to bring him down, but he made it, and I was on my feet yelling my lungs out.

"Touchdown! Touchdown!" I screamed. "We got a touchdown!"

I looked around. No one else was cheering.

"What?" I said. "*What?*"

"Sit down," said Les. "There was a flag on the play."

I stared. The Redskin who had been doing a victory dance between the goalposts suddenly stopped. A referee switched on his microphone and waved his arms, but I didn't understand a thing he said. All I knew was that the touchdown didn't count. Turned out it wasn't even the Redskins' ball. So what did the players do then? Went into a huddle and talked about it.

At school the talk was of the PSAT, Halloween, and the Snow Ball. Because Halloween fell on a Wednesday this year, no one seemed to be planning anything. We were simply too busy, for one thing. Too much homework. And we certainly weren't going trick-or-treating anymore. As for the Snow Ball, I hadn't been asked to go as a freshman or sophomore, and suddenly, as much as I'd liked going to the Homecoming Dance with my girl-friends, I wanted to go to the Snow Ball with a guy. To be asked by a guy. And not just any guy: a senior. And not just any senior: Scott Lynch.

I tried to figure out the odds of his asking me.

Pro: He'd sat next to me for a while at the game.

Con: He was a popular senior; I was a junior.

Pro: The way he smiled at me.

Con: He smiled that way at everyone.

Pro: He'd squeezed my shoulder once.

Con: So what?

When we had our staff meeting on Wednesday after school to lay out the photos and write-ups of Spirit Week, I tried to catch Scott's eye and see if there was any spark. See if his smile lingered a bit.

"Hey, Alice!" he called. "Look at this one."

I went over to the layout table and stood as close to him as I dared. The photos Sam had taken of Mismatched Day and Pajama Day and Wild Hair Day were lined up across the table. Scott was pointing to a close-up of my legs, the one in red stocking and boot, the other in net stocking and heel.

"Yeah!" said Tony, grinning. "Let's use that one!"

"Sold!" Scott said, smiling at me, that luscious, wide, lip-stretching, teeth-gleaming smile. Then, to Don, he said, "Show me your five best shots of the football game and the Homecoming Dance, and let's see what we've got. We'll do a double-page spread." As he passed by me in the narrow space between table and desk, Scott's fingers rested on my arm for just a moment. I wanted to put my hand over his and keep it there forever.

Later, as I wrote down my assignment for the next issue, I found I had made elaborate *S*'s and *L*'s in the margins all up and down the page.

I didn't have Dad's car that day, so after the staff meeting Jacki Severn dropped me off at the corner nearest our house. She was reciting some of the Halloween parody she'd written, which was funnier on paper, I hoped, than it seemed when she recited it aloud. The gist of it was that it was the one holiday of the year when everything was the opposite of ordinary—when ugliest was best, the grosser the better. . . .

"I've got this great idea for the Snow Ball issue," she said just before I got out. "There's this computer graphic of icicles, and I want them hanging from the top of each page, with pictures of couples dancing on the double-page spread."

"Sounds good," I said. "You going?"

"Hope so," she answered. "If the right guy asks me."

I felt sure that her "right guy" was the same as mine, and my heart sank. I trudged the half block to my house feeling about as gray as everything around me. The sky looked more like November than October, and the wet leaves clumped on the sidewalk were depressing. I wished I had *some*thing to look forward to that weekend. That *some*body was giving a party. *Any*thing. It seemed like most of my life now was dictated by something else—namely, school. When to get up, where to go, what to read, what to wear, when to eat . . .

I opened the front door and put my books on the hall table. As I hung up my jacket, Sylvia called, "Alice! In here! Come see what I've got."

"What?" I asked, and walked into the living room.

Sylvia was standing by the fireplace holding a cat in her arms. It was a white cat with irregular patches of black on it, not especially attractive. The eyes were yellow, and the cat was probably about a year old. Not a kitten.

I stared at it. Then at Sylvia. After Oatmeal died when I was in fifth grade, I'd made up my mind that when I got another cat—*if* I got another—it would be *what* I wanted, *when* I wanted one. Dad had surprised me with the cat in the first place, and Sylvia was surprising me now. I didn't want something to love and lose again without having any say in the matter.

"Whose is it?" I asked, unsmiling.

I saw a flicker of disappointment in Sylvia's face at my reaction.

"Well, right now it belongs to one of the teachers at school, but she's having a back operation and asked if I could keep it for three weeks." She bent her head and rubbed noses with the cat. "Her name's Annabelle."

"Oh," I said, and sat down on the couch, making no move to go over and pet it.

"The thing is," Sylvia continued, "Beth—my friend—is going to need a second surgery after this one, and a cat's a little more than she can handle. If we *want* to, she'll let us keep Annabelle. Otherwise, I guess we'll have to find her another home."

"Yeah, a cat's a lot of work," I said.

Sylvia studied me, then sat down on a chair across the room, Annabelle on her lap. "I wouldn't mind the work," she said. "I think I like having one more thing to love."

"Well," I said, picking up a magazine and flipping through the pages. "Whatever you want."

"It's not just what I want, Alice," Sylvia said. "I only agreed to take her because I thought we all might enjoy a pet."

"I already had a cat," I told her. "And I'd sort of like to be in on a decision before it becomes a fact."

"Of course," Sylvia said. "We won't keep her if you don't want to."

"But see? Now I'm the bad guy!" I protested. "I'm put in the position of saying no, and I hate that!"

My voice was too loud, I knew. Annabelle's ears lay back for a moment, then perked up again.

For a short while Sylvia just sat stroking the cat. Then she said, "You're right. I'll see if somebody else at school can take her, and if you're ever ready for a pet, you can choose it."

"Thanks," I said. I got up and started toward the kitchen to get a snack. Suddenly the cat leaped off Sylvia's lap and dived for my ankle. I could feel her claws like pinpricks through my sock.

"Ouch!" I yelled, giving her a little fling with my foot.

Sylvia laughed. "Oh, she was just trying to catch that long string on the bottom of your jeans," she said. "It was dragging on the floor."

"Well, she grabbed my ankle, not the string," I said, rubbing my foot.

"Come here, you!" Sylvia got up and picked up the cat, and I went on out to the kitchen, furious that I had to play the role of spoiler.

When Dad walked in the door that evening and saw Annabelle, he said, "Well! What have we here?"

Sylvia came out of the kitchen and said, "I'm

afraid I should have asked first, Ben, but Beth, at school, is having back surgery tomorrow and I agreed to keep her cat for three weeks. If you think you can stand one for that long . . ."

"I certainly don't mind," Dad said. "A cat on my lap might feel good on a cold fall evening." He looked over at me, and I stuck my nose in my geometry book again, hating myself as I did it, angry at Sylvia for creating the situation in the first place.

I really didn't want to be difficult. I hadn't planned this. But I would like *some* say in my life. I hate when things just *happen* to me. Like, *deal* with it, Alice! So much of my life is planned by others that I can't even choose my own pet?

Things were too quiet at dinner. I tried really hard to pretend that nothing had happened. But as I talked about school, my voice sounded unnatural. Sylvia's was too polite. Dad could sense that something had gone on between us. I looked up once and saw the glance that passed between them and knew right away that when dinner was over and they were alone, she'd tell him everything—like what a snot I'd been.

I guessed right about Dad and Sylvia. Around nine o'clock, when I was sitting at my computer Googling twentieth-century poets, Dad came to the door of my room.

"Al?" he said. "Sylvia says she's not going to keep Annabelle. Is that what you want?"

I lifted my fingers from the keyboard. "Yes. And . . . ?"

"Well, I think she's really fallen in love with that cat. I'm afraid it would break her heart to give it up."

"So? Keep it. Why are you asking me?" I said coldly.

"Because she feels really bad that you're against it."

I whirled around in my chair. "Okay, what do you want me to do, Dad? Just tell me and I'll do it. Go downstairs and say that I always wanted a cat named Annabelle? Why do you even ask me stuff when there's only one right answer? Either I cave and say, 'Great! Let's keep her!' or I'm the bad guy and Sylvia's upset. Do whatever you want and leave me out of it, will you? When there's a decision to be made where I have some real input, let me know."

Dad's voice was strained and matter-of-fact. "Okay," he said, turning, and went downstairs.

That wasn't what I wanted either. I wanted him to stay and discuss it with me. *All* my feelings, not just this. Now, no matter what happened, somebody would be mad. Things were just too tense with Sylvia around! Sometimes it seemed as though she didn't even *try* to fit into the family. Just went off and did things her way.

I went in the bathroom, filled the tub with hot water, and soaked awhile, sinking in up to my chin. For two cents, I thought, I'd go to the Humane Society tomorrow and come home with a dog. *I had no idea I'd fall in love with a dog like this!* I'd say. *It would break my heart to give him up.*

I tried to be really nice to Sylvia at breakfast, and I think she was trying to be nice to me. Dad was all business, like he wasn't going to take sides, and Sylvia and I would have to work it out ourselves.

Annabelle was batting a spool of thread around the kitchen floor. It pinged against her water dish, then sailed into the dining room. It smacked against the opposite wall and came spinning out into the middle of the floor again, making Annabelle jump. I almost laughed, but caught myself in time.

Dad kissed us both good-bye when he left. It was a perfunctory kiss on the top of my head, but at least it was a kiss.

"Life sucks," I told Pamela that day at school.

"Don't I know it," she said. "What happened?"

I told her about Annabelle. "It's not enough that I say, 'Okay, keep it.' I have to be *happy* about it! I have to say I want it! I have to lie!"

"So lie!" said Pamela. "Here's the way I look at it, Alice. You give in on this one, and then Sylvia owes you big-time. Someday you're going to want something from her, and then you can pull out all the stops. All you'll have to say is, 'Remember Annabelle?' and you'll get what you want."

It made sense, but I also realized that if I expected Dad to let me have friends in the car when I drove—to move the date up from December to November—I'd better start making concessions now and quit making waves. But it took some time before I could get the words out.

Sylvia came home late from an after-school meeting a few days later, and we worked together in the kitchen, cutting up beef cubes and celery for stir-fry.

"Listen, Sylvia," I said. "I want to clear the air about Annabelle. She's not my cat, and this is your house as well as mine. If you want to keep her, I really don't care, as long as I don't have to look after her. I mean, as long as we understand that she's your cat, not mine."

"Of course, Alice. But our relationship means a lot more to me than Annabelle. Are you sure of this?"

"Yeah, I am. Someday maybe I'll want to choose my own pet and maybe it will be something *you* don't want, who knows?" I said. "But it's okay. You like this cat, and it's silly of me to object."

"All right. And I'll take the responsibility for her—feeding, brushing, trips to the vet, litter box . . . ," said Sylvia. "Thanks, Alice. I'm really surprised that I'm so fond of her already."

I felt better then. I'd had my say, and even felt I understood Sylvia a little better. Maybe women who'd had hysterectomies and couldn't have children of their own needed pets more than others, I thought.

Dad and Sylvia celebrated their first anniversary on October 18. It was a Thursday night, so Dad left work early, Sylvia came straight home from school, and they got all dolled up and went to the Four Seasons restaurant in Georgetown for dinner, with tickets to a show at the Kennedy Center later. I played the part of the magnanimous daughter who babysat an ugly cat without complaint while they were gone.

Annabelle really was fun when I let myself admit it. I left my bedroom door open, and she sauntered into the room, tail straight up like she owned the place. She meowed a couple of times, then jumped up on my bed and started purring, kneading her paws into my bedspread.

"Go away, you conceited fur ball," I told her, scratching her under the chin. "Who made you Queen of the Universe, anyway?"

It was most fun to watch Annabelle at my window. She was an indoor cat, Sylvia said, never having set foot in the great outdoors. But she quivered and crouched in the pounce position when a bird landed on a branch nearby.

"You don't know what you're missing, kid," I told her. "There's a big wide world out there, and you're stuck inside forever."

On Halloween night, I stayed in to study. I told Sylvia I'd man the front door, though, and I wore a tall black witch's hat. When the doorbell rang, I'd answer with a large bowl of candy in my hands.

First the Milky Way bars disappeared. Then the Mars bars and the little packs of M&M's. Tootsie Rolls were the last pieces chosen.

I was just about to turn off the porch light at nine o'clock, signaling that we were through with the treats, when a group of six rowdy kids came to the door. As I answered, my witch's hat tipped to one side and fell off. I stooped to pick it up, and in that one moment I saw Annabelle slip through the doorway and out into the night.

4

Crushed

"Sylvia!" I yelled. "Annabelle's outside!"

"You let her *out*?" she cried from the other room, where she was grading papers on the dining room table.

"I didn't *let* her out. She slipped through the door," I said. The kids, seeing that I was distracted, reached in with both hands, grabbing candy by the fistfuls.

In the light from the porch, I could see the cat on the sidewalk below, sniffing the air, her quivering tail straight up. But as the children went galloping back down the steps, she disappeared into the bushes.

"Alice, I told you she's *never* to go outside!" Sylvia said, pushing past me in the doorway and hurrying to look over the porch railing. "I didn't want her to even get a taste of outdoors! Now she'll always be meowing to go out."

"Well, then you should have locked her in the basement or something while the kids were trick-or-treating," I said defensively, going out on the porch and down the steps.

"Annabelle!" Sylvia called. "Here, kitty, kitty, kitty!"

Unless she knew something about cats that I didn't, I doubted Annabelle would come just because Sylvia called her name. Do cats even *know* their names, and if they do, do they care?

Sylvia came down, and we crouched by the azalea bushes, parting the branches with our hands, trying to see into the darkness.

"Annabelle?" Sylvia kept calling. "Here, kitty! Here, kitty, kitty, kitty!"

The branches scratched my hands, my cheeks. *I knew this would happen,* I told myself. This wasn't my cat, yet here I was outside in the dark when I had a ton of homework waiting for me.

We moved along the row but couldn't see anything. A car was coming down the street a little too fast, and Sylvia jerked upright, staring at it, expecting, I'm sure, to hear the squeal of brakes and the cry of an injured cat.

"I'll get a flashlight," I said, and went back inside, then came out with two of them, handing one to Sylvia. "Let's check around the side of the house."

"She may have run across the street or even followed a child home," said Sylvia, and her voice had a slight accusatory tone. I didn't answer.

We shone our flashlights on the holly bushes and the rhododendron. I got down on my hands and knees and crawled through to the back, shining my light along the base of the house. The ground was wet, and I came back with muddy knees and with twigs in my hair, but not with Annabelle.

"Oh, Alice!" Sylvia said in dismay. There was that tone again.

"Well . . . ," I said, and paused. "I've got to turn in a paper tomorrow, and I'm not even halfway done. I'm going back inside."

Sylvia ignored me. "She'd walk right in front of a car and not even know what it was. A dog could tear her apart in seconds," she continued.

I took a deep breath and held it. "Maybe if we opened a can of tuna, she'd smell it," I suggested.

"That's an idea," said Sylvia.

I clumped back in the house and found the tuna. I opened it, then brought it out and handed it to Sylvia. She held it out away from her as though it were a magic wand and slowly turned around and around in a circle, like she was casting a spell or something. But no cat materialized.

Still another group of Halloween stragglers was coming up the walk, but we waved them off.

"Well, I'm going back to my homework," I said.

"I'll keep looking," said Sylvia.

Inside, I settled down again with my clipboard and reference books. Fifteen minutes went by. Then twenty. Twenty-five. I began to feel awful, and angry that I did. I remembered how terrible it had been back in fifth grade when I found my cat dead on the kitchen floor. But it was almost more horrible imagining what might be happening to Annabelle this very minute. I wondered if I *should* have stayed out there to help. Then I heard Sylvia's footsteps on the porch, and she came in. No cat.

She headed for the hot air register and stood there hugging herself.

"What am I going to tell Beth?" she asked plaintively. "What if she wants Annabelle back?"

"I don't know," I murmured.

"I'm going to take a hot bath and go to bed," she said suddenly, and leaving her papers scattered on the dining room table, she went upstairs. I heard water running in the tub.

Dad was at a concert listening to one of his music instructors play the oboe, so I was going to get stuck with the job of telling him what had happened to Annabelle. I studied until ten fifteen, when the doorbell rang again. I debated not answering. No kid should be out this late. But I opened the door a crack and peeped out. There stood Lester.

"Trick or treat?" he asked. "Dark chocolate, if you've got it."

I laughed, and he came inside, reaching around me for the candy bowl.

"You came all the way over here for some candy?" I asked.

"No. I had to pick up something at the mall, so I swung by here and saw you were still up. Figured you might have some candy left."

"Take it all," I said. "It'll keep me from eating it."

"Any idea what that can of tuna is doing on your front porch?" he asked. "Trying to ward off vampires or something?"

"No, it's bait," I said, and told him about Annabelle and how Sylvia was so upset, she'd gone to bed.

"*That's* a bummer!" he said.

"I *knew* this would happen, Lester," I said irritably. "Sylvia swore she'd take complete care of that cat, but that's never the way it is."

"I know," said Lester. "Dad said the same thing when I begged for a dog."

"I'm sounding like *Dad* now?" I asked.

"As long as you don't start looking like him, you're okay," he said. "Give me a bag for the rest of the candy, and I'll take it off your hands."

"You're a first-class moocher," I said fondly, but we encourage him because it's one way to guarantee we'll see him now and then. I got a bag from the kitchen and filled it up.

As Les opened the door to leave, he suddenly paused, his hand on the knob. "She's baaaaaack!" he said.

"Annabelle?" I said, moving up behind him.

"And she's got *com*pany!" Lester said.

I stared. There were two cats competing for the tuna can, nudging it this way and that as they fed. One was Annabelle, and the other was a large orange tomcat.

"Omigod, get him *away* from her, Lester!" I cried.

But all Les had to do was open the screen, and the tomcat leaped to the top of the railing and sailed down into the bushes. I ran out on the porch and scooped up Annabelle as Les brought the tuna can back inside.

"Well, well!" Lester said. "Looks like she got herself a boyfriend!"

"Les, what are we going to *do*?" I bleated.

"About what? This isn't Annabelle?"

"Of course it is, but she's never been out of a house before! She's never touched grass or smelled a flower or seen a male cat until tonight!" I told him. "What if she's pregnant?"

"Yep, let a female loose for one night, and she goes wild," Lester said.

"Les, this is serious!" I cried.

Les put on his serious face and shook his finger at Annabelle. "*Bad* kitty! Bad, bad, bad!" he scolded.

I took Annabelle out to the kitchen and let her lick out the tuna can. "Do you think I should call a vet?" I asked. "Should we take her to an animal emergency room or something?"

Les stared at me. "For *what*? A morning-after pill? Are you out of your mind? You don't even know what she did."

"I can guess."

"Maybe the tomcat just smelled the tuna."

"And maybe he smelled *her*. What if she has a litter?"

"So take her to a crisis center! Capture the tomcat and test his DNA!" Les said in exasperation.

There were footsteps overhead, and then the stairs creaked and Sylvia appeared in the kitchen doorway in her robe.

"I *thought* I heard voices down here," she said. Then she saw Annabelle. "Where did you *find* her?" she asked delightedly, kneeling down beside the cat. "Is she okay?"

Les frowned at me and gave an almost imperceptible shake of his head.

"She's fine," I said. "I guess the tuna lured her back."

"You naughty little girl!" Sylvia said, picking Annabelle up in her arms. "You're never getting out again, so I hope you enjoyed yourself!"

"Oh, I'm sure she did," said Lester. "Probably more than we'll ever know."

I was telling Pam and Liz about the Annabelle episode at lunch the next day.

"Can you believe it? Her first time out, and she comes home with a boyfriend," I said.

"Man, I wish *I* had that kind of luck!" said Pamela. "I'll bet he was all over her too!"

Karen and Jill were standing near our table with their trays, looking to see if there was a better option somewhere else. It was raining, though, and most of the kids had stayed inside, so all the tables were taken. The girls took the last two seats across from me.

"Who you talking about?" asked Jill. "Who was all over whom?"

I caught Pamela's eye. "Tom and Annabelle," I said.

"Who are they?" asked Karen, taking a bite of her ham salad.

"Oh, you wouldn't know them," I said. "Sylvia brought Annabelle home one night. Friend of a friend."

Liz was hiding a smile behind her napkin.

"And the minute their backs were turned, Annabelle's out the door. Five hours later she's back with a boyfriend," Pamela said, poker-faced.

Jill set down her Sprite. "She's staying at your place, Alice?"

"Unfortunately," I said.

"What's the boyfriend like? Some bar bum? Did you meet him?" asked Karen.

"Orange hair. Big. You could tell he had only one thing on his mind," I answered, and quickly wiped my mouth.

"And Sylvia just let him come in? He spent the night?" Karen exclaimed. Pamela and Liz and I were trying desperately to keep from laughing.

"No. Lester found them together on the porch and sent the boyfriend packing, but Sylvia will forgive anything," I said.

Liz stifled a giggle, and Jill glanced quizzically at her.

"But what did Annabelle have to say for herself?" Karen asked.

I couldn't keep it up any longer. "Nothing," I said. "She only purred." And Pam and Liz and I broke out laughing.

Jill gave me a disgusted look. "I might have known," she said. "The only girl at *your* table who will ever get some is of the feline variety."

Pamela bristled. "There are other tables in the cafeteria, Jill. Help yourself," she said.

Jill laughed if off as though she'd been joking. But she and Karen continued their conversation in a low voice, and it seemed to be about a lingerie sale at Victoria's Secret—definitely, they appeared to be saying, not for the likes of us.

The day *The Edge* goes to press, we pile in Scott's car and anybody else's car who can drive, and we take the new copy to the printer. Then we go to the fast-food place next door and eat dinner. Meatball subs and fries.

"Come on. We can seat three up here," Scott was saying from behind the wheel. "Alice, you squeeze in between Jacki and me."

He was smiling at me with those incredible eyes. The middle seat was a kind of fold-down affair between the two bucket seats, and I had to sit at an angle, my legs to one side, so that Scott could move the gearshift. That made my upper body closer to him than it would ordinarily be. I was almost leaning against him.

I could smell the scent of his leather jacket, the shampoo traces on his hair, the male-armpit deodorant smell.

"Everyone buckled up?" he asked, turning the key in the ignition. "There's no belt for you, Alice, but if I crash, I'll grab you, I promise."

Crash! I wanted to say. *Please crash. Just a little fender bender, that's all. . . .*

My left hip was pinned against his right hip, my

left shoulder touching his right. I could feel any move he made with the gearshift, every turn he made of the wheel.

Jacki Severn was prattling on and on about the pictures she *wished* we'd gotten to accompany her feature articles this issue, and Sam, in back, was explaining how shots like those were so difficult to get. Tony and the sophomore roving reporter, sitting with Sam, were arguing over one of the referee's calls in the last football game. About the only people in the car who weren't saying anything were Scott and me.

Didn't that mean something? I wondered. Was he conscious of the warmth of our bodies pressed together there in the front seat? Was he thinking about me like I was thinking about him? Ignoring all the chatter and just thinking how close our bodies were right then? I think this was the closest I'd ever been to Scott Lynch in my life, and I loved it—the smell of him, the feel of him, the way he laughed, smiled, breathed. . . .

The printer is way out in Gaithersburg, a thirty-minute drive, depending on traffic, and I wished it were thirty hours instead. I wished it were just Scott and me, and we'd leave everyone else at the restaurant and he'd drive me home and we'd park and . . .

We all trooped inside the print shop and waited

while Scott and Jacki went over a few details with the printer. Then we went next door to the sub place and took a table.

I wanted to sit beside Scott, but Jacki got that chair, so I sat across from him instead. I took a chance and gave him a big smile. "Looks like I got the best seat at the table," I said, smiling knowingly.

He smiled back. "Ketchup?" he asked when our food arrived, and handed me the bottle.

It was like I was waiting all evening for the perfect time to talk to him. I was so aware of him—so full of him—that I hardly tasted my Coke or fries. He had a funny little wrinkle at the corner of each eyelid and three tiny moles at the side of his jaw. There was a faint blond mustache above his upper lip. If you could fall in love with a face, I guess I was in love with his. I wanted in the worst way to run a finger along that mustache. It was crazy. I was crazy for crushing on him like this.

Jacki got involved in a conversation with someone else, and I saw my chance.

"So," I said to Scott. "What do you do when you're not working on the paper?"

"Study," he answered. "Fill out applications for college. What else?"

"Which colleges?" I asked.

"Ithaca, University of Michigan, Ohio State. . . .

I'd like to go into journalism. Either that or architecture, I'm not sure."

"You'd be great at either one, I'll bet," I said. "But what do you do for fun?"

He grinned. "Oh, go to the movies. Go bowling with my cousin. Rock concerts. Jazz. Sailing in the summer. What about you?"

"I love movies too," I said, hoping he wouldn't ask the name of the last one I'd seen. "I like theater . . . I like to write . . . I love dances."

He took another bite of his meatball sub, so I barreled on: "Thanksgiving's so early this year that they moved the Snow Ball up to November," I said. "November thirtieth. I heard that the decorating committee is going all out."

"Yeah," he said. "I heard that too. It's going to be like an ice cave you have to walk through to get in the gym."

"That should be fun," I said, and looked right into his eyes. I was smiling my special smile, just for him. At least, it felt special. I could feel the air on my teeth. I waited. Scott went on eating.

"My dad's manager of the Melody Inn over on Georgia Avenue," I said, hoping I didn't sound desperate. "We've got a great collection of CDs if you ever want to come by."

"That right?" he said. "Thanks. Maybe I will." Then he reached over and swiped the pickle off

Jacki's plate, but she caught him and slapped his hand, and he laughed.

It hurts so much to like someone who doesn't see you as anyone special. I felt right then as though I could have been a doorknob. A chair. A comfortable old shirt, maybe. I wondered if this was what it had felt like to Sam when I broke up with him—that hollow feeling in the stomach. The dryness in the back of the throat. The thick feeling on the tongue, like it's too big for the inside of your mouth. All I wanted to do was go home, curl up, and sleep.

Maybe Jill and Karen were right, I thought. Maybe I *was* a boring Miss Goody Two-shoes and I'd be the last girl on the newspaper staff—no, the last girl in the whole high school—Scott would take to a dance.

When the next issue of *The Edge* came out, there were some leftover pictures from last month's Spirit Week, including the one of my legs with a different shoe on each foot. And on the last page of the paper was a little filler by the freshman roving reporter, titled "Thoughts on Careers from Upperclassmen":

Ann Haung—chemist
Dan Kowalski—criminal lawyer

Scott Lynch—journalist
Holly Morella—business
Erin Healey—physical therapist
Sean Reston—veterinarian
Alice McKinley—bubble dancer

5

Surprise of
the Nicer Variety

The following evening before dinner, Dad and I were doing the final raking of the yard. I had decided that for the month of November, I would focus so much on driving very carefully, obeying the rules, helping out at home, and getting along with Sylvia that Dad would *have* to let me drive with friends along in the car. My six-month probation period would end the last week of December, and Dad had all but promised he'd reduce the probation period to five months.

"Are we still on for the week after Thanksgiving?" I asked pleasantly, plucking a leaf off the sleeve of Dad's knobby wool sweater.

He looked at me blankly. "We had a date or something?"

"The car!" I told him. "You said if I didn't get in an accident for six whole months after I got my license, you'd shorten the waiting period for driving with friends in the car from six months to five months."

"Oh. That," said Dad. "We'll see. If you can go all that time without an accident or a ticket and do your homework, clean your room, help with housework, cook some meals, wash the windows, shine my shoes . . ." He grinned.

"Hey! No fair!" I said.

He laughed. "Concentrate on driving safely, doing your homework, and getting along with Sylvia, and we'll make it November," he said. "The last week, now. Not the whole month."

The fact that he mentioned Sylvia meant either that she had been telling him things that had gone on between us or that he'd been noticing on his own. I hated the thought that they might be talking about me behind my back. But as soon as the rakes were put away, I went inside and e-mailed my girlfriends.

We're on! I typed. *By the last week of November, I can have you guys in the car with me!*

Hooray! Liz e-mailed back. *Let's have another Girls' Nite Out.*

Yeah, seconded Pamela. *But make it special.*

U mean go sumplace special? wrote Gwen.

Pamela: *Yeah. Someplace sexy.*

I circled the last week of November on my calendar, first in red, then green, then blue. There it was for me to see first thing when I opened my eyes in the mornings: the week I would really begin to feel like an adult.

It was a good thing I'd agreed to be on my best behavior because Dad dropped a bombshell the following night. This time he made sure that I was in on the original conversation:

"I got a call today from Frank Kroger," he said, "the manager at the construction company. He's made a new offer, so I want both of you in on the decision."

I looked up from my shrimp stir-fry. "About remodeling the house?"

"Yes. As you know, we were planning to start right after New Year's, but one of their contracts fell through and they've got a crew with time on its hands. Frank said they'll give us ten percent off the initial price if we can start now."

Sylvia put down her fork. "*Now?* Before the holidays? Like . . . ?"

"Tomorrow or the next day," said Dad.

Sylvia gasped. "But . . . we're not ready!"

"They'll be tearing down the back of the house with us in it?" I cried.

"No, they'll leave the back walls intact as long as they can," Dad explained, and added, laughing, "You won't have to undress in front of the neighbors or anything."

"What would we have to do to get ready?" asked Sylvia.

"Keep out of the men's way, mostly, and put up with trucks coming in and out, bricks and lumber in the yard, a Porta-John out by the street, noise. . . . If you think it will be too disruptive over Thanksgiving and Christmas, we'll wait."

Sylvia sat thinking it over. "Ten percent's a pretty big savings, Ben," she said. "It could help us buy new furniture for the family room. But I hate the thought of all that mess at Christmas."

"I know," Dad said.

"We could go live in a hotel for a few months!" I said brightly.

"Great suggestion, Al. That would take care of the ten percent savings," Dad said.

"Well," Sylvia said finally. "We don't plan to have company here for the holidays, so why don't we go ahead with it? What do you think, Alice?"

"If they start now, when will they be done?" I asked.

"Probably February or March," said Dad.

"And it *would* be nice to have it all done before spring," said Sylvia.

To be honest, what I was really thinking about was how I would feel if Scott Lynch *did* invite me to the Snow Ball, and when he came to pick me up, he'd see that ours was the house with the blue

Porta-John in front. But I wanted to be mature and reasonable, and I *especially* wanted Dad to let me drive my friends in November, so I said, "I think it's a good idea to start early too. Let's do it now and get it over with."

The next day I came home from school to find stacks of lumber and a load of cement blocks in our side yard. The day after that a truck delivered the Porta-John. The third day a cement truck was making deep ruts in the yard as it backed up over the curb. Men were pushing a huge wheelbarrow back and forth, and there was constant hammering from the back of the house.

REMODELING BY ACE ARCHITECTS, read a sign.

"Welcome to the madhouse," I said to Les when he came by later to see what was going on.

"They're really going through with it, huh?" he said.

"Yep. The new addition will be a family room off the kitchen and a study off the dining room, with a powder room in between. And a screened-in porch off the family room. Upstairs it will be a master bedroom suite with a bath, two walk-in closets, and a laundry/linen closet."

"Wow!" said Les. "Now that I've moved out and you'll be going to college in a couple of years, they must be expecting a lot of grandchildren."

"Yeah," I said. "Get busy."

I walked to homeroom on Friday hugging my books to my chest. I hate dragging a backpack from class to class. I was thinking how utterly, completely, totally ordinary life was. Really. I was an ordinary girl with ordinary hair and ordinary clothes, making ordinary grades, and I wouldn't even have an ordinary home to remember after I left. It would be changed forever. I was trying to figure out how I felt about that.

On one level I didn't want it to change. I wanted the same old thing I loved to come back to. If anything was going to change for the better, let it be *me,* I thought. My life. My personality. My grades. My future. *Anything.* Let me be remembered as *anything* except Miss Goody Two-shoes—the nice, dull, sweet, obedient, ordinary, dry-as-dust Alice McKinley.

"Alice, Alice, Alice!" Amy Sheldon yelled at me from half a hallway down. "Do you know how many girls in our school have a name beginning with 'A'?"

I hate it when she yells to me like that. I shook my head.

"I don't either. I just thought maybe you knew," she said as she got closer. "But we're two of them. That's one way we're alike!"

I ducked through the doorway of my classroom, glad I didn't have any classes with Amy, and sat down in the middle row, third seat from the back, as always. Mr. Hertzel makes us sit in the same seats each morning to make taking attendance easier. He goes over the announcements, reminders—all the housekeeping details of our school life—and then we listen while the office plays the national anthem and we say the Pledge of Allegiance.

I was only half listening to Mr. Hertzel talk about what was and was not appropriate use of our lockers—decorating with balloons on birthdays was appropriate; painting our lockers was not—when Tony Osler suddenly walked into the room and stopped at the teacher's desk. He was wearing a dark blue pullover with his jeans, an orange-striped shirt collar sticking out the top. Surprisingly cute.

Mr. Hertzel stopped talking and turned to look at Tony.

"Could I speak to Alice McKinley for a moment?" Tony asked, bold as brass.

I stared. *Wha . . . ?*

Mr. Hertzel frowned. "This can't wait till after the bell?"

"Not really," said Tony.

I thought maybe I was supposed to get up and go out in the hall, but Hertzel gave a disgruntled nod and Tony came right down the row, stepping over backpacks, till he got to my desk.

"Alice," he said, leaning down and lowering his voice a little. "Would you go to the Snow Ball with me?"

My God! I couldn't believe it! A senior walking into a junior's homeroom and asking *me* to the Snow Ball, in front of everyone! A junior who still wore braces! I was dumbfounded! Amazed! Excited! Thrilled!

"Okay," I said, my face heating up.

He smiled at me, turned around, and stepping over the backpacks on the floor again while everyone grinned and looked at me, he left the room.

A couple of kids clapped, and even Mr. Hertzel smiled a little.

Karen is in my homeroom, and she looked the most astonished. When our eyes met briefly, however, she quickly looked bored, but I knew that I wouldn't have to tell a single person who I was going to the Snow Ball with. By noon everyone would have heard the news: Miss Goody Two-shoes was going to the Snow Ball with a senior who was definitely *not* an imitation of Patrick Long or Sam Mayer. He wasn't like Scott Lynch, either, I realized with a pang, and now that I'd committed myself to go with Tony, I couldn't go with Scott even if he asked.

You only live once, I told myself. And I knew Pamela or Gwen would say, *You go, girl!*

"Is it true?" Pamela asked when she saw me in the cafeteria. "Karen said Tony walked in the room, interrupting the teacher, and asked you to the dance in front of everybody!"

I smiled happily as we walked our trays to a table. "That's the way he did it."

"You're really going with *Tony*?" Liz exclaimed. "Gosh, Alice!"

"*What?*" I said.

She grimaced a little. "Isn't he sort of . . . you know . . . fast?"

"I don't know. I guess I'll find out," I said flippantly.

"Wow!" said Pamela.

Gwen just gave me a benign smile and went on eating her salad. "Every so often a girl has to go a little wild," she said.

"You *approve*?" asked Liz.

"She didn't ask *me*," said Gwen. "What do I know?"

Strange how that incident in homeroom made a difference, though. I felt more attractive. Older. More sophisticated. It was just so weird, the way Tony interrupted the class. Just took over. Whatever I thought of Tony Osler before, I was as excited as anything now. He always had been sort of flirty with me. Curious about me, maybe.

I saw him in the hall on the way to Spanish that afternoon. He playfully grabbed my arm and pulled me close to him.

"Didn't embarrass you, did I?" he asked.

I laughed. "Not really. I think you shook up Hertzel, though."

"Just wanted to get my bid in before you were asked by someone else," he said. "See you." And he was off.

I wondered what that meant. Had he heard that someone else was interested? Somebody else might ask? I felt a little sick to my stomach. What if that someone was Scott?

But by the end of the day I learned that Scott Lynch was taking a girl from Holton-Arms, the exclusive girls' school in Bethesda. It would undoubtedly be someone who wasn't stupid enough to tell the world she wanted to be a bubble dancer, blowing her one good chance to let guys know she had given her future some thought. I told myself I didn't care. If private school girls were Scott's taste, then I'd never make the grade. And besides, I insisted, Tony would be more fun.

Dad was watching the news that evening when I told him.

"I got asked to the Snow Ball today," I said, curling up on the end of the couch. Dad says that as soon as we build the family room, the TV goes in there.

"Oh?" he said, then listened to the commentator another fifteen seconds and switched the set to mute when a commercial came on. "Who you going with? Patrick?"

"Patrick!" I stared. Was Dad living in a time warp or what? "Dad, I haven't gone out with Patrick for the last two years!"

"I knew that," said Dad, grinning. "But since you're not going out with Sam any longer, I figured maybe Patrick was back in the picture."

"No," I said. "I'm going with a senior. Tony Osler."

"A senior, huh?" Now I had his full attention. "He the same fellow who drove you to that Halloween party last year?"

"Yes. He drove a bunch of us. It wasn't a date or anything."

"How well do you know this Osler boy?" he asked, and kept the mute on even though the commentator was back again.

"Well, this is my third year on *The Edge*, and he's been on the staff the whole time. I guess you could say I know him pretty well."

"Safe driver?" asked Dad.

"We've had this conversation before," I reminded him.

"Anyone else going with you?"

"I don't know yet. We'll probably double with somebody," I said.

"Well, make sure to get all the details. If I know where you'll be all evening, I won't volunteer for parent chaperone," he said, and laughed when he saw the horrified look on my face. "Don't worry. Just like to shake you up a little."

I decided to be the very best daughter I could—until the end of the month, anyway, when I'd have earned the privilege of having friends in the car with me. I took a load of laundry from the dryer and carried it upstairs to iron the collars of some of my shirts. I'm not fond of the "slept-in" look, where the front edges of a shirt are curled and wrinkled.

We leave the ironing board up in Lester's old room, so I called downstairs, "Sylvia, I'm going to touch up a few things. Anything you want ironed?"

"Oh, *would* you, Alice?" she called back. "There are two shirts of Ben's hanging on a closet doorknob and a blouse of mine on a chair. Those and a few of Ben's handkerchiefs. That would be great."

We couldn't see out the back windows of Dad and Sylvia's bedroom anymore because the workmen had stretched a heavy sheet of plastic on the other side of that wall to seal out noise and dust until it was time to take the wall itself down.

Dad and Sylvia really did need more space, I realized. There were two big closets in their bedroom, but one had shelves instead of clothes racks, and we used it to store extra blankets and pillows. Suitcases took up the lower half. The other closet was crammed with Dad's clothes on one side, Sylvia's on the other. I could smell the scent of Sylvia's perfume as I pressed her blouse and put it back in the closet. I wondered what kind of clothes my mom had worn. Whether she would have had so many nice things—the silky dresses, the sling-back pumps, the beautiful sweaters with the gorgeous colored yarns. Les said she usually wore slacks. Was Sylvia sexier? Would Dad remember my mother's scent?

Then I remembered our visit to Grandpa McKinley just before he died—how he mistook me for Mom. "Marie," he kept calling me, and I was glad, for him, to be her.

Well, I told myself as I ironed the clean handkerchiefs, *I'm not her, and I can't be her, and I can't be a replica of Sylvia, either. All I can be is me, whoever that is.*

When I took my own shirts back to my room, I found Annabelle asleep on my bed.

"Don't get too comfortable," I told her. "When their new bedroom is finished, off you go."

6

Speaking of Animals . . .

I was taking Speech as my elective, and was almost as nervous about that as I was about geometry. The problem was that Gwen helps me whenever I don't understand something in Geometry, but no one can take your place in speech. You're so alone up there. At least in geometry, when you have to go up to the board to prove a theorem, all you need to do is get it right. But if you have to memorize Edna St. Vincent Millay's "The Dragonfly" and recite it in front of the class, you not only have to get the words right, you have to think about expression and volume and voice quality and the fact that your armpits are wet and your knees are knocking.

I knew I needed it, though. If my career was going to involve people, it was important to know how to speak distinctly and be comfortable in front of groups. But Mrs. Cary took off two points for each "I mean" or "Y'know" or "like" and it's hard not to include those when you're talking extemporaneously.

In the ten weeks since the semester began, we'd recited poetry so that every word was articulated; we'd memorized lines from a play and presented them with great drama. We'd described the workings of a machine; given instructions for making pizza; and practiced introductions. But last Friday, Mrs. Cary had given us a new assignment:

"Choose a controversial subject, something you feel strongly about, and give a three-minute talk defending your position," she said. "Don't memorize it and don't use notes. You'll be graded primarily on your passion and your persuasiveness—how successful you are in getting us to agree with, or at least understand, your point of view."

I was thinking about that as I walked to second period on Monday morning. I felt strongly about injustice and prejudice and torture and rape and animal cruelty, but these weren't exactly controversial issues, Annabelle notwithstanding. I was pretty strongly against hunting and trapping. But someone could argue that if I wore a suede jacket or leather shoes or a fur-trimmed cap, my heart wasn't really in it.

Then I remembered an article I'd read about a woman who worked in a medical research lab, but she was really a spy for an organization that watches for cruel treatment of laboratory animals and then publicizes it. I still remembered the photo of the cat that was trying to walk again after they'd broken its spinal cord.

When I took my seat in World History, Patrick said, "Ah! The girl with the furrowed brow."

"Yeah," I said. "I'm trying to think of a controversial subject to present in speech class."

"Socialized medicine, the Palestinian cause, capital punishment, statehood for Puerto Rico . . . ," said Patrick.

I looked at him long and hard. "You know what?" I said. "Your brain is so full of stuff from your accelerated program that it's just spilling over."

He laughed. "Is that a problem?"

I wondered if he was still seeing Marcie, the girl he'd taken to the Jack of Hearts dance last February. "Don't you ever think of anything *fun*?" I asked.

"All the time," he said. "Whenever I can squeeze it in."

"Yeah? I didn't see you at the Homecoming Dance. Are you going to the Snow Ball?" I asked.

"No."

"See what I mean? Why not?"

"Because I'm visiting colleges that weekend. A friend invited me to Bennington," said Patrick.

I wanted to ask whether the friend was male or

female, but this was undoubtedly to check out schools, knowing Patrick.

"You going to the dance?" he asked.

"Yes."

"Oh? Who with?" he wanted to know.

"A guy from *The Edge*."

"Sam?"

"No," I said. "A senior. Tony Osler."

Patrick blinked. "Tony? You're going with *him*?"

"What part of 'Tony Osler' don't you understand?" I joked.

"All of him," said Patrick.

"Why? What do you mean?"

"I don't know. He just doesn't seem your type, that's all," Patrick said.

The teacher was looking around now, checking his attendance book.

"So what *is* my type?" I asked. If he said *sweet* or *nice*, I was going to go out and get a tattoo.

"Hmmm," said Patrick. "I'll have to think about it."

All that said to me was that I was so unremarkable, so plain, so vague, so *vanilla*, that I couldn't even be typed. I reached for my history book and buried my face in the pages.

Neither Elizabeth nor Gwen got asked to the Snow Ball, strangely enough. Liz couldn't get up the nerve to ask a guy herself, so she wasn't going. Gwen said she didn't want to ask someone because she didn't want to buy another dress. I was sure I could get a date for Liz in a minute if she'd let me, but she hates that and made us promise we wouldn't. She can't stand the thought of somebody having to be prodded to ask her out.

Pamela, though, got asked by Tim Moss, a guy in her English class, and Tony had said they could go with us. He'd be driving his dad's Buick LeSabre for the night, not his little Toyota.

"So what are you going to wear?" Liz asked me. She didn't seem to mind talking about the dance, even though she wasn't going. But that's Liz. I don't think there's a jealous bone in her body.

"I don't know," I said. "I hate spending money on a dress I'll probably only wear once or twice. But my other dresses don't fit so well."

"What about Sylvia? Won't she help out?" Liz asked.

I shrugged. "I don't know. I just don't feel like asking her. I don't want to be . . . indebted to her, you know?"

"What are you talking about? She's your step-mom!" Liz said.

"I know. But we've got . . . issues," I said.

"Doesn't every mom and daughter? Listen, just

for kicks," Liz said, "let's go to that consignment shop that sells prom dresses."

"*Used* dresses, you mean?" I said.

"Yeah, but who cares? They're clean, and they look like new. If you don't like anything, we'll leave," she said.

We went after school on Tuesday without telling anyone. I'd made sure I had on my strapless bra and decent pants. A little bell tinkled as we entered the store.

A girl and her mom were the only customers present.

"May I help?" asked the clerk. "What size are you looking for?"

"About an eight," I guessed.

She led me to a rack against the wall. There were a dozen dresses in my size, their hems almost touching the floor. "Look through these, and tell me if you want to try anything on," she said, and went back to the counter.

Liz started sliding the hangers backward, pausing at every dress for my reaction.

"Too frilly," I said of a pink ruffled organza.

"Too severe," I said of a midnight blue dress with a collar.

It was easier to reject than to like a dress. We were down to the last three—a red dress with a back cut so low, I'd probably have to leave off my underwear; a gold sparkly dress that looked as though it had belonged to Barbie; and a slim black dress with a halter top and knee-high slits on both sides.

We lingered over the black one.

"It's simple," said Liz. "Non-fussy."

I looked at the price tag. "The price is right!" I said. "I like the top."

"Try it on," said Liz.

We dumped our backpacks in one corner of the open dressing room. There were no cubicles, no doors to close, just a couple of mirrors on the wall. I slipped out of my jeans and top and slid the black dress down over my head and arms.

"Oh! Wow!" said Liz, starting to smile. "Don't look yet." She zipped up the back, then tugged a little on each side around my hips. "Now stand on your tiptoes. Pretend you're in heels," she said.

I turned toward the mirror. There stood a sexy-looking girl with strawberry blond, shoulder-length hair in a black halter-top dress that hugged her hips. I moved one leg to the side, and the slit opened up.

"Sex-y!" Liz said, grinning.

"Slink-y!" I said, turning slowly around.

"You'll need to wear heels and hold your tummy in, but it looks great on you," Liz said.

There did seem to be a slight bulge in front, but

a pair of Spandex panties should take care of that, I decided. I had the typical little bulges of fat on my outer thighs just below the panty line—not a lot. Just enough to show I'm female.

"Buy it," said Liz.

And I did.

Most of the research I did on using animals for experimentation came off the Internet, but it was enough to make me sick. Some of the material was accompanied by photographs, and some pieces were on video.

The day I was to give my three-minute talk, I felt queasy at breakfast and wondered if I was coming down with the flu. I realized finally that having to tell the class about the horrible things I'd been reading made the stories that much worse.

Four of us gave our talks that morning. Brian Brewster argued for lowering the drinking age to eighteen. If you're old enough to marry, to be a father, and to be sent to war, he said, then you ought to be able to have a beer now and then.

Another guy argued against capital punishment and talked about the number of people who had been put to death for crimes they hadn't committed.

A girl, believe it or not, actually got up in front of the class and gave her three-minute talk on why girls should remain virgins until they're married.

A lot of kids clapped for Brian. Maybe half the class clapped for abolishing the death penalty. Nobody clapped for the girl. Then it was my turn.

I hoped I would get through my talk without breaking into tears, because my voice was trembly. I began by saying that animals were not put on this earth for us to use in experiments, especially those in which they suffer a lot of pain. I described the dog used in a military experiment to test the effects of nerve gas, as though scientists didn't already know. As the vapor rose, the dog began licking his lips and salivating, then he lost the use of his hind legs and lay down, whining, moaning. Then he began to drool, and he died.

A couple of girls covered their faces.

Live rats, I told the class, were immersed in boiling water for ten seconds, then infected on the burned parts of their bodies. Others were shaved, covered with ethanol, and "flamed" for ten seconds.

I described the nine rhesus monkeys strapped in chairs, vomiting and salivating from total-body irradiation. The goats suspended from slings and shot with high-powered weapons for military surgical practice. The baboons who suffered artificially induced strokes by removing their left eyeballs to reach in and clamp a critical blood vessel to their brains.

"And for what?" I asked, and ended with, "Some primates eventually go insane from terror and isolation. A few university laboratories have been reduced to animal torture chambers. Since animals can't tell us of their excruciating pain, we have to speak for them and abolish once and for all the use of animals in medical and military experiments."

I sat down and found myself swallowing and swallowing to keep from crying as a lot of kids clapped for me. Why does hearing your own voice crack make you feel even more emotional? Why does the sight of even one girl with tears in her eyes make tears well up in your own?

It wasn't the way I'd wanted to present my argument. I'd wanted to come across as professional, concerned, knowledgeable, articulate, and very much in control. Instead, I felt my legs shaking and I had to pee.

"All right," said Mrs. Cary. "Comments, anyone? How would you rate her delivery?"

"It was very passionate," said a girl.

"Too emotional," said a boy. "I found it distracting."

"Sometimes I missed a word because it sounded like she was trying to speak and swallow at the same time," said another girl.

"Too over-the-top," said Brian. "Like violins

should have been playing in the background. She gave only the worst examples."

"Yeah, but if those things really *are* happening, why *not* tell the worst?" said someone else.

The only thing that saved me from further dissection was the bell. We ran out of time, and Mrs. Cary gave me a B. All I could think of was how glad I was it was over.

Actually, we *were* going to have company for Thanksgiving. My cousin Carol from Chicago—Aunt Sally and Uncle Milt's grown daughter—was coming to Washington with the "nice young man" Aunt Sally had told us about, and they wanted to spend Thanksgiving with us.

Dad hung up the phone after talking with Uncle Milt and relayed the message to Sylvia and me as we worked at the dining room table. Sylvia was grading papers on one side, and I was doing my geometry on the other.

"It will sure be nice to see Carol again, won't it?" Dad said, smiling broadly.

Sylvia just stared at him. "They're coming for Thanksgiving *here*?" she cried. "Ben, the front yard's all torn up! It's so tracked and muddy, the workmen put down boards for us to walk on!"

Dad looked nonplussed. "But the inside of the house is still okay, isn't it?" And when Sylvia didn't answer, he said, "We'll just take them to a restaurant, then. We'll have Thanksgiving dinner out."

Sylvia sighed. "Oh, I don't want to do that. I can roast a turkey. It's just . . . things are such a mess. I was hoping we wouldn't have company here until after all the remodeling was done."

But I was excited. "Carol won't mind at all!" I said. "How long are they staying, Dad?"

"Well, I don't know exactly," Dad said. "Milt didn't tell me."

"But . . . are they staying *here,* with us, or in a hotel and just coming for dinner?" Sylvia asked.

Dad looked crestfallen. "I didn't get that straight, honey. Milt and I got talking about his heart medication, and all he said was that Carol and her boyfriend would be dropping by for Thanksgiving."

Sylvia put her face in her hands, but I was ecstatic. I couldn't wait to see Carol's "nice young man." I was betting he'd be *hot* hot!

"If they stay here, where am I supposed to put them, Ben?" Sylvia asked. "Do I put them in the same bedroom? Are they even engaged, did he say?"

Now we were getting down to the important stuff! I looked from Sylvia to Dad and from Dad to Sylvia.

"Beats me," said Dad. "I guess I should have asked more questions. All we can do is play it by ear."

"I'll help get ready for them!" I said quickly. "I'll put fresh sheets on Lester's bed and help with the pies and the vacuuming."

"We'll all help, Sylvia," Dad told her. "Carol is family. She'll just have to take us as she finds us."

"You're right," Sylvia said. "Just let me concentrate on the rest of these papers, and when tomorrow's over, I'll put my mind on Thanksgiving."

I guess since they weren't *her* relatives—not blood relatives, I mean—she couldn't be expected to go nuts over them. But she could have shown a *little* more enthusiasm.

We got a call from Aunt Sally the day before Thanksgiving. I had just put a pecan pie in the oven, and Sylvia was making the pumpkin.

"Now, I know you're busy," Aunt Sally said to me, "but I wanted to wish you and your family a happy Thanksgiving and say that I hope Carol and Lawrence won't be too much trouble for you."

Lawrence? Carol was dating a Lawrence? I think Lester and I had watched an old movie once, *Lawrence of Arabia*.

"What kind of trouble would they make?" I asked. "We're excited to see them."

"Well, I think we're all a little nervous when we meet someone for the first time," she said.

"Why? Is Lawrence an ex-con or something?" I joked.

"Mercy, no! He's a very nice man, Alice, and I want to get to know him better myself. I don't know how serious they are, but I think they've been seeing each other a lot."

"So what do you want me to find out for you?" I said, knowing exactly why she'd called.

"Why, nothing, dear!" she said.

"Not even how old he is?"

"Well, I'm guessing around thirty, but I could be wrong," said Aunt Sally.

"Should we ask what kind of work he does?" I questioned.

"He's in business, that's all I know."

"Should I ask how much money he makes?"

"Gracious, Alice! That would be rude! Of course, if they ever marry, we'd hope he could support a wife and children," Aunt Sally said.

"What about his family?" I asked.

"I don't know if he has any brothers or sisters, but it might be nice to find that out too," Aunt Sally said, getting enthusiastic.

"Do you want me to ask Carol if they're being 'intimate'?" I tried not to laugh.

Aunt Sally gave a little gasp, and I knew she was probably getting pink around the neck and ears. "Now, Alice, you just stop!" she said. "My goodness, I would never ask anything like that."

"Well, if I find out anything good, I'll let you know," I said.

"Have a nice Thanksgiving, dear," she told me.

"And hugs to Uncle Milt," I added.

Lester came over early on Thanksgiving to bring in wood for the fireplace.

"What do you know about this Lawrence guy?" he asked me as we crumpled newspaper to put under the logs.

"Not much," I said. "Uncle Milt said he's here for a convention or something and that Carol decided to come along."

"That's not much help," said Lester.

"Well, *I'll* bet he's tall and dark with a thin mustache above his lip and that he rides horseback through the desert in the moonlight," I said. "Lawrence of Arabia!"

"*I* think he's five foot two and wears a bow tie," said Les.

The bell rang, and we all turned toward the front door.

7

Lawrence of Arabia

He was big, he was blond, and he was built like a boxcar—not at all what I'd imagined. His head, his jaw, his hands, his entire body were square, and he had shoulders like the frame of a rowboat. I think I saw Les wince a little when Lawrence shook his hand.

"We're so glad to have you!" Dad said, hugging Carol, and then Carol hugged me.

"I've wanted Larry to meet you for the longest time!" she said.

So not even his name would be "of Arabia," it seemed. Larry it was.

Unless they'd left their bags in the car, I guessed they weren't planning to stay overnight. And after all that scrubbing I'd done in the bathroom too!

"So this is Lester!" Larry said. "And this must be the inimitable Alice?"

"Inevitably," said Lester, and everyone laughed.

I wanted in the worst way to sneak off and look up *inimitable* in the dictionary, but I decided to treat it as a compliment and returned the smile.

Dad took their coats, and Sylvia ushered them into the living room. "I thought we'd start with a glass of something in front of the fire," Sylvia said. "I've got some sherry and some sparkling cider. Which shall it be?"

I immediately set to work filling glasses as Carol and Larry sat down on the couch across from Les. I figured that if Larry didn't ride horseback across a desert in the moonlight, then he must play fullback for the Minnesota Vikings, but he didn't.

"I'm in the hospitality business," he told Dad in answer to a question. "Working my way up the ladder in hotel management."

"Now, that's an interesting business," Lester said.

"And practical," Dad added. "There will always be a need for hotels."

I noticed the tender way Larry brushed back a lock of hair from Carol's cheek. The way her hand sought his on the couch between them. I think Dad noticed it too, because he just beamed like a proud uncle. We all liked Carol and wanted life to go well for her.

"What on earth are you guys building out there, anyway, a swimming pool?" Carol asked. "When we walked up your board sidewalk, Larry said, 'Are you sure this is the place?'"

We laughed.

"Isn't it a mess?" said Sylvia. "But it'll be worth it once we're done." And she went on to describe what it would be like—the study, the family room, the master bedroom suite. . . .

"But they forgot one thing," said Les.

Sylvia turned. "Really? What?"

"Hot tub and sauna," he said, and grinned.

We gathered at the table in anticipation of the beautiful turkey Dad carried in from the kitchen. He began to carve while the sweet potatoes and cranberry sauce made the rounds. There's nothing that makes you feel more like family than to sit at a big table passing the food from one person to the next.

After dessert Dad got out some old photo albums with childhood pictures of Carol in them, including one of eight-year-old Carol, her girlish arms impulsively hugging a startled Lester, five, who was standing straight as a mop handle, arms at his sides, his face turned toward the camera with a "what-do-I-do-now?" look. We howled.

"The opportunity of a lifetime." Lester grinned and shook his head. "Gone forever."

Larry told us about growing up in Red Wing, Minnesota, and going ice fishing with his father when the Mississippi froze over. And he and Dad discovered they'd both attended Northwestern University.

I wanted Carol and Larry to stay all weekend. I wanted to hear that maybe Larry was going to be transferred to Washington to run a hotel here and that they were marrying in the spring. Finally Dad said, "You're staying with us, aren't you, while you're in town?"

"Oh, no. We're staying at the Capital Hilton," Carol said, to my disappointment.

But then she looked at me, pursed her lips, and said, "You know, Larry has an early-morning session tomorrow, and he'll be in meetings all day. Why don't I stay here tonight so Alice and I can chat some more? Then I'll take the Metro in tomorrow and be there in time for the business dinner."

"*Would* you?" I cried. "Bunk with me, like old times!"

I saw Larry squeeze her shoulder. "Well . . . I'll miss you . . . but I think I can manage to live without you for one night."

"Great!" Carol said. "I'll just need to borrow some pajamas."

"I might even have an old pair around here somewhere," said Lester.

"She'll sleep in a pair of mine, Les," Sylvia

scolded. "We'll get you whatever you need, Carol."

After we said good-bye to Larry, Carol went out on the porch for a private good night, and then we all gathered in the kitchen to do the dishes and clean up the place.

"Ah!" Carol said when we were finally done and had trooped into the living room to enjoy the fire. "Bring on the marshmallows and the fluffy slippers!"

We had no room in our stomachs for toasted marshmallows, but shoes came off, and Les and Carol and I sat down on the rug. In fact, Carol lay down, a sofa pillow under her head and her toes pointed toward the fire.

"Still working for that nursing association?" Dad asked Carol.

"Yes. I'm the assistant director now."

"Hey, nice! Congrats!" said Lester.

"It only pays half of what Larry's earning, and I'd have to give it up if we ever leave Chicago," she said, "but I enjoy the work."

"Are you still in the same apartment?" Les asked her.

Carol winced slightly. "Not anymore. I moved in with Larry the day before yesterday, and Mom doesn't know. I'm still trying to think of a way to tell her."

"Well, the first time she calls your apartment

and the phone's been disconnected, that should do it," Les said.

"I've just told her my phone's not working," Carol confessed.

"Your mom's a big girl now, Carol," Dad told her. "She can handle it."

"Well, maybe. I'm just worried about how she'll react between the time I tell her and the time she decides to accept it."

Around ten o'clock Dad and Sylvia said good night and went upstairs. Carol sat up and hugged her knees, watching the fire. "What about you, Les?" she asked. "How's *your* love life?"

He told her about Tracy and how that had turned out.

"Gosh, I'm sorry," Carol said. "It's only a matter of time, though, till the right girl comes along."

"How do people know that?" I asked. "How can anyone say for sure that you'll find someone to marry?"

"Statistical probability," said Carol. "And the fact that there are a lot of 'rights' out there. It's not as though there's only one person in the whole world for you to marry."

That was comforting somehow. I think girls sort of grow up with that "Some Day My Prince Will Come" attitude, as though there's one guy out there searching for you, and you worry whether or not he'll ever find you.

At eleven I told Carol I'd go up and use the bathroom first, then get in bed.

"I'll be up pretty soon," she said.

I washed, brushed my teeth, and put on my pajamas. I figured it would be midnight before she and Les said good night, but twenty minutes later I heard Lester's car drive away, and here Carol came, wearing the pair of pajamas that Sylvia had left in the bathroom for her.

"I think I've got a new toothbrush around somewhere that you could use," I told her.

"I don't need it. I keep a fold-up kind in my purse," she said, and crawled in beside me. The only light in the room came from the streetlight.

"So . . . ," I said, turning over on my side and getting ready for a long chat. "How did you and Larry meet? Was it romantic?"

Carol laughed. "Not very. I was at this nursing convention in Boston. I'd been out for a drink with two of my girlfriends after a long day of training sessions, and I went back to my room in the hotel about midnight. I'd only been in the room once, when I'd signed in and taken my bags up, and I couldn't remember the number. So I got out the 'welcome slip' to see what the number was. The clerk had written it down, but I mistook a nine for a seven. And there I was, at half past midnight, trying to open the door of Room 607 instead of 609."

"How embarrassing!" I said.

"I'm turning the handle and pushing and trying to put the card in upside down and everything else I could think of. And finally, down the hall, the elevator door opens and this man starts toward me. I was terrified. I mean, here I am out in the hall all by myself in the early morning, and I can see he's heading straight for me."

"What did you do?"

"I stepped over to the fire alarm box on the wall and put my hand on the lever. When he gets about twenty feet away, I say, 'If you come any closer, I'll pull it, and I'm not kidding.' And he says, 'Miss, believe me, I'm here to help you,' and just then the door to 607 opens, and a man in his shorts and T-shirt says, 'What the hell do you think you're doing?'"

"Which one was Lawrence?" I asked eagerly.

"The man in the hall, the one in the suit. The guy in the room had called the desk and said someone was trying to break in. Larry was manager-in-training that weekend, so they sent him up to see what was going on."

We both laughed. "Oh, Carol, I can just *see* you!" I said.

"The guy in the shorts says to Larry, 'Stop her

before she wakes the whole floor,' and Larry says, 'Miss, I think you have the wrong room. Could I see your card, please? I'm the manager.'"

"And then what?" I asked.

"He opens the door to Room 609 and tells me if I just calm down, he'll treat me to dinner the following night. I was embarrassed right down to the bone!"

"And did you go to dinner?" I wanted to know.

"No. I had other plans and told him I'd be going back to Chicago the day after. He said, 'Well, I'll be working in Chicago after I finish here in Boston, so why don't you give me your phone number and we'll do it another time?' And we did. About four months later I get a call from a Lawrence Swenson, and after that we started going out. And fell in love."

I sighed dramatically. "I hope I'm that lucky someday."

"Well, I can think of easier ways to meet someone, but it's a story we laugh about now," said Carol.

We were quiet for a moment or two. Then I asked, "So why'd you move in together? Why don't you just get married?"

"Because I want to be sure," said Carol. "I had one bad marriage, and I don't want another. I keep reminding myself that I thought I was in love then, too, so I want to make sure I'm not deluding myself a second time."

I thought about that. "Some people live together for seven or eight years and *still* don't know if they're ready to marry," I said.

"I think if you have to question yourself that long, you're *not* ready," she said. "Larry would get married tomorrow if I gave the word. But I want to wait a few more months to be certain. I wouldn't hurt that man for the world."

She had been lying on her back all this time, and now *she* turned over and faced me. "So...what's new with you? Are you going out with anyone special?"

"Not really," I told her. "But I've got a date for the Snow Ball—a guy named Tony."

"Yeah? Nice?"

"Well . . . yeah. I guess," I said.

"You guess? Is he hot? Is that the attraction?" asked Carol.

I grinned. "Yeah, pretty hot. And he's a senior."

"Aha! Has your dad met him?"

"Yeah."

"And?"

"Dad's not too crazy about him, but I had a long talk with Tony last year. He's a different person when he talks about himself and his feelings and everything," I said. "He just seemed to need someone to really open up with."

"Hmmm," said Carol. "Hot and needy, huh? That's a lethal combination."

"Why?"

"Oh, he makes you think you're the only one who understands him. And then he's in your arms, and you're stroking his forehead, and one thing leads to another. . . ."

I laughed nervously. "We're just sort of friends. Nothing like that. We're on the newspaper staff together."

"Uh-huh . . ."

"I had no idea he was going to ask me. He just walked into homeroom one morning and asked to speak to me. And in front of everyone, he asks if I'd go to the dance with him."

"Wow!"

"Yeah. I was like, 'Omigod, and he's a senior!'" I said.

"Uh-huh . . ."

"That was pretty exciting."

"Sounds a little like me and my sailor," Carol said. "I was sitting in this deli near campus, and I could see this sailor at another table, looking at me. My girlfriends had left before I did—I was studying for a test—and he came over and asked if he could sit down."

"Were you thrilled?"

"Sure. You know—a man in uniform, all that stuff.

We talked awhile—he was stationed in Chicago—and he asked if I wanted to go for a walk. There was a little park nearby. I was through with classes for the day, so I said sure. I mean, what can happen to you out on the sidewalk on a warm March day? We got along real well and started going out. He was wild and crazy and made me laugh. It was so much more fun than sitting in class, studying for tests, that four weeks later, when he was on leave, we eloped. I left the university, and we got married and went to Mexico for a honeymoon. I sent Mom and Dad a postcard, letting them know. And I never realized how deeply that hurt them till I was older."

"They didn't like him?"

"They didn't even know him. Had never met him. I'm their only child, and I didn't even include them in the wedding."

"Oh, man. And then?"

"After a year or so, he was still wild and crazy, but I didn't laugh about it anymore. I found out he was seeing other women, and after the divorce it took me a long time to get my confidence back. I started going to night school, taking business courses, and eventually got my degree and a job as secretary for this nursing association. And . . . I've been there ever since."

"And now you're the assistant director! Yay for you, Carol!" I said.

She rolled over on her back again and pulled the covers up under her chin. "Yeah, I have to tell myself that now and then when things are rough. 'If you survived that marriage and that divorce, you can survive anything,' I say. Looking back, I think, 'Was that really me?' A girl who would leave college and marry a guy she'd only known for four weeks?"

"It must have been, because you did it," I said.

"One part of me, anyway," said Carol. "It's like I didn't even know the rest of me—the other part. Had to find that out the hard way."

"Well, I hope you and Larry will be very happy and you'll love living together and you'll get married and you'll never be sorry," I said.

"And I hope you have a great time at the dance and that all your hotshot fella does is talk," she said.

"Well, I hope he does a *little* more than that," I told her.

8

The Quarrel

It was as though the last week of November, circled on my calendar, was a blinking neon light. My eye fell on it as soon as I entered my bedroom. It was like "the first week of the rest of my life." I could drive the car with friends in it and go wherever I wanted. Well, almost. Around the area, I mean. And, of course, the Snow Ball was Friday night.

Just as he'd promised, Dad let me have the car that Monday, and I drove Liz to school, but I could hardly wait for a "Girls' Night Out."

"Where shall we go?" I asked the others in the cafeteria.

"Did we decide on a night?" asked Liz.

"Yolanda wants to be in on it too," said Gwen, referring to her friend from another school who hangs out with us now and then.

"Great," I said. "I can fit three in the backseat."

"I heard about this student hangout in

Georgetown where they card you but put a bracelet on you if you're under twenty-one. You can sit at the tables like everyone else, but they won't serve you alcohol. Great band," Pamela told us.

"Yeah, that's Edgar's!" said Gwen. "My brothers love that place."

"Let's do it!" said Liz.

"There's a cover charge, though," Pamela told us. "Let me get the details, and then we'll decide."

"And dress like college girls!" said Liz. "I know just what I want to wear."

"*Hot* college girls!" Gwen corrected. "College girls out on the town!"

I felt as though everything about me was different—my walk, my talk, my voice, my face, my hair. . . . Little by little I was getting inducted into adult life, and it felt very, very good.

On Tuesday, Liz's mom drove us to school, and as soon as we got inside, Pamela came racing down the hall toward us.

"Did you check your e-mail last night?" she asked me.

"No, I went to bed early. Why?"

"We're on for tonight!" she said. "Can you do it? There's no cover charge on Tuesdays, and some guys from St. John's are going to be there!"

"I think I can do it!" I said. "Liz?"

"Probably, if we're not out too late," she said.

"We can go early and eat there," Pamela told us. "They've got sandwiches and stuff."

We asked Gwen at lunchtime, and she said she could make it. Everything seemed to be falling into place, like the gods had prepared the way.

"Tonight it is," I said, and we set a time when I would pick each girl up. We'd split the parking fee in Georgetown.

All day I mentally tried on jeans and tops and belts and shoes. I felt like I could scarcely wait to get to college. To be a college student. It was so completely satisfying to be the driver for Girls' Night Out—driving around, picking everyone up, tooting the horn in the driveway, my high-heeled shoe on the brake pedal. Dangly jangly earrings, I decided. Earrings and heels—and the tightest jeans I owned, most definitely.

Sylvia wasn't home yet when I got in the house. I took my books up to my room and worked on geometry so I wouldn't have to do it later. Did a work sheet for history, started reading *I Know Why the Caged Bird Sings* for English, but I was too excited to concentrate. I decided I'd rather drive Dad's car. Sylvia's was nicer, but Dad's was smaller and a little easier to handle, and I'd be driving into D.C.

Every so often my computer would ding, and I'd check the e-mail.

Heels? asked Gwen. *Yo says stilettos.*

Whatever uv got, I replied

See if you can stay out til midnight, Alice, Pamela wrote, *in case we want 2 do sumthing with the guys after.*

Fat chance, I thought.

At five I showered and put on fresh makeup, my best jeans, and a silk shirt. Everything but my heels. When I heard Sylvia in the kitchen, I padded downstairs barefoot.

She had rolled up the sleeves of her blouse and was rinsing off spinach leaves at the sink.

"Well!" she said. "You sure look spiffy!"

I smiled. "Where's Dad?"

"He's in Baltimore at a conference," she said.

"Baltimore?" I asked. "When will he be home?"

"Around ten, I suppose. Why?"

"Oh no!" I cried. "I wanted to use his car. Sylvia, can I drive yours tonight?"

She glanced over at me, hands on the colander. "Why, no, Alice! I'm going to a teacher's retirement dinner."

"Tonight?" I wailed. "Oh, Sylvia, I promised my friends! We're having Girls' Night Out, and we heard about this fabulous place in Georgetown, and there's no cover charge on Tuesdays!"

"Well, this is the first I've heard about it," she said, giving the colander another shake and setting it down on the counter.

"It's the last week of November, remember? I've been waiting all this time to have friends in the car with me, and there's no cover charge on Tuesdays, and some guys from St. John's are going to meet us there. . . ."

"One of the other girls will have to drive, I'm afraid, because I've got to have my car," Sylvia said. "I'm sorry."

I was desperate. "But can't you go with someone else or take a taxi? Just this one night?"

Sylvia turned and faced me, glancing quickly at the clock, and I could see she was in no mood to argue. "No, I can't. I'm taking Beth, and she's recovering from back surgery. I've got my car seat adjusted especially for her, pillows and everything. You'll just have to go with someone else."

"But there are medical taxis!" I said. "You know, for handicapped people. You could call one of those and—"

"Alice, I am not putting Beth in a taxi. I told her I'd pick her up, and I'm taking my car," Sylvia said firmly.

Tears welled up in my eyes. "How can this be happening?" I cried. "You and Dad both knew I've been looking forward to this week for a long time! For months! I even have it circled on my calendar!"

"If you reserved our cars for the entire week,

nobody told us," said Sylvia, moving past me to get something from the refrigerator. She sounded impatient and irritated, but not half as angry as I was.

I wouldn't give up. "It just seems like it would be easier for you and Beth to go with someone else than for me and four of my friends to completely rearrange our plans," I said, selfish as it sounded.

And it certainly sounded that way to Sylvia, because she snapped, "Well, it's not! And if I were you, Alice, I'd quit the arguing and start calling my friends to see what else we could work out."

I already knew the answer to that. I stormed out of the kitchen and on upstairs and grabbed my cell phone. There was no point in calling Liz because she only has her learner's permit. I called Pamela's number.

"You're *kidding*!" she cried. "*No*, I can't get the car! Even if Dad was home, he wouldn't let me drive to D.C., and anyway, he's out with Meredith. Alice, you've *got* to make her let you. She *owes* you one, remember?"

I called Gwen.

"No deal," she said. "Dad's out shopping at Best Buy, and Jerome's the only brother here. He's got a sports car, seats two. We'd still need a second car."

"What are we going to do?" I asked, holding back tears. "Yolanda? Can she drive?"

"Don't even think it. She's having a huge fight with her folks. I think we'd just better pack it in, Alice. We'll do it another time."

"But I'm all dressed! I did my nails and everything! Even my toenails!" I wailed.

"So did I. Bummer."

"There's *got* to be a way!" I said. "I'll call Lester."

"Good luck," said Gwen.

I called, but he wasn't home. George, one of his roommates, answered and said that both Les and Paul, the other roommate, were out for the evening. I was almost too angry to cry.

Sylvia appeared in the doorway of my room. "Alice, I've left a shrimp and spinach salad in the fridge for your dinner," she said.

"I don't want it!" I said. And then, "It just seems to me, Sylvia, that since I caved on the subject of your cat, you could do this one favor for me! This is *huge* for me! Everyone's counting on it."

"If you let me know something in advance, sure," said Sylvia. "But not tonight, and I'm sick of arguing about it." She turned and started down the hall.

I felt the blood rushing to my face, anger almost choking me. "And I'm sick of you!" I said, leaping up to slam my door, and I found myself stepping in something warm and mushy. I looked down to see that Annabelle had been in my room and had thrown up on my rug, right next to my high-heeled shoes. *On* one of the shoes! And Beth, the woman who was ruining our plans for this evening, was the one who had given her to us.

I went ballistic. I yanked open the door and screamed, "And take your cat with you! She puked all over my shoes! I never wanted her here, and you know it!"

Sylvia turned around and stood looking at me. It wasn't the calm, beautiful face of the teacher I'd loved back in seventh grade. In fact, there was a flash of anger I hadn't seen before.

"You don't have to scream to make a point," she said, carefully enunciating each word.

"Well, nothing else works!" I cried. "Everything is *your* way ever since you moved in here. The cat, the cooking, the remodeling—*every*thing! If you think *I'm* unreasonable, you've forgotten what it's like to be sixteen and have four other girls depending on you."

"Then perhaps sixteen is too young to have any empathy for a woman in pain from back surgery who's going to be driven as carefully and gently as I can manage, to a teacher's retirement dinner that she has been looking forward to for a long time," said Sylvia icily.

"I *do* have empathy, but you could go in a taxi

for the handicapped, and you know it. All you have to do is call one!" I said.

"And if you and your friends want to hire a taxi to take you to Georgetown, all *you* have to do is call one," Sylvia said.

I lunged for the door, my toes still squishy with cat puke, and slammed it. Then I opened it and slammed it again as hard as I could. I heard plaster fall between the walls.

I sat down on the bed breathing hard and crying from both rage and shock at what I'd said. Sylvia knew that we could never afford a taxi to take us all the way to Georgetown. Half of me knew that I had behaved abominably, and the other half knew that this was long overdue, that always, *always*, whatever I wanted came last. I grabbed an old T-shirt beside my bed and wiped the cat puke off my toes. I wanted to take it out in the hall and shove it in Sylvia's face.

Liz called and said that Pamela had called her. "It's off, then?" she asked.

"I don't know, I guess so," I said as I heard Sylvia's car drive away. "I'm so angry, I can't even think."

"Well, maybe it's for the best," Liz said. "I've still got some homework to do." But I knew she was disappointed.

Gwen called and said that she and Yolanda were going to rent a video. Then Pamela called to see if

Sylvia had changed her mind. I told her what had happened.

"Shit," she said, and hung up.

I was too angry to concentrate. Every time I put my mind on my history book, I could see only words in front of me . . . letters . . . and I found myself reading the same paragraph again and again.

Of course Sylvia was right. I knew it even as I was yelling at her. I hadn't told either her or Dad that I wanted the car for that night because I hadn't known until that morning that we were going. And I was a selfish pig for suggesting that she and her friend change their plans just for me.

At the same time hadn't she and Dad known how much this week meant to me? Hadn't I been talking about it forever—about being able to drive my friends somewhere? How many times had they heard me mention "the last week of November"? How could they not have realized I'd want a car— *any* car—every chance I could get?

As my breathing slowed, I tried to calm down. But every time I looked at my carefully polished nails, tears rolled down my cheeks again. The guys from St. John's knew we were coming. Pamela had passed it on. They'd be waiting for us, and here we were, stuck at home. I looked down at the cat puke on my rug and felt the surge of anger once again. I just wanted to do something to get even . . . I don't know what. Running away was the first thing that came to mind, ridiculous as that was. Just go somewhere and sit for five hours and make them worry. I remembered when Pamela had had a fight with her dad once, and I'd smuggled her into my bedroom. Her dad went nuts looking for her. Maybe Sylvia wouldn't even care.

I got up finally and cleaned up the vomit. Fortunately, I was able to get it off my shoes without it leaving a stain. I took off my clothes, my silk shirt and tight jeans, and hung them up, putting on my pajamas instead. I felt drained. Exhausted. Also a little scared. If Sylvia told Dad what all I'd said to her, I bet he'd move the date for the end of my driving probation period back to December or even later.

Around nine o'clock I went downstairs and ate a bowl of cereal, ignoring the salad Sylvia had left for me. I watched TV for a while but turned it off when I heard Sylvia's car in the driveway.

She came in and, without a word, put her car keys on the mantel. Her light brown hair was windblown, and she looked trim and tailored in a periwinkle blue blouse with matching slacks and a black sweater.

I took a deep breath and said, "Sylvia, I'm sorry

for spouting off earlier. I was just really mad."

"I guess I was pretty mad too," she said, turning. We studied each other, knowing there was a lot more to say. I had expected her to immediately offer me a hug or something, but she didn't.

"I just . . . I guess I thought that everyone . . . like you and Dad . . . knew how much I'd been looking forward to this week. That I'd want a car as much as possible."

"You're not made of glass," Sylvia said, and she sounded tired. "We can't know what you've planned unless you tell us."

Was she going to forgive me or not? I wondered. There was still a slight edge to her voice.

"Well . . . whatever," I said flatly. "But I would like to ask a favor—that you not tell Dad about our . . . our argument."

She didn't answer right away. Seemed to be considering it. "It's something he should know, perhaps," she said finally.

"No, I don't think it is. I think it's something we have to work out ourselves," I told her. "And I'd really appreciate it if you didn't mention this to him."

She looked at me for a moment as if debating it still, and in that moment we heard his steps on the front porch.

"All right," said Sylvia. "I won't."

Dad came in and took off his coat. "Feels a little like snow out there," he said, "and if it does, I'm sure glad I'm not back on the beltway." He smiled at me, then at Sylvia. "Oh, it's good to be home," he said, and, to Sylvia, "Nice of you to wait up."

"I just got home a few minutes ago," she said, and I saw a hidden message in the glance she gave him. I knew then without a doubt that the minute they were alone, she would spill the whole story. I didn't know whether to stick around as long as I could to keep her from telling him or to go to bed. If I stalled, she'd only tell him later, so I decided on bed.

"I think I'll go on up, Dad," I said, going over and kissing his cheek. "Hope you had a good conference."

He gave me a quick hug. "It was okay. Too long, though. Speakers could have said what they had to say in half the time."

"G'night, Sylvia," I said, and went upstairs.

I know she'll tell him! I thought. She was lying through her teeth! I went into my room, closed the door just hard enough to be sure they had heard it, and then, with my light out, I carefully opened it again and crept to the top of the stairs, listening for the sound of their voices.

Instead, I heard them going around turning out lights. The click of a lamp. The clank of the dead bolt on the front door. They were coming upstairs! Sylvia would tell him after they went to bed!

Suddenly a wild impulse swept over me. I reached back and silently closed the door to my room, then went down the hall into their darkened bedroom and opened the door of the blanket closet. Pushing the suitcases to one side in the lower half, I crawled in and pulled the door almost closed, all but the last inch. It took only five or six seconds for me to realize that this was a mistake. A terrible mistake. But it was too late, because they were coming down the hall, and the next thing I knew, they were in the room.

9

On Impulse

I couldn't believe what I was doing. Couldn't believe I was sitting on the floor of their bedroom closet, hugging my knees, watching Dad take off his shirt and tie, Sylvia remove her sweater and start to unbutton her blouse.

". . . not worth your time?" Sylvia was saying.

"Not worth a whole day and evening, that's for sure," Dad said. "Heard a few things that will be helpful in the store, but I don't think I'll go to a management conference again. How did the dinner go?"

I held my breath.

"Well, we got off to a rocky start . . . ," Sylvia began.

My anger began to swell.

". . . Beth is really in a lot of pain. I don't think she should be trying to get out and do things so soon, but she wanted so much to attend Millie's dinner. I'm glad Joyce went with us, because I needed help getting Beth out of the car."

I began breathing again. Maybe she'd tell him after they got in bed. But then her voice might be so soft, I wouldn't be able to understand what she was saying. I'd probably hear Dad, though, and he'd explode!

"You're a sweetheart," Dad was saying, and he went over to put his arms around her, caressing her back. She was in her slacks and bra now. "You look tired, honey."

"It's been quite a day," said Sylvia.

They moved out of my field of vision then, and when Sylvia passed in front of the closet again, she was in her knee-length nightgown. She went across the hall to the bathroom, and I could hear water running, the lid of a jar dropping onto the counter. The sliding of the medicine cabinet door. Five minutes later Sylvia came back into the room, and Dad crossed the hall in his shorts.

My heart pounded. What if they needed an extra blanket? What would I say if he opened the door? What *could* I say that he would ever understand? I was sixteen, not six.

When Dad came back, he turned the lock. My eyes widened. The lamp went off by their bed, and I heard Dad's grateful sigh as he climbed in and lay down. Only a small night-light near the baseboard gave any light to the room.

". . . come here," I heard Dad say.

Murmurings.

". . . not that tired . . . ," said Sylvia.

Dad said, "I'm so hungry for you . . ." And I knew they were going to make love! The look that had passed between them down in the living room didn't mean that there was something waiting to be said, but that yes, it was a good night for making love. That's why they had both come right up.

Omigod! I should leave! I shouldn't be here! I told myself, my head throbbing from guilt and shame.

Another murmur from Dad. An answering murmur from Sylvia.

"Let me help," Dad was saying.

A little giggle from Sylvia. "I think my arm's caught in the sleeve."

He was taking off her gown!

There was no way I could leave the room without unlocking their door, and even in my bedroom at the end of the hall, I often heard that loud *click*. I sat with my hand over my mouth, my eyes as big as coat buttons, horrified. Rustlings and murmurings . . . murmurings and rustlings . . .

My face felt so hot, I thought it would melt. My mouth, my tongue, my throat were dry. I sat with my forehead resting on my knees, my eyes shut tight with embarrassment. And then . . . the bed began to squeak, a rhythmical squeaking, and I put my hands over my ears. *I should not be listening!* This was a horrible invasion of their privacy. If Sylvia thought I'd been bad before, this was bad beyond belief.

I pressed my hands against my ears harder, harder, tighter and tighter, and kept whispering in my head, *Don't listen, don't listen, don't listen,* to drown out anything that might slip through.

I'm not sure how long I sat there like that, shutting out all the sounds that I could. Five minutes? Ten? I was supposed to be getting more mature as I got older, and this was one of the worst things I'd done—worse than anything I'd done in grade school.

Finally, my hands aching from the pressure of pushing against my ears, I relaxed my fingers and found that the squeaks and rustlings had stopped. Only an occasional murmur came from the bed.

". . . every inch of you," Dad was saying, his voice relaxed and sleepy.

And finally there were footsteps on the floor. I saw the shadowy silhouette of Sylvia's nude figure slipping into a robe, and then she left to go into the bathroom, leaving the door to their room ajar behind her.

I waited fifteen, twenty seconds and was grateful for the sound of Dad's deep, steady breathing. I pushed the closet door open a foot more, then crawled out on my hands and knees, pushing it almost closed again behind me. With my heart in my mouth, I crawled across the rug, through the doorway, and on down the hall toward my room.

The bathroom door opened before I could open my own door, and I crawled behind the stair railing, cowering in one corner. But the bathroom light went out before Sylvia stepped out into the hall, and I heard her footsteps once again and the closing of their bedroom door.

I went inside my own room and buried my face in my pillow. I felt as though I were running a fever, my head was so hot. The shame of what I had done! The shame of it!

Then another sound. The *click* of the front door. Soft footsteps. Silence. After a minute or two the sound of someone rummaging through the refrigerator. Lester!

I leaped off the bed and hurried downstairs, practically falling on the last step, and threw myself into the kitchen.

"Lester!" I whispered, holding on to the edge of the table. "I've done an awful, terrible thing!"

He was holding a glass in one hand, orange juice container in the other. "Are the police on the way?" he asked.

"*Listen* to me!" I gulped. "I just . . . I just . . ."

Something about my face—the flush of it,

perhaps—caught his attention, and he put the orange juice on the counter. "What's wrong?" he asked. "You sick?"

It came out in breathy spurts. "I was mad at Sylvia . . . and wanted to see if she'd tell Dad . . . what I'd said to her, and I . . . I hid in their closet, and they just had sex."

Lester put down the glass. "You *what*?" he said, disbelieving.

"It's awful, I know! I didn't realize they were going to do it. I wanted to hear what she told him after promising me she wouldn't, and she *didn't* tell him. They made love instead, and I *heard*!"

Lester kept staring at me, shaking his head. "I can't believe you did that," he said.

"I can't either," I wept. "How am I going to tell Dad?"

"What?"

"I've got to apologize, and he'll be furious," I continued.

"No," said Les.

I looked up. "What?"

"You don't have to tell him. And you shouldn't."

"*Why*, Lester? It's a terrible thing I did. I'll never feel right again if—"

"Al, listen to me." Lester came over, took me by the shoulders, and sat me down in a chair. "For once you've got to be an adult. You're never going to mention this to either Dad or Sylvia. This is something you've got to keep to yourself."

I just stared at him. "I'll never be able to face them again! Every time I look at them, I'll remember, and—"

"And you won't say a word," Lester said sternly.

"I've . . . I've never kept big things from Dad before," I cried. "I have to know he forgives me."

"This is going to be one of the most grown-up things you'll ever have to do, Al," said Lester, "but you've got to deal with this yourself. You've got to save Dad and Sylvia the embarrassment of knowing you were listening to something very, very private. It's not like they were in the next room and you couldn't help but overhear. They had every reason to believe they weren't within hearing distance of your room."

I shook my head. "I'll never feel good about myself again if I have to keep this all bottled up," I cried.

"Yes, you will, because you'll be a better person, knowing how absolutely wrong you were tonight."

If I thought it would be hard to tell Dad what I'd done, somehow it seemed a lot harder *not* to confess. I suddenly wished I were Catholic. If I were Catholic, I could go to a priest and tell him what I'd done, and he would tell me how many Hail

Marys it would take to be forgiven. At least, I think that's how it works.

"Lester," I said plaintively, "pretend you're a priest."

"*What?*"

"I want someone to tell me I'm forgiven."

"You're forgiven."

"You're not God."

"Then pray to God."

I sank back in the chair, arms dangling at my sides. "What makes me do stuff like this, Les?"

He was rummaging through the refrigerator again and pulled out a slice of pound cake. "I don't know," he said. "Mixed-up chromosomes or something. Anyone saving this pound cake?"

"You can have it," I said.

"What's with the shrimp and spinach salad?"

"You can have that, too," I said. And as Lester began to eat, I said, "None of this would have happened if you had been home this evening when I called and had agreed to drive five girls to Edgar's in Georgetown."

"If I had been crazy enough to drive five girls to Georgetown, I'd be the one with the mixed-up chromosomes," said Les.

I got down some graham crackers and drank a little milk. "Where were you this evening, anyway?" I asked.

"Took a woman to the movies, if you must know. Just a friend, not a date," Les said. "I wanted to get something to eat afterward, but she had to get home. And since we were in Silver Spring, I naturally thought of stopping here after I left her off. If I'd known you were upstairs hiding in a closet, I would have come earlier and dragged you out."

"I guess you're right about never telling them," I said. "I'm glad you came by, Les. It's always good to talk about things with *some*one."

I put my glass in the sink, and as I started for the stairs, I heard Les say, "Go, my child, and sin no more." And I smiled for the first time that evening.

It was a strange couple of days, those days before the Snow Ball. When I woke in the mornings, it seemed as though hiding in the closet were just a bad dream—that it couldn't possibly have happened. Then I knew that, no, it really was. It really did. It really had.

I was quieter than usual, but I was good around the house. I helped without having to be asked. Did everyone's laundry, not just mine. Had salads waiting in the fridge when Sylvia came in. Set the table. But I kept finding it hard to look right at Dad and Sylvia when we were talking, as though they suspected. Maybe I had left the suitcases all pushed to one side, and they guessed. Maybe I'd left the closet door open a little too wide.

But once, as I was putting fresh towels in the bathroom and peeked into their room, I saw that the closet door still remained open the same few inches, and when I had a chance, I pushed all the suitcases together again. I don't think they ever noticed. It was, though, as Lester said, a secret I'd have to carry with me all of my life. The only redeeming thing was that I had, supposedly, become a better person because of it. Of that, I wasn't so sure.

By Thursday evening, however, I was a little sick of feeling guilty. My friends had simply put our plans to go to Georgetown on hold, and now I was thinking about the Snow Ball the next night. Liz and Gwen were going to spend Friday evening at Molly's, they told me, having a "foodless" party, as Molly gets nauseated so easily. They were going to bring over balloons and *Saturday Night Live* videos, and Gwen and Liz were going to demonstrate the steps tŏ some new dances. I hoped that I would be that generous when a dance came along to which I wasn't invited: spend the evening with someone who was too sick to go.

When Sylvia came home from school Friday, I'd already showered and was in my underwear and strapless bra, doing my hair. She tapped on the bathroom door, and I cut off the dryer.

"Anything I can do to help?" she called.

"Well . . . you could zip me up once I'm in the dress," I said.

When my hair was dry, I curled it, then let it cool down while I put on my dress. Just as Liz had done, Sylvia pulled the material down around my hips where it tended to bunch.

"This is really a knockout, Alice!" she said. "I don't know if we ought to let Ben see you in this or not. He might forbid you to leave the house!"

We laughed together then, but somehow her laugh seemed forced, and I wondered if she felt the same way about mine.

I was ready before Tony got there. He was late, in fact, and that made me feel a little strange. Then I realized he probably didn't want to have to spend any more time than necessary in the same room with my parents. I noticed the relief on his face when I answered the door.

"Come in and let Sylvia take a picture," I said.

Tony was wearing a black tux with a red ruffled shirt. I'd never seen anything like it. He looked like a bullfighter or a flamenco dancer or something, but with his tux and my dress, the red made a nice contrast.

And then we were out the door, and Dad was calling from the porch, "Take good care of her, Tony." And I could not believe that he added,

"Drive with both hands on the wheel." Talk about embarrassing! I'll bet even Dad was embarrassed after he said it.

Tony started the car, then slid one hand over to my knee and laughed. "Now, where *else* did he think I'd put my hand?" I laughed too and let him keep it there.

Pamela was in a salmon-colored satin gown and black stiletto heels. It had thin spaghetti straps and was cut low in front. If she leaned over too far, I swear she would have popped right out of the dress. Tim, her date, was in a midnight blue tux and smelled of aftershave.

I felt very adult and sexy as the Buick glided along the streets, and a singer's sultry voice came over the speakers. There was no snow yet. There rarely is this early in Maryland. None that sticks, anyway.

"I wonder why they hold the Snow Ball so early if it never snows?" said Tim. "Why don't they wait till January?"

"Maybe it's like some primitive ritual," I suggested. "Like a rain dance. If we put on costumes and perform a dance, it'll snow."

"Hey, you ought to write a story about that for *The Edge*," Tony said.

We had reservations at an upscale Thai restaurant

in Bethesda, and I think we were about the two most attractive couples there. Everyone was looking at us and smiling, and I thought how great it was to be sitting in a room full of adults, being served like adults, Tony and Tim paying with credit cards like anyone else. Then it was on to the dance.

The entrance to the gym was just as I'd heard it was going to be: Couples entered one at a time through a Styrofoam cave—something like an igloo—with fake icicles hanging down around them, and stepped out onto the gym floor with swirling, snowflake-shaped strobe lights flashing across the floor and the roof of the gym.

Tony checked my jacket—Sylvia's, actually—then whirled me out onto the dance floor. He held me so close, I felt like we were a grilled cheese sandwich. But I liked the scent of his cologne. Liked his firm grip. Liked that at last I was wearing the shoes I couldn't wear to Georgetown last Tuesday. Liked that being in Tony's arms helped make up for not meeting new guys from St. John's.

Then we were cheek to cheek during a slow number, and Tony whispered, "Oh, baby . . ." in my ear. I closed my eyes and enjoyed the throb of the music, the beat of the drum.

When the band took its first break, Pamela and I went to the girls' locker room, where girls had gathered to repair their hair and discuss their dates.

"Oh, man!" Pamela said. "You two looked *hot* in more ways than one. And this was only the first set!"

"What do you mean?" I asked.

"The way you guys were dancing. If you don't have the hots, he sure does."

I brushed it off. "It's a dance! What do you expect?" I said.

Jill and Karen were there looking fabulous, as usual, and I think Jill was surprised to see me in a black halter-top dress.

"Something of Sylvia's?" she asked innocently.

"No," I said. "I bought it."

Karen looked me over quizzically. "I could swear my aunt had a dress just like that. I know she did! Same size and everything, but I think she gave it away."

"Imagine that," I said, and moved off. I wouldn't let anything ruin my evening.

Couples were still arriving when we went back upstairs, and just as the band started up again, someone else came through the ice cave and stood staring at the couples merging onto the dance floor.

It was Amy Sheldon, and she was alone.

10

In the Buick

"Well, look what the wind blew in," Tony said.

We could have danced together or apart on the next number, and Tony chose together. I could see Amy over his shoulder, standing at the entrance in a pale green dress with a voluminous ruffled skirt.

"Looks like a head of lettuce," said Tony. "She is one weird girl."

"Just a little slow," I commented.

We were swallowed up by the other dancers, and I couldn't see her anymore. We danced past Jill, her arms around Justin's neck; past Lori and Leslie, both wearing white tuxedos; past Karen and her date; everybody looking more glamorous than we'd ever seen them in school. Then I caught another glimpse of Amy, looking a little dismayed, talking with one of the teacher chaperones.

The next number had a South American beat, and the teachers who had been standing on the sidelines before now moved slowly, unobtrusively, around the edge of the dance floor. Tony chuckled. We knew what they were looking for—"grinding," which the principal had already announced would not be permitted: couples thrusting their pelvises together front to front or back to front. One girl tested the limits by turning her back to her partner and bending over slightly, but it was a fun dance and the band was great.

"Hey, Tony! Nice shirt, man!" said Mark Stedmeister, who was there with Penny.

Pamela caught my arm at one point and told me that one of the thin straps on her gown had snapped loose, so the next time the band took a break, we went to the locker room again, where teachers had put out a supply of safety pins and tampons and Band-Aids.

As we entered the restroom, we saw a small crowd of girls at one end, all gathered around a girl in the middle. I felt my throat tighten when I saw it was Amy.

"Where did you get that *beautiful* dress?" one girl gushed as the others stifled their laughter.

"It's so . . . so *springlike!*" said someone else. Amy was smiling back, glowing with their attention.

"With all those ruffles, doesn't she look like a . . . a Christmas tree?" said the first girl.

"More like a cupcake," said another, and now

some of the girls were giggling openly, but Amy didn't get it and smiled even more broadly.

"Let me pin that strap for you, and then I'm going over to rescue her," I murmured to Pamela as the girls chattered on.

We found the pins, and I slipped my fingers down the back of Pamela's dress to fasten the end of the strap in place.

"You're going to have to be careful not to make any quick movements, or it might come undone," I said. "I doubt the pin will hold all night."

"The dress is so tight, I think it could stay up by itself," said Pamela.

I glanced at her breasts bulging out over the top. "I wouldn't count on it," I said.

When the strap was secure, I turned to find Amy and saw that she was going back up the stairs to the gym, the gaggle of girls following at her heels. Then my eye caught a long trail of white fluttering down the back of her dress, and suddenly I picked up the hem of my skirt and ran after them.

On ahead, I saw that, on the long trail of toilet paper pinned to the back of Amy's dress, someone had printed in black eyebrow liner, DON'T I LOOK STUPID?

Just as Amy reached the floor above, I pushed through the crowd and grabbed her shoulder.

"I think your tag is showing," I said, stopping her. "Here. Let me fix that for you."

Amy smiled and dutifully stopped as the other girls cast sullen smiles at me and went on by.

"Spoilsport," one of them murmured.

I crumpled the paper up and threw it in one corner, but Amy was blissfully unaware.

"Gosh, Alice, you look so pretty!" she said. "Who'd you come with?"

"Tony," I said. "Tony Osler."

"Oh," said Amy. "Well, I didn't know you were supposed to come with a date. I thought there would be lots of singles here, like at proms and stuff."

"Well, there's no rule against it," I said. "Who drove you?"

"My dad. He's coming back at eleven to get me." She sighed and looked at the big gym clock. "That's a whole hour from now."

We moved around the line of couples waiting to have their pictures taken.

"Alice," she said suddenly, "would you be my partner for the photo? Dad gave me the money." She opened the ruffled matching purse in her hand and pulled out a twenty-dollar bill.

"But . . . I . . . ," I began awkwardly.

"*Please?*" said Amy. "If I'm all by myself, it won't look so good. We don't have to hold hands or anything."

I saw Tony coming toward me, motioning for me to get in line for the photo.

"All right," I said to Amy. "Stand behind us, and after Tony and I have our picture taken, I'll go up there with you."

"Thanks!" she said. And then, to Tony, "Hello, handsome!"

Tony rolled his eyes and moved over beside me, then groaned when he realized Amy got in line behind us.

"It's a beautiful gym, isn't it?" she babbled on. "The decorations almost make you feel cold! I mean, when I came through that igloo, I had to touch the icicles to see if they were real."

Tony put his arm around me and turned me toward the front of the line, but Amy went right on talking: "I like your dress, Alice. It's really sexy. Isn't she sexy, Tony? I don't think I look sexy, but I think I'm pretty in this dress. It was my aunt's. I think it was a bridal dress. No, maybe a bridesmaid's. Always a bridesmaid, never a bride. That's what they say."

We watched Jill and Justin stand before the sparkly background of snow and ice, Jill looking like a movie star, her slim waist accented by the silver lamé dress she was wearing. Justin had started wearing a small goatee, and they looked so grown up.

When it was our turn, Amy called out, "Next!

Step right up and get your picture taken, Mr. and Mrs. Tony Osler!"

I felt my face turn crimson. Tony turned to Amy and said, "Put a clamp on it, will you?" We stepped up on the low stage and posed in front of the snow scene, but I could tell that my face would show up orange-red in the picture. I wanted to wait till my face had cooled, but it was too late. The photographer was already positioning our shoulders just so.

When we were finished, Tony started to lead me away, but Amy stepped up on the platform.

"Just a minute," I said to Tony. "I promised Amy . . ." I could barely face the camera, I was so embarrassed. The other couples stared.

"What the . . . ?" Tony said.

The photographer looked confused.

"Just take it," I told him, my face redder still.

"O-kay!" he said, putting us shoulder to shoulder. I heard giggles from some of the girls. "Looks good to me!" said the photographer. "Hold it right there."

"Thank you, Alice," Amy said as she followed me off the platform, but all I wanted to do was get away, and Tony obliged by sweeping me out onto the dance floor and into the crowd.

"That's enough of that," he said.

I put my cheek against his and didn't look for Amy again.

• • •

Tony wanted to leave early and go to a party at a friend's house, but I'd promised Dad I'd tell him if we went anywhere else, and I knew he'd give me the third degree. Would probably want to talk to the friend's parents. It just wasn't worth it. I told Tony I couldn't. I could tell he was disappointed, but he was a gentleman about it, and we stayed almost to the end of the evening, leaving a little before midnight.

I had a one o'clock curfew for the night, but Pamela's was twelve thirty, so we headed straight for her house. Tony parked beyond it so that she and Tim wouldn't have an audience when they said good night. As though they hadn't been saying and kissing good night in the backseat for the last twenty minutes.

Once we dropped off Tim at his house, however, Tony said, "We still have a half hour left," and parked beside a soccer field. The LeSabre had a bench seat in front with controls on the steering column. Tony pushed a button, and the front seat slid noiselessly back six inches. He kept the CD player on as well as the heater. I lay back in Tony's arms with my legs curled up on the seat.

"You smell good," he said.

"So do you. I think you're wearing my brother's favorite men's cologne," I told him.

He kissed me, one hand slipping under my wrap and around to my bare back, caressing my skin. "I've liked you ever since you joined the newspaper," he said. "Jealous as hell of Sam when you were going out with him. Didn't work out, huh?"

"Sam's a nice guy," I said simply.

"But . . . ?"

"He's a nice guy," I repeated, laughing a little. I wasn't about to trash-talk Sam or any other boy.

"Okay," said Tony. We kissed again. He was an excellent kisser—slow and gentle at first, then harder and more urgent as he hugged me tighter. . . . I nestled my face against his neck, letting scenes from the evening play back in my mind. The way Jill had looked at me in the halter-top dress, as though Miss Goody Two-shoes had finally managed to surprise her. The remark Karen had made about her aunt giving away a dress just like mine. The embarrassment I'd felt standing beside Amy to have our picture taken.

Well, right now MGT was sitting—lying—in a Buick LeSabre with a senior in a tux, who was gently caressing my right breast through the material. I felt the tingle of excitement each time his finger approached my nipple, withdrew, touched it, withdrew. . . .

I drew a sharp breath and felt the muscles of his face draw into a smile.

"Like that?" he asked, doing it again.

I didn't answer; just let him do it some more. He reached behind my neck and undid the fastener of the halter top. Then he slowly pulled it down, exposing my strapless bra. Just as slowly, he undid the bra and let it drop on the floor. I was lying in his arms with my bare breasts looking up at him, and he leaned down and kissed them.

It was exciting and a little scary to feel the wetness in my pants, my nipples tightening and standing up straight, as if they were begging for more. I drew in my breath again when his hand explored my thigh—investigating the long slit in my dress, tickling me gently behind one knee as the music played on.

"Oh, baby," he breathed in my ear. I wished he would think of something else to call me but "baby," but I liked the urgency in his voice. Then his hand was under my dress, moving up my thigh to my panty line. I knew it was almost one o'clock, and I gently took his hand and pulled it away.

"I've got to get home," I whispered, and we kissed—a hard, almost biting kiss from Tony. I reached down for my bra, my arm crossing his lap, and I could feel the hardness inside his trousers. He fastened my bra for me and hooked the closure on the halter top.

We slid the car seat forward again, and Tony

turned the key in the ignition. But when we got to my house, he smiled and said, "I think I'd better not get out in case your dad waits up. You know . . ." He motioned to the front of his pants.

"Okay," I said, and smiled at him. "'Night, Tony. It was a great evening. Thanks."

"'Night, baby," he said. "*Next* time . . . !"

Dad had left the lamp on in the hallway, but otherwise, the living room was dark. I took off Sylvia's wrap and hung it in the closet.

A minute later I heard soft footsteps on the floor above. Dad appeared at the top of the stairs in his pajamas. "You back, honey?"

"Yeah," I said.

"Anybody with you?"

"No. Tony's gone on home," I answered.

"Have a good time?"

"Yeah, we did. I'll tell you about it in the morning," I said.

"Okay. Now that you're safely home, I can go to sleep," he said.

"G'night," I called.

My body still felt flushed and excited. I picked up the hem of my skirt and went quietly upstairs, then slipped the dress up over my head and hung it in the closet. My bra came off . . . my shoes . . . my underwear. . . . I crawled into bed and relived

the scenes in the car. Tony's arm around me . . .
his finger on my nipple . . . up my thigh to my
panty line. . . .

My own fingers caressed my breasts under the
blanket. Then my stomach, then between my legs,
and finally I finished what Tony had begun in the car.

As my breathing returned to normal, I gradually
opened my eyes to the darkness of my room—the
shadows cast by the streetlight. I wasn't such a
Miss Goody Two-shoes anymore. It had been
exciting being in the car with Tony, letting unfa-
miliar hands explore me. I shivered again just
thinking about it. *Next time . . .*

11

Edgar's

I rode in with Dad the next morning to my part-time job at the Melody Inn and decided to tell him as much as I cared to about the dance before he had a chance to ask. If he had to prod things out of me, he'd figure there was more beneath the surface, which, of course, there was.

"The gym was all shimmery with glitter, just like a mountain snow scene," I said, "and the band was great."

"You went to a restaurant first?" he asked.

"Yeah. Thai. One in Bethesda. It was really good," I said.

"And . . . after the dance?"

"Well, we stayed almost to the end, the music was that good. Then we dropped off Pamela and her date, and Tony brought me home," I said.

Dad turned at the corner of Georgia Avenue and drove another block before he asked,

"You didn't invite Tony to come in?"

"No. It was almost one, and I'd danced practically every dance. I was tired," I said.

"Well," Dad said, "I'm glad you had a good time. I guess I'm going to have to get used to your going out with boys I hardly know."

I smiled. "Guess so, Pops," I said.

The store had been decorated for Christmas during the week, and I found the Gift Shoppe—the little section under the stairs—wreathed in evergreen and tiny twinkly lights.

"If I stand behind this counter, I'm going to feel like I'm onstage," I said to Marilyn, Dad's assistant manager. She's married now and happy as a clam.

"Just wanted to add a little excitement to your boring Saturday job," she explained.

"Well, this is your first Christmas as a married woman," I said. "Now, *that's* exciting. What are you getting Jack?"

"I've been saving up for a new guitar for him—a really good one," she said. She and Jack are both folksingers. "Ben says they go on sale next week—the Christmas bonus sale—and with my employee discount, I think I can afford it."

Dad had ordered a lot of extra stuff for the Gift Shoppe because people who've never been in our store will come in looking for Christmas gifts for musician friends. In addition to bikini underwear with BEETHOVEN on the seat of the pants and long silk scarves like the keyboard of a piano, we had coffee mugs with Mozart's face on the side; music boxes with dancing bears on top; tie clips in the shape of a clef sign; earrings like tiny violins; T-shirts with part of the "Hallelujah Chorus" on the front; and little wind-up drummer boys. Customers came in as soon as we opened, and we were busy all day.

David, the young man who started working for Dad about a year ago—the one who's trying to decide if he should become a priest—shared a sandwich with me at the little table and chairs we keep for employees back in the stockroom.

"Now, why do I think that last night was special for you somehow?" he asked, studying my face.

It took me by surprise, and I instantly felt my cheeks redden, as though he'd seen through the window of the Buick.

"I—I don't know. Why?" I said.

"Hmmm. Must be your hair," he told me. And then I remembered there was still some glitter in it, and I relaxed.

"You're right, it was," I said. "The Snow Ball at school."

"Nice time?"

"Yeah," I said. "Great band. So how are things with you?"

"I'm going home for Christmas," he said. "New

Hampshire. I want to talk over my decision with my folks. See how they feel about it."

"Your decision about the priesthood?" I asked.

He nodded. "To tell the truth, I also want to visit a woman up there that I've been serious about for a time. See how I feel about giving her up, if I go that route."

"How can you do that, David?" I asked. "What about *her* feelings?"

"That's what I need to discuss," he said thoughtfully.

"I don't mean you shouldn't become a priest, but . . . I mean . . . if you're serious about someone, how can you just give her up?"

"Because I might be even more serious about the church. If I'm married to a woman but have a love affair with the church, it's not fair to the woman. If I join the priesthood and have an affair with a woman, it's not fair to the church. I've got to figure out which I love more."

"But a lot of married men are ministers!" I protested, rooting for the woman, whoever she was.

"I know," said David. "But until the Vatican decides otherwise, it's a choice I have to make."

I rested my chin in my hands. "Why is life so complicated, David?" I asked.

"To keep us from being bored," he said.

• • •

Liz wanted to hear all about the dance and invited Pam and me to sleep over on Saturday night.

Pamela was as happy as I'd seen her in a long time and kept saying, "Tim's so *nice*! I didn't realize a guy that cute could be so nice."

"Wow! Talk about stereotypes!" I said. "Cute guys have to be players, and plain guys have to be nice?"

"No, it's just that he's so quiet at school—you don't notice him much," Pamela went on. "He doesn't stand out in a crowd. But get him one-on-one, and he's funny, he's smart, he's thoughtful. . . . Isn't it strange how some people get along better with just a few people around, and some people enjoy a crowd?"

"Just goes to show how labels don't mean a thing," I said.

"But what we really want to know is how did he say good night?" asked Liz, and that broke Pamela and me up.

"What? . . . What?" she kept asking, poking at us.

"What you really want to know is how far he got, Liz, not how he said good night," I said with a laugh.

"Well, that, too," she confessed.

"From the sounds in the backseat, I'd guess they'd been saying good night for the last half hour before we got them home," I joked.

"Hey, he's a good kisser," said Pamela.

"French kisser?" asked Liz, all ears.

"Yeah," Pamela said dreamily. "French and Irish and Italian and Russian, all put together."

"What's *that* supposed to mean?" I asked.

"That he kisses everything in sight—my lips, my ears, my neck, my shoulders. . . ."

"And . . . ?" we urged her on.

"That's as far down as he went," said Pamela.

"*Listen* to us!" I said. "We're worse than guys. We give guys a bad rap if they kiss and tell, and we're doing the same thing."

"Yeah, but we're not spreading it around school," said Liz. "This is just among girlfriends. And so . . ." She grinned at me. "How about you and fast-track Tony?"

"Well, he got a little farther than my shoulders," I said, grinning.

Liz and Pamela crowded closer and glanced at the bedroom door to make sure it was closed. "*How* much farther?" Pamela wanted to know.

"We did a Liz-and-Ross in the front seat of his car," I said. That's what we've called it ever since Camp Overlook the summer before last, when Ross, this boy she met at the camp, kissed Elizabeth's bare breasts—the furthest either Pam or I had ever gone with a guy at the time.

"Ah! The halter-top dress!" said Liz.

"Ummm, nice!" said Pamela, imagining it. "If you had seen them on the dance floor, Liz, they were as close as the pages in a book. Hot, hot, hot."

"You really like him?" Liz asked me.

I cocked my head and paused a moment. "I sure liked what he was doing."

"And the slits on the sides of your dress?" asked Pam.

"He got up as far as the panty line, and then it was time for me to go home," I said.

We all sat soaking that in for a while. Finally Liz broke the silence: "Does this mean the three of us are 'experienced' now?"

Pam and I howled again. No one can say things quite like Elizabeth.

"We're not 'used merchandise,' if that's what you're thinking," I said. "And we're still virgins."

"But for how long?" asked Pamela.

We put a pillow over her face and turned on the TV. But I was wondering the exact same thing. *You really like him?* Liz had asked. *I sure liked what he was doing,* I'd answered. And it didn't take what I'd learned at that sex education course at church to know that there was a difference.

It was awkward seeing Tony at school on Monday. There were only two boys in the whole school who had touched parts of my body I'd never allowed anyone to touch before—Sam and Tony. Sam Mayer was always so much a gentleman that I never worried he'd talk about me to other people. But Tony?

I avoided the hall where his locker was located and ducked in an empty classroom once when I saw him rounding a corner. But at lunchtime he came looking for me in the cafeteria, and I'll have to admit it was exciting to have a senior interested in me. When his eyes met mine, I could tell immediately what he was thinking. I tried to pretend it was the last thing on my mind.

"Hi, Tony," I said, hoping to sound casual, while my friends watched intently.

He smiled down at me and put his hand on the back of my neck, his fingers caressing. "Hi, baby," he said. "How ya doin'?"

Liz had left the table to use the restroom, and Tony slid into her seat. He put his arm casually around my shoulder, one finger stroking the side of my face, and I felt the familiar tingle in my groin. I liked having his attention. Liked the way Jill and Karen at the next table kept glancing over, then pretended they hadn't.

"How'd you like the dance, Tony?" Penny asked from across the table.

"Grrrrreat!" he said, giving my shoulder a noticeable little tug to show everyone it was me who made it great.

People went on discussing the dance then, and Tony concentrated on me. He was rubbing my earlobe between his fingers. "So . . . ," he said, lowering his voice. "We going out next weekend?"

"Where to?" I asked.

"Does it matter?" he said.

I laughed nervously. "Of course it matters. Dad has this thing about 'purpose' and 'destination.'"

"Okay," said Tony. "Purpose: to be with Tony. Destination: uh . . . Tony's house? If my folks aren't home?"

"Yeah, right," I said.

The bell rang, and he gave my waist another squeeze. "Okay. See ya," he said, almost too abruptly, and left. I stared after him, wondering if I'd been *too* casual, *too* unresponsive, *too* inhibited. A senior had just asked me *out*, and I hadn't acted very enthusiastic. Then I reminded myself that he hadn't asked me *out* so much as he'd asked me *over*. There was a difference.

"Alice," Gwen said, nudging my arm. "That was the bell."

I picked up my tray and carried it to the counter, then followed the other girls into the hall.

We did our postponed Girls' Night Out that Tuesday. Dad let me use his car after getting out a map and showing me the best route to Georgetown. "If you get off on a side street, you'll find it's pretty narrow," he told me, then rapped me lightly on the head. "Please try not to dent my car."

"I'll drive slow," I told him, "and we're going to pay to park in a garage, so I'm not going to try to parallel park in Georgetown."

Once everyone was in the car, I was surprised myself that Dad let me go. With one or two friends, maybe, but not four—three in back and one in front. Liz sat with me and read the directions from the map.

Everyone was chattering and laughing and making a lot of noise, and the first thing I did was go through a stop sign. The girls shrieked and laughed.

Okay, I told myself. *This is serious.* "You do the talking, Liz. I have to concentrate," I told her.

I know you can cause an accident by going *too* slow and making cars go around you. But I followed the speed limit, and—forty-five minutes later, with Liz holding the map—I finally merged into one horrific traffic jam on Wisconsin Avenue in the Georgetown section of D.C.

It was easy to see why the area was so popular. People crammed the sidewalks, meandered through traffic in the streets, and cars moved at a crawl, people leaning out of windows, shouting to each other. Snowflakes fluttered through the air, which added a holiday touch. I think every shop was open, every display window lit up. Pamela and Gwen and Yolanda in the backseat were calling our attention to funky dresses in store windows, lace-up boots, fur-trimmed jackets, beaded T-shirts, but all I wanted was to get Dad's car to the parking garage without bumping into anybody.

When the car behind me gave us a little tap with its front bumper, I almost freaked out and wondered if I should get out to inspect it, but Gwen assured me it was a bumper tap, nothing to worry about. When I finally pulled into a parking garage, I could feel a trickle of sweat roll down my back and under the waistband of my pants.

We walked five abreast along the sidewalk, and I let out a loud "Who-eee!"—glad to be free of the car I'd waited so long to drive.

"We're here, girlfriends!" Pamela said. "And we're *babes* tonight!"

Yolanda, with her cinnamon skin, probably looked the best, in five-inch knee-high boots so tight, they fit like stockings. I don't know how she could even walk in them. Her fake fur jacket had a hood that fanned her face and certainly attracted a lot of attention.

"Look!" she cried, pointing to a guy with a pot-bellied pig on a leash. "Omigod, where else would you see *that*?"

"People are probably saying the same thing about you!" Gwen teased.

It was like we were in New York all over again, five suburban girls going ape over the sights of the city.

At Edgar's we lined up with the others and obediently accepted the "under twenty-one" bracelets when we were carded at the entrance. We took one of the few available tables and ordered our drinks— all nonalcoholic, of course. Gwen ordered nachos and potato skins for all of us, and we wolfed them down but made our drinks last.

The band lived up to its reputation. Pamela went for the lead guitarist. "He is so *hot!*" she purred, one leg crossed seductively over the other, her high-heeled shoe balancing on the end of her toe.

Seated on a sort of platform at the back of the room like we were, we could see everyone who came in—what they were wearing, who they were with.

"You know what?" Gwen said between numbers. "We are the most dressed-up girls here."

Stunned, we looked around. She was so right. We spotted a few women in dresses and heels, but almost everyone else had come in loafers and jeans and denim jackets.

"We've got 'suburbs' written on our foreheads, practically," Pamela lamented.

"They *definitely* know we're in high school," said Liz. "I'll bet most of these people are George Washington or Georgetown U students. Maybe we ought to leave and go buy some loafers." As if we would.

The guys from St. John's never showed up, probably because Pamela had forgotten to tell them we were coming, but the room was almost too crowded for anyone else. The man at the door was shaking his head at the people outside. Six guys managed to squeeze in just before the door was closed and were trying to beg extra chairs from nearby tables so they could sit together in the back.

Pamela asked if they'd like to share our table.

"That's a table?" one guy said, seeing that it was scarcely big enough for our drinks. "Sure! Thanks!"

We scooted out to make our circle larger so the guys could crowd their chairs in. One guy was still left without a chair, so Liz gave him hers and sat on his lap. They turned out to be nice guys, students from GW, who were showing an out-of-town friend a good time.

It was pretty clear to me that they had come to hear the band, not to pick up girls, because they were talking music among themselves, and Gwen guessed they were music majors. None of them made a move, none of them did more than a little flirtatious teasing, and when they decided to move on, none of them asked for our phone numbers, and we concentrated on the music again.

Suddenly Liz gasped, "Look!"

The five of us turned to see ten guys wearing nothing but sneakers and Santa Claus caps come streaking through the club. They were coming, in fact, right toward our table, and they were singing "Santa Claus Is Coming to Town." In harmony!

Everyone started cheering and clapping, and—as we gaped in surprise—the first two men lifted the caps off their heads and plunked one on Gwen's head, the other on Pamela's. We shrieked with laughter.

As the men disappeared out the exit, people were saying, "Who *were* they? Who *were* those guys?"

The emcee said, "Well, folks, we've just had a visit from the University Men's Glee Club, showing their naughty parts and doing their bit for Children's Hospital." More laughter and cheering. He looked at us. "I know you'd like to keep them, girls. The caps, I mean. But if the two of you would please go around the club collecting money for the hospital, the men will return tomorrow—fully clothed—to pick them up. Thank you."

Pamela and Gwen had a great time going from table to table, holding out the Santa Claus caps. Almost everyone put a dollar or two in them, and the manager came over and explained that it was an annual thing. The guys discovered they could collect three times the normal amount if they streaked through the clubs naked, no matter how beautifully they sang.

"Did we pick the right night, or *didn't* we?"

Gwen said when the girls came back, breathless, having turned in the caps with the money.

"And to think that we saw it on Mulberry Street!" Liz said, quoting an old Dr. Seuss book, and we laughed some more.

I looked at Liz and realized how far she'd come from the girl she had been back in junior high, complaining that she had never seen a naked man or boy in her entire life. She had seen statues and paintings, of course, but not a live nude male. And, trying to be helpful, I had gone through stacks of *National Geographic,* paper-clipping photos of naked men in other cultures, but they always seemed to have a spear or shield in front of the very thing Liz most wanted to see.

She caught me grinning at her. "What are *you* thinking?" she asked.

"Just happy thoughts. You and nude men and all that," I said, and she gave my ankle a kick.

We decided at last to leave and visit the shops, and we soon discovered that heels aren't good for walking, much less shopping. But we bought some great earrings at a ceramics shop and watched Yolanda buy an outrageous thong at a sexy lingerie store.

Finally we went back to the garage, pooled our money to pay for the parking, and I confidently drove us home, knowing that with each block we traveled away from Georgetown, traffic would be lighter, the distance from home would be shorter, the roads more familiar. And then it was back to our old neighborhood, and I was very, very glad to be home.

"Both your car and your daughter are back without a scratch," I announced as I came inside and gave Dad his car keys.

Dad gave me a small smile. "That's good to know," he said, but his face looked tired. Serious. *Now* what had I done? I wondered. For half a minute I thought that somehow he'd found out about Tony and me in the car. Then he said, "We got some disturbing news tonight, Al. Milt's had a heart attack and is in the hospital for a coronary bypass tomorrow."

I stood without moving. "Is . . . is he going to live?" I asked.

"Carol said not to worry, that his condition was stable. But she thought we would want to know," said Dad.

I sat down slowly and looked over at Sylvia, who was curled up at one end of the couch, hugging her knees, then looked back at Dad. "Four people I know have had heart problems!" I said shakily. "Mrs. Plotkin died; Uncle Charlie died; Grandpa died; and now Uncle Milt!"

"Milt's alive, Alice, and expected to live."

"But if it could happen to him . . . ," I began, and couldn't finish.

Dad understood. "Care to sit on my lap?" he said. I hadn't heard him say that since I was nine or ten. Like a child, I obeyed. I went over and sat on his lap, leaning back against him. My eyes were welling up already. "I know it's scary," he said, patting my leg, "and maybe you're afraid it will happen to me." I sniffled. "Well, Milt's been having heart problems for some time now," Dad went on, "and I'm doing what I can to lead a healthy life. I'm taking blood pressure medicine and watching my cholesterol, so I expect to go on living for some time yet."

"But so did Uncle Charlie," I mewed. "He thought he would go on living so long, he got married!"

"I know. His death surprised us all. But if I have any say about this, I'll be here to watch you get married someday and to play with my grandchildren."

I swallowed. "Are we going to go to Chicago to see him?"

"Carol says she doesn't think it's necessary. They got him to the hospital quickly after his attack, and the doctors feel they've minimized the danger. She'll let us know if we're needed. Right now she's with Aunt Sally, and she'll stay until Milt's home again."

I was quiet for a while, my head against the side of Dad's face. "The awful thing about life," I said finally, "is that we have to die."

"Yep," said Dad. "All the more reason to enjoy every single day we have. Did you have a good time tonight?"

I got up and went over to sit on the couch beside Sylvia. "Yes, except we were vastly overdressed. I bought some ceramic earrings. . . ." I took them out of my purse and showed them to Sylvia.

"Ooh, I may ask to borrow these sometime," she said. "They're beautiful!"

"And we shared a table with some college guys who weren't very interested in us," I said.

"Even better," Dad said, and smiled.

"But I don't think I want to drive to Georgetown again anytime soon," I told him. "Traffic was awful."

"Then that was a good introduction to city driving," said Dad. "I'll admit I had some second thoughts when I watched you drive away. But I'm glad you're home safe. My car, too."

When I went upstairs, I lay facedown on my bed for a while and thought about Uncle Milt and Aunt Sally. About Carol and what she must be feeling about her dad. What should I say to Aunt Sally when I called? What should I say to Uncle Milt?

I wished I could put a magic bubble around each person I loved and protect them always. And then I remembered that once Dad had said the same thing to me. *About* me. And I loved that he loved me that much.

12

Taking Chances

Tony hadn't come near me at all on Tuesday, and he didn't come by my locker on Wednesday morning, either. I knew he was in school because I saw him with some other guys outside the physics lab. My fear that he'd ask me out—ask me *over*—gave way to fear that he wouldn't. When I'd seen him on Monday, Miss Goody Two-shoes had opted once again to be the cautious junior, the inhibited Sunday-school girl, the unexciting Alice McKinley. It was like being on a seesaw. You can feel like a child and an adult, one right after the other.

The weather was freakishly warm for December 5, almost springlike, though we knew it wouldn't last. After geometry I sat by the window in World History, the sun warming my arms, eyes half closed. Patrick slid into the seat next to me and glanced over.

"What's this? Hibernation?" he joked.

"Yeah," I said dreamily. "Wake me when it's spring. This sun feels so *good*!"

"Heard you went to Edgar's last night," he said. "Pamela was talking about it before school this morning. Have they got the same band—Blood and Tonic? I heard them once, and they were great."

"Yeah, same band," I said. "I didn't know you took time to do anything fun, Patrick."

"Hey, a guy's gotta live!" he said, and then the teacher started talking, and the class began.

Later, as Pamela, Liz, and I went down the corridor to the cafeteria, we saw that kids were taking their lunches outside and eating on the steps. Sitting on the walk.

"Yes!" said Pamela. "Let's sit on the sidewalk and bake in the sun."

Up ahead we saw that one of the office staff was taping up photos of all the couples who'd had their pictures taken at the Snow Ball. They were arranged in two long rows, one above the other, with a sign that said you could pick up your copies in the office.

"Omigosh, let's look!" Pamela squealed as we walked along the rows of smiling couples.

The office secretary taped up the last one and took her empty box back to the office.

"There's Jill and Justin," said Liz. "My God, look at that dress! And Karen!"

"Here's me and my date," said Pamela. "Not bad!"

"Lori and Leslie," I said, moving on. "Penny and Mark. . . ."

Some of the couples looked a little geekish, but most were more glamorous than we'd ever thought they could be. And then, right in the middle of the second row, was the photo of Amy and me, my face the color of sunset, Amy looking pleased and proud.

"Alice?" Pamela said, coming to a dead stop. "What happened? Where's Tony?"

I glanced frantically around. The photo of Tony and me was farther down, separated by eight or nine pictures. If anyone missed it, they'd think I came to the Snow Ball with Amy. I could feel my face burning all over again.

My first impulse was to take the photo down, but then it would be obvious one was missing. "Amy came alone and begged me to be in her picture with her," I explained tersely. "Come on. Let's get lunch."

Blindly, I made my way over to the cafeteria line, paid for a sandwich, and went outside with Liz and Pamela. I found a space on the concrete wall by the steps and hoisted myself up, wishing that the sun could evaporate me, that I could just disappear. It was chilly without a jacket, but the sun felt delicious, and I let my legs dangle, face turned toward the sky.

There was a low roar in the distance, gradually getting louder as a motorcycle came into view and careened slowly up the curved driveway in front of the school, a definite no-no.

Tony and a bunch of guys went over to look. A few girls, too. The cyclist seemed to be a friend of Tony's, because Tony gave him a slap on the back. It was a sporty-looking cycle, a Kawasaki Ninja, bright yellow with orange streaks and a black seat.

"Looks like it belongs in a circus!" Liz commented from the steps below.

Tony turned around to call to a friend, then saw me sitting on the wall.

"Hey, Alice!" he yelled. "Come and get a look at this."

My heart began to race. I put down the rest of my sandwich and slid off the wall.

"Alice . . . ?" Liz said, but I kept going.

At the curb Tony introduced me to his friend Steve. "Hey," Tony said, "how about taking her for a ride?"

Steve grinned at me. "Sure," he said. "Hop on."

Everyone was looking at me.

"I—I don't have a jacket," I said.

Tony slipped off his leather jacket and put it on me. It was too big, and I had to shake my fists to get my hands out. But I put one leg over the seat behind Steve, clutching his shoulders, and sat down.

"Hug me around the waist," he said, and I had barely put my arms around him when the motorcycle roared off, tipping so far to one side that I was sure we were going to fall over.

If Steve was saying anything, I couldn't hear him. Anytime I tried to look around him, the wind blasted my face, and I had to bury my forehead against his back to keep things out of my eyes. I felt as though my hair were flying off my head, and my fingers had a death grip on the sides of his jacket. I didn't know where we were headed— Georgia Avenue, maybe—but every time the cycle leaned to one side, I tried to lean the other way to keep us upright.

"Relax!" Steve yelled when we stopped at a light. "Just go with the flow. You like it?"

"Uh . . . yeah!" I gulped. "Great bike!"

"Got a twin-cylinder four-stroke engine with dual overhead cams," he said.

"How long have you had it?" I asked.

"'Bout a month," he said, and I lost the rest of the sentence because the light changed and we were off again, weaving in and out of traffic. I wondered if he could feel my arms trembling on either side of him.

"Aren't I supposed to be wearing a helmet?" I called.

"What?" he yelled.

"A helmet!" I called back. "Aren't I supposed to be wearing one?"

"Yeah, but I left my extra at home. You enjoying this or not?"

I guess I wasn't sounding positive enough. "Love it!" I lied. "Great day for a ride."

"Yeah. We've got an event coming up New Year's Day, if it don't snow. I know a fella you could ride with!" he shouted.

"Oh, sorry! I'll be out of town," I lied again.

At the next light he said, "Well, I better get you back," and when we got the green, he careened around a corner. I don't know if our feet scraped the ground or if I only imagined it, and by the time we got back to school, the bell had rung and people were going inside. Tony was still waiting at the curb.

"How was it?" he asked, helping me off the cycle. I took off his jacket and gave it back.

"Great!" I said. "Terrific motorcycle."

Tony and Steve gave each other a sort of salute, and then Steve took off again.

"So! Decided to live dangerously for a change, huh?" Tony asked me, giving my waist a quick, almost impatient tug.

"Hey, life's always dangerous," I said.

"You only live once. Gotta do what the spirit moves you to do," said Tony. And when we got inside, he said, "See you at the staff meeting after school."

I guess, just like me, Tony had two sides to his personality, maybe more. Once when he drove me home from a staff meeting, he'd just wanted to talk—about how he feels he's a disappointment to his dad, who'd hoped he'd be a big sports hero or something. But because of his heart defect, he has to settle for being a sportscaster or sportswriter, and maybe he won't even get that kind of job. This week he's Mr. Hot Stuff, the Wandering Hand Guy, friend of Motorcycle Guy. Which was he, really, or was he both? Would the real Tony Osler please stand up? And then, the bigger question: Who was I?

In speech that afternoon Mrs. Cary faced the class. "Most of you did a pretty creditable job of choosing a topic you strongly believe in and giving a persuasive talk," she said. "A number of you backed up your talks with excellent research. We heard sales pitches, you might say, against the death penalty, for lowering the drinking age, for spreading democracy in the Mid-East, against using animals in research, pro-abortion, against gay marriage—we covered a wide range of topics here in class."

We basked in her praise.

She continued: "Most of you are taking this class because you want to be able to stand up before a group and speak easily, naturally, without too much nervousness."

"I took it because I couldn't get mechanical drawing for my elective," some guy said, and we all laughed.

"Well, that's legitimate," Mrs. Cary said. "But to be a good communicator, you also have to be a good listener. You have to be able to sift through what you're hearing to sort out the logical from the irrational. So here's your next assignment: I want each of you to take the same subject you chose before and give another three-minute talk, this time taking the opposite point of view."

There were surprised groans and protests, but she went on: "So if, for example, you argued against capital punishment, now you have to defend it to the best of your ability. And once again, you'll be graded on how well you research your argument and how persuasive you are in presenting it to us."

"You should have told us about this assignment before we decided on our topics!" said the girl who had argued in favor of chastity before marriage. "This isn't fair!"

"Not fair to examine some of your beliefs?" asked Mrs. Cary. "I'm not asking you to change your minds. But teaching you to *think* is more important than teaching you facts, in my book. The assignment is meant to help you examine a topic from another perspective."

I picked up my books at the end of the period and stalked out of the room. After all I had read about the suffering and torture of animals used in medical research, I now had to *defend* it? Brian and I practically collided going out the door. He had to give a three-minute talk on why we should *not* lower the drinking age.

Amy Sheldon caught up with me halfway down the hall.

"Alice!" she called, and came running alongside me. "I've been meaning to ask you a question." Her voice was particularly loud and irritating.

"Yeah?" I said, not even slowing down.

"Do you think there's something wrong with me because I'm fifteen and I still haven't started my periods?" she asked.

"How should I know?" I said impatiently, rudely. "Talk to your mother! Ask your sister! Ask your aunts! I'm not a doctor." And I shoved through the glass doors at the end of the hall and clattered on down the stairs to my locker.

• • •

By the time I got to the staff meeting, Tony had seen the photos in the hall, and he wasn't happy about the one of me and Amy.

"I took it down, what do you expect?" he said.

I was relieved, to tell the truth, but what I said was, "Amy will be disappointed. She'll be looking for her picture."

"Then she can go to the office and buy a copy," he said. "That made *me* look like a jerk. What d'ya want people to think? We went as a threesome?"

The staff was debating which photos from the Snow Ball we should publish in the next issue of *The Edge*. Not the photos taken by the professional photographer, but the candid photos caught by Sam and Don. We obviously couldn't use them all. Scott suggested selecting a few of seniors with seniors, since this was their last year to attend the dance, but after that was settled, he still seemed unhappy with the paper.

"We're just doing the same old stuff, month after month," he said. "We need to come up with something different. A real story. An exposé or something."

"About the Snow Ball?" asked Jacki.

"Forget the Snow Ball. Something that'll get attention. Make waves."

"Like what?" asked Don, who looked like a

linebacker. "Follow a teacher after hours and report on his nightlife?"

"Something offbeat but with a purpose," Scott said. "Everybody think about it. If you get any ideas, call me. There's still a big hole in the paper we need to fill by the deadline on Monday."

Tony drove me home after the meeting in his Toyota. When we got to my street, he pulled over to the curb and parked a block away. Then he reached for me across the gearshift, which was awkward enough, and kissed me. His right hand slid under my jacket, felt its way up my side, and cupped my breast, squeezing and stroking.

"See you, baby," he said, letting me go, and as soon as I was out of the car, he rode off.

I don't know when I'd felt so down on myself. Tony . . . the picture of Amy Sheldon and me together at the dance . . . the MGT and DD tags that Jill and Karen had labeled me. . . . People might even drag up stuff from last semester— how I'd taken a sex ed class at my *church*! I felt depressed and angry and confused and sad—a whole soup of emotions, all at the same time.

At dinner I heard myself saying, "Why hasn't Lester been over for dinner lately? It's like a morgue when he's not around." I was instantly sorry because it really wasn't true.

Dad looked at me sharply. "Ex*cuse* me?" he said.

"I'm sorry," I apologized. "I just miss his jokes." And then, when neither Dad nor Sylvia replied, I added, "I've had sort of a bad day."

"Well, so have I, so don't take it out on us, please," said Dad.

I swallowed the bite of potato I'd just taken and looked around the table. "Uncle Milt's not worse, is he?"

"No, Sal said his surgery today went off without a hitch. We should know more in a few days. But our plans to rent the store next to us fell through, and I really wanted that space for an annex," said Dad.

"Oh, I'm sorry," I told him, and we continued eating in silence.

Finally I said, "Do you think the owner would reconsider?"

"We don't think so," Sylvia said. "He's going to rent the space to a restaurant."

That sounded interesting, and I wanted to ask what kind of restaurant, but that didn't seem appropriate. I knew Dad's heart was set on expanding the store. After dinner he said he had a headache and went upstairs to lie down.

"I'll do the dishes," I told Sylvia.

"Oh, I'll help. Sometimes it's good just to be doing something with my hands instead of my brains," she said.

I carried plates and silverware to the sink while Sylvia rinsed them off and placed them in the dishwasher. Finally I said, "Did you ever feel like saying, 'Will the real Sylvia Summers please stand up'?"

Sylvia looked at me and smiled a little. "About once a day in high school. In fact, a few times in college, as I remember."

"It's sort of what I've been feeling lately," I told her. "Like sometimes I don't even know myself."

"Want to talk about it?" she asked.

"Not particularly," I said.

"Okay." She went on stacking plates.

"Anyway, that's why I've been sort of irritable, I guess," I explained. "Sort of uncertain."

"I know the feeling," said Sylvia. "Sometimes when we try to please too many people, we get caught up in things that just aren't us."

"Well," I said quickly, "I don't plan to repeat what I did today, that's for certain."

Sylvia looked at me intently. "Well, whatever it was, I'm glad," she said.

13

The City at Night

There's one cure for feeling so completely lousy and low that I can barely stand myself. That's finding someone who's a lot worse off than I am and concentrating on her for a while. The first person who came to mind, other than Amy Sheldon, was Molly, so I drove over there after dinner.

The thing about Molly Brennan is that she's always lived "in the moment," whatever it was. As a member of stage crew, Molly gave one hundred percent to each performance. She was one of those girls who, when she was talking with you, made you feel like you were the most interesting person in the world.

She'd never had a boyfriend, never had a date, never been kissed, but was simply too busy to care. "It'll happen when it'll happen," she'd tell us. "I'm ready!" Meanwhile, she joined clubs, worked on committees, took flute lessons, learned to scuba dive, got good grades, had a zillion friends, and . . . got leukemia.

The hard part about visiting someone who's seriously sick is you feel you have to say something encouraging. Something cheerful. Something funny. And if you don't *feel* encouraged or cheerful or funny, you wonder what good your visit will do. And then you find out that just being there is what's important, even if you don't say anything. If you don't do anything but hold somebody's hand, it's something.

"She's had a rough week," Mrs. Brennan said when she met me at the door that night. "She's made it to only a few classes this semester, and she's really too sick to go at all. She's discouraged."

"Shall I go on up?" I asked.

"Go up and ask if she wants you to stay. She'll be honest. At least she'll be glad you cared enough to come by," Mrs. Brennan said.

Molly was asleep when I came in. I just sat by her bed and watched her sleep. Sat looking at her bulletin board—at her blue ribbons and trophies and pictures and photos and notes and silly little mementos—what a full life she'd had before.

She stirred and sighed, flopping one arm over the edge of the bed. Her eyes fluttered, opened slightly, closed, then opened wider, staring at me.

"Hi," I said. "Just wanted to come by and say hello to Sleeping Beauty."

She smiled. "My mouth tastes like gym socks," she said, her lips dry, sticking together.

"Day-old socks or week-old?" I asked. She closed her eyes again.

"I feel yucky," she said finally.

"I know," I told her.

"My bones ache and my gums are sore and I feel like I'm going to upchuck and I have no energy at all."

"We all knew it was going to be rough, but I guess you're the only one who can tell us just how rough," I said.

"Yeah," she said. "This morning I was thinking about all the lousy times in my life: the time I got stung by a nest of hornets and my face was swollen for a week, and the time I lost my best friend's key chain . . . the bone I broke in my foot . . . the usual miserable things that happen to a person in a normal life. . . . And I would gladly relive them all just to trade in what I've got now."

"I can understand that," I said.

She was quiet for a while. Then she asked, "What are they saying . . . about me at school?"

"That you're sick and you're getting treatments and that you're a fighter," I answered.

Molly's mouth turned down a little at the corners.

"I always thought I was too, but now I'm not so sure." A single tear rolled down her cheek.

I reached over and stroked her hand. "*I'm* sure, Molly," I said. "You're going to give this old thing everything you've got."

I didn't feel any better when I left Molly's, but I saw life with a little more perspective. I called Gwen, though, and told her how afraid I was for Molly.

"You don't think she'll die, do you?" I asked shakily. "I thought you said the doctors were optimistic." Gwen had had a high school internship with the National Institutes of Health last summer when Molly was sent there for evaluation, so she knew some of the inside stuff.

There was too much quiet at the other end of the line.

"Gwen?" I said.

"I don't know," she answered. "Maybe I was wrong."

I stared blankly at the wall. "What do you *mean*?"

I heard her sigh. "You know how they tell you that when you're sick and you go for the results of your tests, you should always take someone with you?"

That was news to me. "No . . . ," I said.

"Well, you should, because if it's serious, they've found, you'll only hear about thirty percent of what the doctor tells you."

"And . . . ?" I said.

"When I saw Molly in our lab and she told me she had leukemia, I asked the doctors afterward just how serious lymphoblastic leukemia is—the kind she has. What they said was that usually this is a disease in younger children, and the cure rate for them is especially high. What I heard was that the cure rate is high. What I blanked out was that the cure rate for people Molly's age maybe isn't that good." I heard Gwen swallow.

"Gwen!" I gasped. "How long have you known this?"

"Since September," she said in a small voice. "I've been doing some reading, asking questions. . . ."

"You never *told* us!" I said accusingly.

"I know. I got everybody optimistic, and there are still a lot of reasons to be optimistic for Molly. But I thought she'd only be in treatment for a year, and it's the first big block of treatment that can last for a year. She'll be in different stages of treatment for two or three years."

"Oh, Gwen!"

"I feel awful," she said. "Guilty and sad and everything that goes with it. I had no business saying anything at all. But there *are* things in her favor. Technical things . . ."

Just like Gwen said, my brain didn't focus on

"things in her favor." It focused on "two or three years." I started to cry.

"It's just hard . . . to know what to say to her anymore," I wept.

"Tell her she's in the best possible hands, which is true," Gwen said. "Tell her that her doctors are experts at this stuff. Tell her that if one drug doesn't work, they'll try something else. And hope, Alice. Hope is powerful medicine."

"I want her to live, Gwen," I said.

"So does everybody. Have you ever met one person who doesn't like Molly Brennan?" Gwen said.

The more I thought about Molly, the more I thought about life and making every day count. And making every day count meant taking chances. Maybe I *didn't* take enough chances. Maybe that's what got me the MGT image with Karen and Jill, not that they were my role models. What if I *had* run away for a while that night I was so mad at Sylvia? In fact, what if I'd called Liz to go with me, and we'd both disappeared for a day or so? We sure wouldn't be DD after that!

Suddenly, without even running it past the automatic censor in my brain, I picked up the list of staff members for *The Edge* and called Scott.

"Whuzzup?" he answered. I could hear his TV in the background.

"It's Alice," I said.

"I know," he said.

"Busy? I could call back."

"No. It's okay." I heard the TV cut off.

"I was thinking about a story we could do for the paper," I told him. "Why don't I go out some night with another girl and pose as runaways in Silver Spring. No money. No ID. Then I'll write up the story."

"You want me to get expelled?" said Scott. "I couldn't assign something like that. You could get beaten up or worse!"

"Then send some guys along to keep an eye on us—take photos," I said, my mouth running on ahead of my brain, hoping that Scott would volunteer.

There was a pause. "I don't know . . . ," he said. "What exactly would we be trying to say?"

"Well, a lot of kids have miserable home situations, and even if they don't, I'll bet everyone's had a big quarrel or something where they just really wanted to take off for a day or two," I said. "We could show the reality of what it's like being out in the city at night with nowhere to go. Or we could show what resources *are* available without getting the police in on it."

"Wow," Scott said. Another pause. Then, "Who would you get to go with you?"

"Oh, I know someone. She'll do it!" I chirped hopefully.

"Let me think about it, and I'll call you back," he said.

Yes! I thought, my heart pounding, and immediately phoned Liz.

"Listen, DD," I teased.

"Don't call me that," she said.

"Well, that's the way some people think of us," I told her. "So . . . you want to do something wild and get your picture in the newspaper?"

"And get grounded for the rest of my life? Not particularly," she said.

"Okay. *Without* your folks knowing about it, but showing everyone at school just how gutsy we can be?" I said.

Now she was interested. "Doing what?"

"It'll be an article for *The Edge,* but they won't use our names. Two girls sneak out late at night and, watched over at a distance by two guys to keep them safe, pose as runaways. We won't have any identification or money on us, and we'll see just what help is available to two girls at night in Silver Spring."

There was a three-second pause. "I'll do it," said Liz.

"You *will?*"

"It's wild and exciting and fun, and we're doing it for a purpose," said Liz. "When?"

• • •

When Scott called back, I could hear the excitement in his voice. "Here's the deal," he said. "I didn't even check with Miss Ames because I can guarantee she'd say no. Too dangerous, and the school would be responsible if anything happened. So you're on your own. I've called around, and Don and Tony have agreed to be your backups—keep an eye on you—and Don's going to get some night photos if he can, silhouette-type. We've got to keep you anonymous. I can't actually assign this—can't condone it. All I can say is that if you turn in a good story, we'll run it, with a statement saying we didn't give our permission but felt it was worth publishing."

"Deal!" I said excitedly.

"The guys'll call you and set it up for Friday. If you can turn in the copy Monday morning, we can get it in this edition. And, Alice," he added, "be careful."

The dead bolt on our front door makes a loud *click* when you turn it, so we didn't lock it after us. Liz and I went down the steps in the darkness. She had come over to spend the night on Friday, and we'd carefully prepared our "look." Old baggy jeans that looked as though we'd slept in them, because we had, in preparation. Wrinkled T-shirts. Smudged jackets, dirty sneakers, dirty hair, no makeup.

Dad and Sylvia had gone to bed around ten

thirty, so we called Tony on my cell phone one hour later and told him we'd meet him and Don at the corner.

"Ready?" I asked Liz as we checked ourselves one last time in the mirror.

She put a folded piece of paper on my bed.

"What's that?" I asked.

"Just in case," she answered.

"Can I read it?"

She didn't say no, so I picked it up.

> Dear Mom and Dad,
> If anything happens to me, I did this to be helpful to any girl who's alone in the city at night.
> Love,
> Liz

I decided that Liz's letter was explanation enough if we disappeared, and we crept noiselessly down the stairs.

Tony's Toyota was parked at the corner. "Where to, girls?" he asked when we climbed in. "Where's this undercover operation going to take us?"

"Let's say we hitchhiked here from some other place in Maryland, and they let us off in Silver

Spring," I said. "I think the first thing we'd need is a restroom."

"Alice the Practical," said Liz.

"Okay. There's a twenty-four-hour Texaco just off Georgia, I think," Tony said, and off we went.

There's not a lot of activity at midnight in Silver Spring, I discovered. Tony parked a block away from the gas station, and we all got out. The guys stayed about twenty yards behind us, and Don had his camera set for night photos.

Liz and I went inside the Texaco. A young man was sitting behind a bulletproof glass enclosure and looked up when we entered.

"Could we have the key to the restroom?" I asked.

He studied us for a minute, a small bulge between his lip and his cheek where he'd tucked his tobacco. "Water's off," he said. "Sorry."

I could tell right away he didn't want us using his restroom.

"Aren't gas stations supposed to be available for travelers?" I asked.

"You got a car?" he asked.

"No, we're walking, but look, we're not going to sleep in there," I told him.

"Or use drugs," put in Elizabeth.

"We just want to clean up a little and use the toilet. And we really, *really* need to go," I told the man.

He reluctantly took a key down from the wall

and slid it through the change slot in the glass wall. "Five minutes," he said. "You're not out in five minutes, I'll use the master key."

Liz and I went to the bathroom. Of course there was water. When we brought the key back, I said, "Do you know anywhere we could stay for the night? Any shelter for women?"

"Don't you got no place to sleep?"

"No," Liz told him. "And we haven't eaten since this morning."

"Well, I don't know where you could sleep. But here . . ." He pushed a package of peanut-butter cheese crackers through the slot, and I think that Don, outside, got a picture. We thanked the man and started off again.

"You taking notes?" Tony asked.

"Mental notes," I told him. "Liz will help me remember the details."

"I'm hungry," she said. "What if we really *hadn't* eaten all day? Let's go to the all-night diner and ask if there are any leftovers we could have."

We walked the five blocks to the diner. There were a couple of workmen eating the blue plate special and an elderly man with a piece of lemon pie.

"Help you?" asked the middle-aged woman behind the counter.

"We don't have any money," I began, "and—"

The waitress cut me off. "Sorry. We don't give food away." She took another swipe at the counter with her rag, her face in a frown beneath the hairnet.

"Well, we were wondering if we could wash dishes, maybe, for a sandwich. We haven't eaten since this morning," Liz told her.

"We can't allow customers behind the counter. Insurance regulations," the woman said.

"Could we wipe tables, then? Stack trays?" Liz wouldn't give up.

"You see any tables need wiping? See any trays?" she asked. "You girls don't look very malnourished to me. I suggest you go back home and get your act together."

It was embarrassing. It was as though she saw through us. As we left the diner, Don got a photo of us, the woman glaring after us in the background.

It was almost one now, and a light rain was starting to fall. Liz and I huddled together in the doorway of a store, and the guys stood on the steps of a building across the street.

"What exactly are we doing now?" Liz asked.

"Keeping out of the rain," I said.

A police car came by. The cop in the passenger seat looked over at us, and the car slowed. It turned around in the intersection and cruised slowly back again. The driver rolled down his window.

"You girls need any help?" he called.

"Should we ask him if he knows of a shelter?" Liz whispered.

"No. We're minors. They'd take us in," I whispered back.

"We're okay," I called. "Just keeping out of the rain."

"It's late," the officer said. "Really shouldn't be out on the street like this." He nodded toward Tony and Don on the other side. "There are a number of people around who would probably like to know you better," he warned. "I'd go home if I were you."

"Oh, those guys are okay. We know them," Liz said.

"You know those fellas over there?" the policeman asked.

"Yeah, they're friends of ours," Liz said.

"They're just keeping an eye on us," I told him. This time the driver turned off the engine, and both police officers got out of the car.

"Omigod!" I said to Liz. "They must think we're hookers and that Don and Tony are our pimps!" I stood up and ran toward the cops, who were now walking across the street. "They're okay! They're okay!" I called. "It was all my idea!"

The policemen looked at us, then at the guys. The camera didn't help. I had to explain how we were researching an article for the school paper and the guys were along for protection. Don and Tony had identification as staff members on *The Edge*, but Liz and I had nothing and wouldn't give our names.

"Well, I'll tell you what. This sounds just crazy enough for me to believe you," the first policeman said. "But there's been some gang activity going on that we're watching out for, and I wouldn't want you getting involved in that in any way, shape, or form. You kids call it a night and go home, and we'll let it go."

"Okay," said Don. "Thanks." We walked down the block and all got in Tony's car.

"I guess that about does it," said Tony.

"No!" I protested. "We've still got to be turned down for someplace to sleep. I mean, what if it was five above zero and it was snowing and . . ."

"I know a home where some priests live," said Liz. "We could try there."

"Let's do it," I said.

"Then we can go home?" Don yawned.

"Then it's a wrap," I promised.

Liz directed them to the rectory, and once again, Tony parked a block away. Liz and I got out and started toward the house. We were halfway up the block when we heard a car cruising down the street, slowing when it got to us.

"Oh no, the police are back," I murmured, but when I turned around, it was a light-colored van with some guys in it. Men.

"Alice!" Liz said shakily.

"Keep walking," I said.

"Hey, girlies," a guy called, hanging out the passenger side, "What's the hurry?"

We didn't answer.

The driver leaned over and yelled, "Wanna go someplace for a beer?"

When we didn't respond, he said, "Hey! Don't act so friendly!"

I remembered the guys who had followed us on the boardwalk last summer—how scared I'd been then and how we'd ducked into a stranger's house where all the lights were on. There were no lights now. Not even at the priests' house, and I had no idea how many men were in the van.

"Hey!" the first guy yelled again, and this time the van came to a stop. "It sort of hurts my feelings when a girl won't even give me the time of day." He started to get out, and we started to run. My heart was beating like crazy, and Liz was making frightened little bleating noises. There were pounding footsteps behind us, and someone grabbed my arm—not to stop me, but to speed me on. It was Tony, and Don stood like a wall between us and the van at the curb.

The men in the car hooted, and the first guy got back in again. "They got their big brothers looking out for them. Let's go," he said, and the driver gunned the motor and off they went.

My chest hurt with both the running and the fright. Even Tony was out of breath.

"Now, *that's* got to go in the story," he said.

"If I ever stop shaking!" I told him, and my voice trembled.

"They could be back, possibly with more," said Tony.

"This is our last stop," I promised. "Then we'll go home."

Liz pressed her finger to the doorbell, and we heard the *ding-dong* from inside. Don and Tony waited on a porch across the street.

"Oh, man!" I breathed out. "What if there had been a whole gang of men in that car, Liz? What if even Don and Tony couldn't fight them off?"

"Don't even think it, don't even think it, don't even think it," Liz murmured. "I'm nervous enough already."

We must have rung three times and stood there for five or six minutes before a light finally came on inside. An elderly man answered the door without speaking. I felt embarrassed for waking him.

"I'm sorry," Liz said hesitantly, "but we don't have anyplace to go, and we're afraid to be out on the street. Some men just tried to pick us up, and we were wondering if we could possibly stay here just for tonight."

The man opened the door wordlessly, and we stepped inside. He motioned us to his study, then came in and lowered himself into his chair, one arm leaning on the desk, nodding toward the sofa against one wall. He was in his pajamas and robe.

"I'm very tired," he said, "so I'm not quite coherent, but somehow I get the feeling that you girls haven't been out on your own for very long. Am I right?"

We sat down. "Yes," I said, wishing he would hurry and tell us to go home so we could call it quits.

"Problems at home? Fight with your parents?" he asked sleepily.

We nodded.

"Is there someone you'd like me to call?" he asked.

"No. We don't want anyone to know where we are," Liz said. "It's really very complicated, but you wouldn't turn us away if you knew the whole story. It's not that we're desperate, we just need to know if we could stay here overnight."

"If men are out there trying to pick you up, it sounds pretty desperate to me," the priest said. "There's the sofa for one of you, and the other will have to sleep in a chair. Bathroom down the hall. We'll be waking you at seven in the morning, because I have an eight o'clock mass and appointments starting at nine."

He stood up and pulled the belt of his robe a little tighter around him. "Good night," he said, and walked unsteadily back into the hallway, slowly climbing the stairs.

Liz and I stared at each other.

"That's it?" I said. "What are we going to *do*? The guys are out there! They want to go home!"

"Turn the light off and on and signal to them?" she suggested.

"Are you nuts?" I said. "We've got to leave, Liz!"

"I'll write a note," she said. I rolled my eyes and rested my forehead on my arms while Liz took the priest's memo pad and wrote:

Dear Reverend,
I'm afraid we came on false pretenses, because we're really doing a story for our school paper about what happens to homeless girls in Silver Spring and where they can go to get help. We promise not to use your address in the story, but thanks for your kindness.
E and A

We turned off the light behind us and carefully opened the study door. Except for a dim hall light, the house was dark, and we tiptoed step by step over to the big front door with the little stained-glass window at the top.

"What if it sets off an alarm?" Liz asked.

"Liz, we've got to leave, regardless!" I insisted.

I put my hand on the doorknob and turned it.

"Good night," a voice behind us said, and we wheeled around to see the priest sitting up there on the landing, leaning wearily against the wall. "Next time you get an idea like this, bag it, okay?" he said. "Promise me you'll go straight home, and I won't have to tell the police I'm worried about you."

"We promise!" Liz said, and this time we meant it.

We all trooped back to Tony's car. We'd talked about going for coffee or something afterward, but we were simply too tired.

"Hope my photos turn out," Don said. "I'd like to get at least two or three we could use."

"Thanks, guys," I said. "I think we'll get a good story out of this."

"Remember to mention the two fabulous hunks who saved your lives," said Tony.

Fifteen minutes later, at quarter past two, he dropped Liz and me off at the corner, and we slipped back into my house.

No one was up. No light was on. No message from Dad or Sylvia. But the note Elizabeth had left on our bed—the "just in case" note—was gone.

14

Secrets

When I rode to the Melody Inn with Dad the next day, he wasn't very talkative, but that was fine with me. I didn't know what he knew—*if* he knew—and I was too sleepy to try to sort it out. I hadn't had more than four hours of sleep. Liz had gone straight home that morning and back to bed. I leaned my head against the seat, my eyes closed, hands in the pockets of my jacket. Once the store opened, phones would ring, customers would mill about asking questions, clerks would call to each other, kids would troop to the practice rooms upstairs with their instruments for Saturday-morning lessons. It was good now just to soak up some quiet. But it was a jumpy kind of quiet with Dad lately, and any little thing could set him off.

He parked behind the store as usual, and we went inside. Marilyn was plugging in the coffeepot as we passed, and she studied us both.

Later, when she brought money over to my cash register, she asked, "Everything okay?"

"Okay how?" I asked.

She gave a little shrug. "Between you and your dad?"

"Sure," I said. "Why wouldn't it be?"

"No reason," she said quickly. "Your dad's been a little edgy lately."

"Yeah, we've noticed. The annex thing," I said.

"That too," said Marilyn. I looked after her, puzzled, as she took the box of twenties, tens, and ones over to David's cash register.

Halfway through the morning, a friend from school came in to buy new strings for his guitar. We stood there talking a few minutes, and even though I edged toward another customer who was looking peeved and impatient, I didn't stop our conversation. Suddenly Marilyn seemed to appear out of nowhere and waited on the woman.

When both the woman and my friend were gone, I said, "I know, I know, I shouldn't have spent so much time talking."

"Yeah, you really need to be a little more careful right now, Alice," she said. "Don't do anything more to upset them."

More? I thought. *Them?*

"Anything other than what?" I asked.

"Just stay on good terms with them till things

blow over," Marilyn said, and then, "Your dad needs me over there. I've got to go."

"No, wait!" I said. "Stay on good terms with *who*? What are you talking about?"

And over her shoulder Marilyn said, "Sylvia knows." She crossed the floor.

I stared after her. What did she mean? Knows *what*? Knows where Liz and I went last night? Knows about Tony and me in his Buick? About me hiding in their *closet*? Was I living in a fishbowl or what?

I tried to get Marilyn's attention after she'd finished helping Dad with a sale, but she avoided me. I waited till I saw her go in the stockroom for something, then followed her back.

"Marilyn, what were you trying to tell me?" I asked.

"Oh, me and my big mouth," she said. "I just don't want you to get in any more trouble, Alice. Just a little tip from me to you, okay?"

I felt my scalp turning warm, but I had to ask. "What do you mean, any *more* trouble?" If I had to die of embarrassment, let it be here with Marilyn, not a stranger.

"Your dad's grumpy lately because he didn't get the annex, and he's been jumping on everyone," Marilyn said. "If he saw you chatting up that guy and ignoring another customer, he'd be on your case in seconds flat."

"So what does that have to do with Sylvia?" I asked. Nothing was making sense.

"Listen, Alice," Marilyn said. "Sylvia dropped by over lunch on Wednesday because Ben had left his glasses in her car. We both saw you on that motorcycle with a guy during school hours. . . ."

I felt as though my brain had broken into a dozen pieces and was trying to realign itself. "That was just . . . it was only . . . I didn't even know him!" I said, every phrase making it sound worse.

"I've got to get back out there," Marilyn said, reaching for the violin bow a customer had wanted, and quickly ducked through the curtain to the main room.

I stood there trying to remember the route the motorcycle had taken. Yes, I think it had turned onto Georgia Avenue, and I could well imagine we might have gone as far as the Melody Inn. And yes, it was over the lunch hour, and we'd stopped for a light. . . .

My throat felt dry as I went back out to the Gift Shoppe counter and pressed the START button for two girls who wanted to see the earrings in the revolving glass case. *Why didn't Sylvia say anything to me about the motorcycle incident? What's she waiting for?*

When I'd wrapped up the girls' earrings and made the sale, I went over to where Marilyn was looking up an order. "Just tell me this," I said. "Does Dad know?"

"I doubt it, because Sylvia and I were both looking out the window, trying to decide if it was you, and Sylvia said, 'Don't tell Ben.' And, of course, I haven't."

All afternoon it haunted me. All I could figure was that somewhere, Sylvia was keeping score, tallying up my misdeeds, so that someday, when she really wanted to wallop me, she'd have all these grievances at once to tell Dad. And it probably included last night. She'd undoubtedly tucked that note Liz wrote in a drawer. It was ridiculous and childish and completely unfair to suspect this, yet I couldn't help it. It was as though Sylvia were a ticking time bomb.

Well, I thought angrily, *at least I'm shaking off that MGT reputation.* How many other girls had been invited to climb on the back of a stranger's motorcycle and ride off into the noonday sun? And yet, all the while I knew, *This isn't me.* Just like all the while Tony was playing with my breasts and I was enjoying it, I knew, *He's not the one. Not really.* You can do things, say things, feel things that—down in your heart of hearts—you know you aren't serious about, and yet, it's like a big deal to everyone else who reads a lot more into it than is really there.

At school, when Liz had finally asked me what all had happened that noon on the motorcycle, I'd said, "We rented a motel room, made mad love, and he dropped me off at school again in time for the bell, what else?" She'd laughed, and so had I. But Sylvia, I felt sure, wasn't laughing.

As soon as I got home from work that afternoon, tired as I was, I wrote up my story and e-mailed it to Scott. He was probably out for the evening, because an hour went by, two, three, and there was no response. Then, just before I went to bed, I got this:

> Alice, you're a wonder! It will probably
> get us both in hot water, but I love it.
> Hope the photos turn out. S.

I knew I'd treasure that one e-mail forever (*Alice, you're a wonder!*), but why couldn't he have added, *But I'd love to be in a hot tub with you!* or something?

Lester finally came by for dinner that Sunday night.

"Where have you *been*?" I asked as he slid in across from me at the table.

"You mean I've been missed?" he asked.

"When you go close to two weeks without even *calling* . . . !" I scolded.

Lester grinned and reached for the scalloped potatoes. "Okay, so I met this girl."

"Thought so!" said Dad.

It had been four months since Les and Tracy broke up, and now he was back in circulation again.

"Can't keep a good man down, can we?" Sylvia joked.

"Did you meet her in grad school, Les?" I asked. "Not one of your instructors again, is she?"

"No, no. She's an aerobics instructor, actually, and a part-time student. I just know her from the gym. We've been going out some. Nothing serious."

"Well, we've missed you," said Sylvia. "Have some salad, Les."

He helped himself. "I heard about the annex deal, Dad," he said. "That's a bummer."

"Oh, I'll survive," said Dad. "I was just so sure we'd get it. The owner seemed to like the idea. But I guess the restaurant folks wined and dined him, and he liked their idea more."

"On the other hand," said Lester, "it's possible that people who come to the restaurant will discover your store."

"That's what I told him," said Sylvia. "He could put up a schedule of music classes in his window. Show people that here's a place a kid can get trombone lessons. Where you can hire a good piano tuner. Buy a guitar. It's not all bad."

"Anyway," said Dad, "that's water over the dam. But while you're here tonight, Les, I thought it would be a good time to call Sal and see how Milt's doing. He left the hospital today."

"Sure," said Les.

I hate group phone calls. You never know whom you're talking to next, and you have to keep the whole conversation generic. When Aunt Sally's on the line, though, all Dad has to do is hold the phone away from his ear and her voice comes through loud and clear. It's like she's addressing a school assembly.

"Milt's sleeping right now, Ben, but he's just doing fine!" Aunt Sally was saying. "The doctor says he's like a new man, and if we continue the medication and diet, he could live out his normal life span."

"That's just great news, Sal! It really is," said Dad, pleased. The rest of us cheered in the background so that Aunt Sally could hear us.

"And Carol's staying for a few days more," Aunt Sally continued. "Her phone hasn't been working in her apartment, so she brought a suitcase here, and it's so good to have her! She's out right now, and I think she's bringing home some take-out food."

Les and I exchanged looks, knowing that Carol still hadn't told her folks that she'd moved in with her boyfriend. Secrets, secrets . . .

"Sometimes," Aunt Sally went on, "good things come out of bad, and I think we've become closer as a family because of Milt's heart attack. Is Alice there, Ben? I want to say something to her."

I reluctantly took the phone. I love my aunt, but whatever she had to tell me, I didn't want the whole family to hear.

"Hi, Aunt Sally," I said. "We're so glad that Uncle Milt's home now."

"So are we," she said. "I just wanted to say, Alice, that things like this make you realize that every day is precious. Each day is a gift to be enjoyed to the fullest. But when I was waiting outside the emergency room for Milt, I wrote a poem, and I want to share it with you. You always did like my poems, didn't you?"

To tell the truth, the only poem of Aunt Sally's I remember is one about sorting clothes on wash day.

"Of course," I said, and held the receiver out so everyone could hear.

Aunt Sally cleared her throat and began:

> "When scorching looks and angry words
> Between you two have passed,
> Just remember, ne'er forget
> Each breath may be his last."

Les and I exchanged wide-eyed looks.

> *"Or you may die, and loving words*
> *Are sealed inside your head.*
> *They'll never reach his longing ears*
> *Because your lips are dead."*

Sylvia put one hand over her face.

> *"So cherish every kiss and touch*
> *And welcome each new day,*
> *For winter claims us, one by one,*
> *And takes it all away."*

I waited, wondering if there was more. When the pause lengthened, I said, "Aunt Sally, that . . . that's . . ."

"Awful!" Les whispered, holding back laughter.

"So . . . sad!" I said. "Uncle Milt isn't going to die!"

"But there were all these thoughts going through my head when we went to the hospital, Alice, and I wanted to write a poem about the guilt I was feeling for every argument we've ever had and how I'm pledging my life to just enjoying the good things and not nagging him about the little stuff."

"That's wonderful, Aunt Sally," I said, and handed the phone to Les.

• • •

Later, when Dad and Sylvia were watching a program, Les and I did the dishes.

"So what's the new girl's name, Les, and what's
she like?" I asked.

"Name's Claire: two arms, two legs, brown hair,
blue eyes. . . ."

"When do we get to meet her?" I asked.

"I'll have to give that some thought," he
answered. "See if she's the family type."

"Is she at all like Tracy?" I asked. "Do you have
a lot in common?"

"Oh, I wouldn't say we've made much progress
in that department, but she's good . . . uh, very
good . . . at other things."

I decided not to ask any more.

That evening, as I was searching for a slipper
under the bed, I found a sheet of notepaper,
scrunched and mauled, with tiny holes and tears
in it. I fished it out and flattened the paper. It was
the note that Liz had left on my bed the night we
crept out to do the story. We must not have
closed the door completely after us when we left
my room, and Annabelle, coming in to sleep on
my bed, had evidently found the note and toyed
with it. I never appreciated her more.

We got my story in by the Monday deadline, took
it to the printer, and the paper came out on Tuesday:

<u>Edge Exclusive</u>
This newspaper neither assigned this story nor gave its permission, but when it was submitted to us, we felt it deserved to be read. The photos accompanying the article are intentionally dark to protect the identity of the writer.

THE CITY AT NIGHT
by Anonymous

Who has never felt, even for a moment, the urge to run away? To simply walk out of a bad situation and take a breather? To see what two girls might be up against on the streets of Silver Spring in the wee hours of the morning, a friend and I—followed at a distance by two guys to keep us safe—slipped out around midnight on a Friday night. . . .

That was the way my article began, and after telling all that had happened to us, I ended with:

What we learned was that anyone wanting to escape a bad situation at home needs to have moxie, moola, and—most of all—a plan and a place to go. Because streets can be mean after midnight, even in Silver Spring.

Wow! That story made a real splash. Did Liz and I want everyone to know we were the girls in the story? Does the sun rise in the east?

When Pamela read it in the cafeteria, her eyes grew wide and she immediately turned to me. "Who *were* they, Alice? You must know!"

Liz and I exchanged glances over our salads, and Pamela saw. She grabbed the copy of the newspaper again and studied the photos.

"That's *you*, Alice!" she said, pointing to the profile of me in the doorway of the gas station, trying to get the key. And to the others, she announced gleefully, "It was *Alice*! Wow! Alice! And you *wrote* this, I'll bet! Who was the other girl?"

"My lips are sealed," I said, grinning.

"Wait a minute," said Gwen. She took the newspaper out of Pamela's hands and her eyes traveled down the page. "Whoever it was knew a house where priests live, so she's probably Catholic."

All eyes turned to Elizabeth. Jill and Karen positively stared.

"*Elizabeth?*" cried Penny. "You and *Elizabeth*? Man, you guys could have been raped, you know that? You could have been killed!"

"Who were the guys?" asked Jill.

"Now, *that*," I said, just to savor the moment, "will remain forever a mystery."

• • •

It was raining that afternoon—a cold December rain—the kind that feels as though it could turn to sleet, but I didn't care. I was on cloud nine. All afternoon the news had traveled around school that Liz and I had been the girls in the story, and kids gave me high fives and hugs.

"You got a car?" Tony asked me. "I'll drive you home."

I was grateful for the offer, because the bus had long since left. Miss Ames had called the newspaper staff in for a conference with the principal, and they let us know that while the story was a good one and provided some useful information, we should not expect that we could publish whatever we wanted just by printing a disclaimer. All of us, but especially Scott, had to promise that we'd run the paper—the whole paper—by Miss Ames in the future before it went to press. We promised.

"Everybody's talking about the story," Tony said when he slid in beside me. "I think everyone knows now that it was you."

"Good!" I said, and laughed. "It probably took me as long to count the characters and lines as it did to write the piece. I don't know how you always get your sports write-ups in on time."

"Computer program," said Tony. "If you know the typeface, the number of characters needed per line, lines per column, and number of columns, you just feed in the information, click 'Enter,' and the computer takes your material and does the rest."

"Amazing," I said.

"We'll stop by my place, and I'll show it to you," Tony said. He turned left at the corner instead of right.

"Who's home?" I asked.

"Mom'll be there soon," he answered. He turned left again farther on and finally into the driveway of a large house. "C'mon. I'll give you a demonstration."

I gave him my suspicious look, and he laughed. "Hey, this is *school*. This is *learning*. Jeez, does everything you do have to be an assignment? Don't you ever do anything just for fun?"

"Of course," I said, and old dry-as-dust Alice followed him into the house.

Tony lives in a more upscale neighborhood than we do. Actually, our house is, or used to be, the most modest house on the block. But Tony's ranch-style had a big lawn. The master suite and study were at one end, he showed me on a quick tour, with the family room and Tony's bedroom at the other. We said hello to the maid in the kitchen, then headed for Tony's end of the house.

I felt that warm flush at the sight of Tony's unmade bed—a pair of Jockey shorts on the floor. We went over to his computer.

Tony sat down and pushed a few keys. He found the article he'd written about our last football game against Churchill, then got up and told me to sit in his place.

"Click on 'Times New Roman,'" he said, and I did.

"Now specify thirty-four characters per line . . ."

I obeyed.

"Then fifty-one lines per column, and press 'Enter.'"

I did, and suddenly Tony's article disappeared, only to reappear in column form. He showed me how to add a heading and even wrap the type around photos.

"Oh, wow! I've got to get this!" I said.

He was standing behind my chair, hands on my shoulders, and he let them slide down my body until they reached my breasts. He bent over me, thumbs circling my nipples. Instantly, I felt the warm wetness between my legs.

"Tony . . . ," I said, laughing a little. He pulled me up out of the chair, turned me around, and kissed me. Without letting go of me, he reached out and slid a CD in his player, and a slow song began, a woman singing a love song.

"Just want to relive a little of the Snow Ball," he said, and started dancing with me, hands on my behind. We danced right over his Jockey shorts, in fact, and as we moved away from the bed, I relaxed a little and swayed to his rhythm.

We danced slowly around his room, our bodies together, and I could feel him getting hard.

I heard a voice from the hallway, a door closing. I startled and pushed away.

"It's the maid leaving," he whispered in my ear. We were alone in the house then.

"Your mom . . . ?" I questioned.

"Shhhh," he whispered, and we kissed again.

The next time we got near his bed, he nudged me down on it and lay beside me. "Oh, baby," he said.

I wanted to say, *Please don't call me that. I'm me. Alice.* But even thinking it, I sounded like Little Miss Sunday School.

My breasts again. He didn't try to unfasten my bra this time. Just reached up under my top and clumsily pushed my bra up over my breasts. It was sort of awkward, the way we were lying across his twin bed. Only our backs and hips were on it, our legs off the edge, feet on the floor. I thought of Aunt Sally's admonition to keep both feet on the floor and almost smiled when I thought of the trouble you could get in with feet firmly planted.

Now Tony was trying to get me to lie on the bed lengthwise, but I didn't like the thought of being pushed back against the wall, so I resisted. Then he was unzipping my jeans, tugging at the sides till they were down past my hips, and his hand was inside my underwear, finding my slippery place. I felt the swelling sensation in my vagina.

"Oh, baby, you're creaming for me," he said. "You want it as much as I do."

He didn't say he wanted *me*, I noticed. He wanted *it*. So did I, honestly, but not, I think, with Tony.

"Tony, your mom . . . ," I said again.

"She won't be home till six," he whispered. "Shhhh."

That was an hour away! I tensed but then gave in again and let his finger explore me. Then it was *in* me, and his other hand was tugging at my jeans, trying to get them all the way off. I was wildly excited.

"Baby . . . baby . . . ," he murmured breathily.

He reached over and yanked at the little drawer on his bedside table, pulling out a condom. "I'll put on a glove," he said, and unzipped his own jeans. Condoms at the ready, in his bedside drawer? Was I just one of his "babes" in a long succession of girls?

"Tony," I said, dislodging his finger and trying to pull up my jeans.

Another door opening somewhere. Closing. Footsteps in the house.

"Tony!" I said, panicking.

"It's only my dad, and he doesn't care," Tony said.

I edged away from him.

"He won't come in. He never does. Trust me," Tony said.

"No," I said, scooting back.

"Baby, don't leave me like this," Tony said, pulling me against him again and putting my hand on his penis. He squeezed my hand a couple of times, and a few seconds later he came.

"Oh, baby, oh, baby," he kept breathing in my ear. "We got a good thing going here. We could be so good together. . . ."

"Tony?" his dad called from out in the hall.

"Got company," Tony yelled back, still breathless.

I wasn't sure, but I think I heard his dad chuckle. "Just wanted to know if you were home," he said, and the footsteps went away.

I got up, pulled up my jeans, and zipped them. Reached under my shirt and pulled my bra back down over my breasts. "I've got to get home. I can't stay any longer," I said.

He wiped himself off with a corner of the sheet, then stood and zipped up, grinning at me.

I was embarrassed when we walked through the high-ceilinged living room.

"Alice, this is my dad," Tony said. "Dad, this is the girl I took to the Snow Ball."

"How you doing, Alice?" Mr. Osler said, and he went back to his newspaper.

Tony talked about his dad as he drove me home. How his dad had been big man on campus when he was in college. "A girl on each arm," his dad used to brag. And I began to get the picture—that if Tony couldn't be the sports hero his dad had wanted him to be, he'd try for big man on campus with the girls. Again I wondered, Who was he, really? Who was I?

When we got to my house, he said, "This was just a warm-up, baby. Next time I'll give you a taste of the real thing."

I smiled. "Your *next* girl, Tony," I said, and kissed him good-bye.

Back at home, while Sylvia was preparing dinner, I lay on my bed thinking about that scene with Tony. The awkwardness of the way we were lying, clothes half on, half off, my bra pulled up over my breasts. A narrow twin bed. I couldn't help thinking about Dad and Sylvia in their own bed, in their own room. Comfortable. Relaxed. Unhurried. Trusting, and in love.

Usually, I wanted to rush right to the phone and tell Pam or Liz or Gwen or all of them when something racy had happened to me. This time I didn't. Not for a while, anyway. Sometimes you don't tell your friends everything, either. I felt like there was a lot to settle in my own mind about what I wanted and what I didn't.

I liked sex, that's certain. I liked a boy to kiss my breasts, to run his hands up and down my sides, to thrust his tongue in my mouth, to explore my slippery place and finger me. I was eager, I'll admit, for whatever came next. But I was going to be choosy. It wouldn't be lying sideways, with my bra yanked up like a rape scene. It wouldn't be in a guy's bedroom with his dad just down the hall. It wouldn't be with a guy who called me "baby" and was adding me to a long list of girls, condoms at the ready.

Why couldn't my hormones understand that? I wondered. Why couldn't they all stay quiet until I was with the right guy at the right time in the right place, and then go crazy? I was surprised to find myself smiling just a little. That would make a humorous subject to write about someday, but it sure wouldn't be for the school newspaper. Or maybe not for anywhere that my parents could read it.

There are things you keep from your parents. Some of them they should know, perhaps, like that night in Silver Spring, but you never tell them because you realize afterward just how dangerous they had been. And you know you won't repeat them. Each time something like that happens, you gain an experience, a little independence, but it's at a price. Growing up also means growing away, I discovered. After our night out on the town, I felt charged and elated that we had pulled it off. At the same time, there was a sort of homesickness inside me, like . . . well . . . that I was leaving a little girl behind. That I probably would never sit on my dad's lap again, as I had the other night. That there was a necessary distance between us now. Like, you can be excited and sad at the same time. And times like tonight, what happened between Tony and me—I wouldn't tell Dad at all.

15

What Happened Next

I still hadn't finished the assignment for Mrs. Cary and couldn't delay any longer. She was going to start calling on us to give our talks the next day and, as Les would say, I just had to "suck it up." But how could you give a persuasive speech about something you didn't believe in?

I'd done most of the research last week, starting with Google. No, to tell the truth, I'd started with Gwen. "Tell me one medical breakthrough that's come about through animal experimentation," I'd asked after explaining my assignment to her.

"The Rh factor in infants," she'd told me.

"What?" I asked.

"Blue babies. I learned about it at the hematology lab. A blood disease of newborn infants when they have a different blood type from their mothers. Doctors learned how to correct it by operating first on dogs. Go to Google and type in 'medical discoveries using animals in research.'"

The list of medical breakthroughs in front of me was long. By experimenting initially on dogs, for example, researchers had created the heart-lung machine that is used to keep patients alive during heart surgery. Operating on baboons, surgeons had learned how to remove cancer cells in bone marrow without destroying healthy cells. Pigs had played an important role in studying the healing process of burn victims. . . .

Of all the medical research involving animals, one article said, 92 percent of it was not painful. But what about the 8 percent that was? How could anyone stand by and watch a rabbit or a guinea pig suffer? And what about labs where the technicians were careless and needlessly let animals suffer?

I ran it past Dad at breakfast the next morning.

"There's no question that there should be stricter controls over laboratory experiments, Al," he said, considering it. "I've read some of those horror stories too. But if a critical experiment is needed, and it's a choice between a dog having to suffer or your uncle Milt dying, which would you choose?"

"Was Uncle Milt . . . ?" I began.

"Well, he's had heart surgery," said Dad.

I sat perfectly still. "Have they . . . have they ever

discovered anything about . . . about leukemia from animals?" I asked.

"I don't know, Al. But if they had . . . if there was . . ."

I sighed. "I'd have wanted them to try whatever they could to save Mom. Or Molly."

Something dramatic happened in speech class that afternoon. I was the second one up, after a guy who argued against legalizing marijuana. I was halfway through my talk when I saw a woman slip through the door at the back of the room and quietly take an empty seat.

I saw Mrs. Cary crane her neck a little to see who it was, smile quizzically, then turn her attention back to me. I don't think any of the other kids noticed.

When I'd finished, but before the critique began, Mrs. Cary stood up and said to the woman, "I'm sorry, but I don't know your name."

Everyone turned to see whom she was talking to. The woman was short, a little stocky, dressed in a brown jacket and pants, with a bright-colored scarf around her neck.

"I'm Jennifer Shoates's mother," she said, rising from her chair, "and I'd like to talk to you about the completely irresponsible assignment you gave my daughter."

The quiet in the classroom was almost eerie. This was something I'd never seen before—well, not since second grade, anyway—a mom coming in to protest. Jennifer, the girl who had spoken against sex before marriage—sitting in the second row—turned as red as a cherry tomato.

We knew that Mrs. Shoates hadn't stopped at the office first because she wasn't wearing a visitor's pass. I'm not sure just how she got by security. All eyes were on Mrs. Cary now, to see how an experienced teacher would handle this.

"I'd be glad to discuss this in conference," Mrs. Cary said politely. "If you'd stop by the office, they can—"

"She's supposed to give her talk today, and you have no right to assign such a personal and irresponsible assignment," Jennifer's mom said.

"Mrs. Shoates, you're welcome to visit as a guest, but this *is* my classroom, and I'm afraid you need to follow my rules here," Mrs. Cary said. "We can put Jennifer's talk off for another day, if you prefer. . . ."

"Mo-*ther*!" Jennifer protested, and I wondered if a face could actually explode, her cheeks were so bright. "Just let me get this over with. *Please!*"

We held our breath. Mrs. Cary waited. Finally Mrs. Shoates sat back down.

It was strange, but I'd lost all stage fright,

because I knew that everyone was thinking about the woman at the back of the room, not me.

"Okay, class. Comments on Alice's talk? How well did she do convincing us that animals are truly needed for research?" Mrs. Cary asked.

"I'm still not convinced that those experiments get the study they need before they're approved," one guy said. "I think she should have focused more on that."

"But that wasn't the point," another boy said. "The question is, if they *were* approved and monitored carefully, do the results justify using animals in that way?"

A girl said, "If *my* grandmother had cancer, wouldn't I want every possible study to be done that might save her?"

Mrs. Cary allowed another two minutes for discussion on my topic, and then it was Jennifer's turn. I took my seat, and Jennifer went to the front of the room.

If we hadn't felt sorry for Jennifer when she gave her first talk promoting chastity, we ached for her now. I did, anyway. If my dad ever came to school and threw a fit like that, I'd crawl under the desk. I mean, we're in high school now. How long is Jennifer's mom going to fight her battles for her? How can Jennifer become independent if her mom takes over when things get tough?

Jennifer's voice was a little too soft. Too shaky. She began by saying that she still felt that virginity before marriage was best. But there might be some situations where having sex would make sense. I stole a look at Mrs. Shoates, and she was shaking her head. Jennifer plowed on.

If a man or woman was physically disabled, she said, and they weren't sure they could have sex, maybe it was best to try first before they married. And if an elderly widow would lose her husband's annuity if she remarried, maybe it was forgivable if she had sex with another man without marriage if they had a loving relationship. But people who lived together before marriage had higher divorce rates than those who didn't.

Jennifer stood stiffly at the front of the room when she had finished, and I could tell she was purposely avoiding looking at her mother.

"Okay, class. Comments?" Mrs. Cary said.

"I thought she was supposed to be defending sex before marriage. How did those statistics about divorce rates help out there?" asked Brian.

"Yeah, what about couples who have sex but *don't* live together? What about that?" asked someone else. "Jennifer's argument was supposed to be about virginity, not just having sex."

The chair at the back of the room squeaked again. "I cannot believe I am listening to this discussion in a Maryland public high school," came Mrs. Shoates's voice.

"Mrs. Shoates, I'm going to ask you to use your guest manners and let my students do the talking," Mrs. Cary said. "I think your daughter can handle this herself, and it would be good to give her that opportunity."

I raised my hand. "I think Jennifer should be congratulated for examining another point of view under extremely difficult circumstances," I said.

Mrs. Cary nodded.

"But she only used extreme examples as opposing points of view," a girl said. "What about all the reasons two younger persons might want to have sex without it doing any harm?"

The chair at the back of the room squeaked again.

Jennifer said, "Maybe sometimes it's good to wait for the things that are most important to you. Maybe instant gratification shouldn't apply to *every*thing you want in life. I think maybe it makes it a little bit special to wait."

"That's also a good point, Jennifer, although you're back now to your original argument," Mrs. Cary said. "But I'm afraid our time is up, and we need to go on to our next speaker. Jay, your last talk was on teaching evolution, so let's see how persuasive you can be for creationism."

I realized then that Mrs. Shoates had left the room, and I felt quite sure she was on her way to the principal's office.

I was glad to see Lester hanging around at dinnertime that evening because I wanted to tell everyone what had happened in speech class.

"That Mrs. Cary is one brave gal," said Sylvia. "I'm not sure I'd take that on."

"You'd never come to school and embarrass me like that, would you, Dad?" I asked.

Dad grinned. "No. I just embarrass you in front of family."

"I remember when *you* came by school one day, Les, when I was being bullied on Seventh Grade Sing Day," I said. "But you didn't embarrass me, you *saved* me. Denise Whitlock said she'd stick my head in the toilet if I didn't sing all the verses to the school song."

"Yeah, I do sort of remember that," Les said. "Figured you needed a little help when I saw they'd backed you up against a car in the parking lot."

"That was one of the nicest things you ever did for me," I said. "Maybe someday I can return the favor."

"Doing what? Rescuing *me*?" he said.

"You never know," I told him.

• • •

When we got to speech class on Thursday, something wasn't quite right. Mrs. Cary's mouth. Her eyes, maybe.

"I've been informed that we have to suspend our assignment for the time being," she said.

"Whaaaaaat?" The exclamation came from all corners of the room.

"It's really all I can tell you right now," she said. "Someone will be doing an evaluation of it, and they'll make a decision."

All eyes turned to Jennifer Shoates, who sat like a stone, her face a pale pink.

"And so," Mrs. Cary said quickly, "we're going to do a reading of *Waiting for Godot*, by the Irish playwright Samuel Beckett. There are five roles, and we'll take turns reading the lines."

We didn't want *Waiting for Godot*. We didn't want an Irish playwright or reading lines. We had started the second part of an assignment we thought we were going to hate, and it was one of the most intense and thought-provoking assignments we'd ever had. We wanted to see it through. Jennifer must have been feeling our laser stares, because they seemed to pin her to her seat, keeping her motionless.

Mrs. Cary began the new assignment immediately, passing out paperback copies of the play and assigning the parts of Estragon and Vladimir and

Lucky and Pozzo and the boy to various students. We were stunned.

When the bell rang at last, Jennifer was the first one out of the classroom, but some of the rest of us gathered outside in the hall.

"We know who's behind *this*, don't we?" Brian said.

"How can she do this?" I asked. "How can one parent decide what the rest of us can or can't do?"

"Look. My aunt has a friend who works in the school office," one of the guys said. "I'll find out what's going on and e-mail you guys. Give me your addresses." We did, then we walked off, grumbling among ourselves.

That evening the news traveled from one student to another by IM. Mrs. Shoates hadn't gone to see the principal the day before as we'd suspected. She'd gone home and called the superintendent, and he'd said that a supervisor would come out around noon on Friday to discuss the matter with Mrs. Cary, Mrs. Shoates, and the principal and that the assignment would be suspended for the time being.

One guy wrote:

> Let's organize a walkout Friday when the super shows up.

Another said:

```
Hey, let's take the whole day off in
protest!
```

But I suggested that we have a demonstration over the lunch hour when the supervisor was there, carrying signs saying how we felt. That seemed to go over well, and we set to work.

I told Dad and Sylvia about it, and I thought they'd try to talk me out of it. But Dad only said, "Don't try to stop the supervisor's car with your bodies, please."

And Sylvia said, "'Polite' and 'orderly' are the passwords, Alice. Don't give the principal any other reason to side with Mrs. Shoates."

I called Lester next and told him what we were going to do.

"Ah! A little civil disobedience, huh?" he said.

"If it's something I really care about, I can be as militant as anyone else," I said.

"You carrying an AK rifle or what?" he asked.

"*Signs,* Lester! Signs saying what we stand for," I told him.

"Go, Alice!" said Lester.

When lunchtime came on Friday, we took our homemade signs from one of the student's cars in the parking lot, where we'd stashed them before school that morning, and gathered on the sidewalk outside the front entrance. We'd told everyone to use thick black markers and print in big block letters. The pieces of cardboard were assorted sizes and colors, but they expressed what we felt: DARE TO THINK; SUPPORT CONTROVERSY; WHAT'S WRONG WITH DEBATE? WE LOVE CARY; DISCUSSION NEVER HURT ANYONE; WHO'S AFRAID OF LEARNING?

Somebody must have alerted the press, because a reporter showed up from the *Washington Post* and another from the *Gazette*. I had told Scott about it, and he made sure that Don was out there with his camera too, taking pictures for *The Edge*.

We were orderly. Polite. We didn't block the driveway or keep anyone from entering the school. When a car with a MONTGOMERY COUNTY PUBLIC SCHOOLS sticker on it pulled into the parking lot, we were pretty sure it was the supervisor and began to chant, "Keep our school . . . free to think! Keep our school . . . free to think!" The supervisor stared at us, at the signs, then she quickly parked and walked in a side entrance.

The principal came out on the steps and looked us over, seeming more puzzled than angry. "Anybody want to talk about this?" he called out, coming down the walk.

"We're just showing our support for a great teacher," somebody said.

"We want to show that we think the assignment

Mrs. Cary gave us was a good one and that one person shouldn't be allowed to dictate what the rest of us can learn," I told him.

"I guess I'm a little surprised that an ordinary parent conference, which is an everyday occurrence at most schools, should become public knowledge," the principal said.

"Mrs. Cary doesn't know anything about this demonstration, but the Freedom of Information Act should apply to students too," a guy said. "We have a right to know what's happened to an assignment that involved us."

We stayed outside through the lunch period and through fourth period as well. We figured we'd get detention for that, but it was worth it. When the bell rang for fifth, though, we went back inside.

When we got to Mrs. Cary's sixth-period class, she simply smiled, welcomed us back, and asked who was ready to give their three-minute persuasive talk. We cheered.

What we found out later was that the principal and supervisor felt the same way we did even before the protest, but they wanted to give Mrs. Shoates a chance to formally voice her concerns about the assignment.

Another thing we students agreed on—most of us, anyway—as we left the room after class was that Jennifer shouldn't have to suffer anymore. It wasn't her fault that her mom had caused a problem, and we shouldn't treat her like a freak. No girl should have to be accountable for the behavior of her mom. And I wondered if my own mother would have done anything like that to embarrass me. I think I would gladly have suffered what Jennifer went through, though, if only I could have *had* my mom.

Mark Stedmeister called me at the Melody Inn on Saturday and said that some of the kids were going to the old Steak House in Gaithersburg for dinner—our last get-together before the holidays. He wanted to know how many cars we could count on.

"Tonight?" I said. "Not mine. Dad's going to be working late here at the store, and Sylvia wants to do some shopping."

"Want to ride with me, then?" he asked. "I'm picking up Penny and Pamela. Liz can ride too if she wants."

It sounded like a good idea, and I told Dad where we were going. At seven that night, Liz and I got in Mark's car, and he set off for Penny's, then Pamela's. The Steak House restaurant was a sort of run-down place that was probably scheduled for demolition. The staff was mostly college kids who worked evenings, and though the food wasn't anything to rave about, it wasn't too expensive and the portions were huge.

Jill and Justin didn't show up, but Karen came with Keeno. Patrick didn't make it, and neither did Gwen. Brian and a few of his friends from school were holding a long table for us when we got there, so it was sort of the old gang and sort of not.

Pamela, Liz, and I shared the deep-fried onion rings, and we ordered steak sandwiches and Cokes. Mostly the talk at the table was about finals, the PSAT, what we were going to do over winter break, and who had already been out looking at colleges.

"Patrick, of course," I told them.

"Jill's waiting to see where Justin's going, and then she's going to apply," said Karen, who had the scoop. "Except that Justin's parents don't like her and want him to study in England or something."

"Really?" said Liz. "Why don't they like her?"

"Jill says they told Justin she just wanted to marry into money," Karen said. "I'll bet they don't realize that Jill and Justin have been going together almost longer than any couple in school, but that doesn't satisfy his folks. Jill said she and Justin have a plan, but I don't know what. It's all she'd tell me."

I noticed that down at the end of the table Brian was pouring beer into an empty glass, then slipping the bottle back in the gym bag on the seat beside him.

Pamela laughed. "That's the real reason the guys like to come out here. If you bring your own, the waiters look the other way."

I didn't know if Brian's folks knew he was raiding their beer supply or knew and didn't care. I figured they didn't care. Mark didn't appear to be drinking, though.

It was only nine when we finished at the Steak House, and Keeno said we were all invited to his cousin's birthday party in Germantown.

"How far is that?" I asked. "I have to be home by midnight."

"Only eight miles or so. We don't have to stay long," Keeno said. "I've got some gag gifts for him. His birthday was yesterday, but they're having a party for him tonight."

"So why weren't you there this evening?" Liz asked.

"Oh, I said I'd come by later with friends. He isn't really a cousin. Sort of a second or third cousin, actually. But he's a lot of fun."

Liz looked uncomfortable, but she had to be back by midnight too, so we were going to hold Mark to that. We followed the other cars.

Keeno's friend lived out beyond Germantown in a wooded rural area, and it took longer than I expected to get there. By the time our cars found the address and we made our way through the crush of people just inside the door, filling every room, it was after ten and had begun to snow. I figured I could stay until about eleven fifteen, and then I'd tell Mark we had to leave.

If there were any adults present, I didn't see them. Brian was goofing off, using a quart jar as a beer stein. There were as many beer bottles on the kitchen table as there were Coke and Sprite cans, and the floor was sticky.

Keeno had the usual gag gifts for the birthday boy—fly in a fake ice cube, plastic vomit, dog turds—but the guy was plastered and didn't appreciate them, so Keeno tried them out on us. It was when he put his hand up the back of my sweater, though, and pulled out a pair of black panties that he made me laugh.

"What are you? A professional magician?" I asked.

"Magic fingers," he said, letting them creep up under my sweater again, trying to unhook my bra. I laughed and slapped his hand away.

Several guys came up to me during the next hour and asked for my name and phone number. Liz's, too. I tried to think of a composer who sounded credible. J. S. Bach, maybe. I said I was "Janice Bach" and gave them the number of the Melody Inn. Liz thought it was hilarious. She gave them Jill's number.

Around eleven fifteen Liz and Pamela and I went looking for Mark. Some kids were going upstairs together, and I hoped I wouldn't have to look for him there, but Brian said he and Penny and Karen had headed out to a movie.

"What?" we cried.

"Relax!" he said, his voice a little too loud. "There are plenty of cars. Pu-len-ty!"

He told us to get in one of the cars out on the lawn—that those three were leaving now, taking kids home. Pamela and Liz and I went out on the porch. It was snowing lightly, and all the cars, bushes—everything—had been frosted with a quarter inch of white.

"C'mon, we've got room," someone called from one of the cars.

Liz was closest, so she ran over, bracing against the wind, and got inside. Some more girls ran past us and then some guys. I wasn't sure which of the cars Pam got in, but somebody yelled, "We can still squeeze in one more."

I stepped through the snow as the first car backed out into the street and crawled in the back-seat of another just as Brian came around the hood to the driver's side.

"Whose car is this?" I asked in the darkness, as all the cars looked alike in the snow.

"Brian's," said a guy up front.

I got out. "No, I'm going with someone else," I said.

"Hey, Al, get *in!*" Brian yelled. "It's snowing! Close the fucking door!"

"No . . . I've . . . I've got a ride," I said, and headed back to the porch, my heart pounding. *Damn Mark!* I was thinking. How could he drive us out here and then go off to a movie? I started looking for Keeno and went over to a window to see inside. Keeno was on the couch with a girl. Kissing. Very deep kissing, evidently. Great! *Now* what should I do?

Dad had said that if I was ever in a place I shouldn't be and needed a ride, I could call, no matter what time it was. But Germantown? *Should I call Les instead?* I wondered as I watched Brian's car go roaring off, snow flying out behind it.

It was coming down thicker now, and the noise was so loud in the house, I knew I'd better call from the porch. I fished in my bag for my cell phone. Some of the kids went down the steps and started a snowball fight.

Thunk! A snowball hit the front door.

Thwack! Another hit a post.

And then—a sound I will never forget—a high, horrible squeal of tires and then . . . *CRASH!* Metal against metal.

"Omigod!" someone yelled. "It's just down the road." And people began to run.

Conversation

Someone dashed past me and jumped into another car out front. Then another. Motors raced, and two cars went speeding toward the sound of the crash. People on the porch held cell phones to their ears and everyone was asking, "Where are you? . . . Can you see anything? . . . Who's car was it? . . . Was it Sheryl's? Was it Brian's?"

I sank down on the steps and sat trancelike, unblinking, as the falling snow coated the part of me unprotected by the roof—my knees, my legs, my feet. *Which cars were Liz and Pam in? Were they together?* I felt as disconnected from this house, this party, the noise, the crash, as my shoulders were from my knees. Frozen solid.

"Yeah?" a guy behind me was saying, cell phone to his ear. "Oh, Christ! . . . Oh, man! . . . What about Sunny? . . . Yeah."

I jerked around. "What about Liz Price or Pamela Jones? Were either of them in that car? Who was hurt?"

"A kid, that's all I know," the guy told me.

"Has anyone called for an ambulance?" I screamed. And then we heard a siren.

"Oh, shit!" said the guy with the cell phone.

A guy out on the lawn, the one with the U OF MARYLAND sweatshirt, came racing back up the steps. "Get rid of all the bottles, man. The minute they know there was a party, they'll be breathing down our necks. Jeez! Where'd I leave my jacket?"

There was bedlam in the house. Someone came out the front door dragging a garbage bag full of bottles and cans and handed it to me.

"Take it over to the woods and leave it there," he said, pointing fifty yards off.

"Were Pam or Liz in that car?" I cried.

"I don't know! Take the damn cans, or we'll all be in trouble!" he yelled.

People were pushing past me out the door. We heard another siren, then another.

"Grab your stuff and let's get the hell out," somebody was saying from inside.

Car doors slammed. Engines started. People who had been to the crash came running back. People in the house were running out.

I dragged the bag through the snow, leaving a

telltale trail behind it. Parking it behind a fir tree, I started back toward the house, pulling out my cell phone to call home, but was blinded by the light from a police cruiser as it careened around a bend in the road and pulled right up on the lawn.

"Stay right where you are, everyone!" an officer yelled, getting out the driver's side while the passenger door opened and a second policeman appeared. "We just want to ask some questions. Don't anyone take it in his head to go out the back door, 'cause we've got that covered too." The second officer was already going around the side of the house as another squad car pulled up.

I was shaking. Not just my hands, but my whole body. An officer came over to me, pulling out a notebook.

"Name?" he asked.

"A-Alice McKinley," I answered.

"Age?"

"Sixteen."

"Where do you live?"

I gave him my address.

"Do you know what just happened out there?" he asked me.

"We h-heard the crash," I said. "Were people hurt?"

"Yes, I'd say they were," the officer said. "How'd you get here tonight?"

"A friend brought me," I said.

"Know whose house this is?"

"N-No."

"Where's your friend?" asked the policeman.

"He left early with some others to go to the movies. I was looking for a ride home. I'm supposed to be home by midnight," I explained.

The officer looked at his watch. "Well, seeing as how it's two minutes after, you're not going to make it, are you?" He looked at the trail I'd made in the snow, my footprints beside it. "You been drinking?"

"No. Just Sprite."

"I want you to get in that car over there," he said. "Sit in the backseat. And hand me your cell phone, please. You'll get it back."

"I've got to call my dad!" I protested.

"We'll call him for you," he told me.

I felt sick. I knew right away that he didn't want me calling any of the other kids, all of us deciding on the same story to give the police—who was drinking and who wasn't, who was driving and who wasn't. I sat in the police car hugging myself, trying to stop the shaking, but it only got worse. I watched the police bring a guy over, the boy who had told me to drag the cans to the woods.

As he slid in beside me, I asked, "Do you know Pamela Jones or Liz Price? Were they in the car? Were they hurt?"

"I don't know anything, and you don't either,

got it?" he murmured. Then, "I think Brian's killed somebody, so just be quiet."

I thought I was going to be sick. "I didn't know anything to begin with," I said, trembling. "I don't even know where I am."

A third cruiser pulled in, and more kids were rounded up. When we got to the police station, Keeno and a few others were already there, looking dazed and disoriented.

"Were Pam or Liz in the car?" I whispered to him as we came in.

"I don't know," he whispered back.

"Where's Brian?" I asked him.

"Rescue squad took him to the hospital," he said, but then a policeman interrupted. One by one we were taken to a desk and asked questions.

"Did you go anywhere else before you came to the party?" a policeman asked me.

I told him about the group of us who went to the old Steak House restaurant in Gaithersburg.

"Did anyone at the Steak House serve alcohol to Brian Brewster?" the policeman asked me.

"No," I said, knowing that was only half of the truth, but I decided to answer just what I was asked.

"Did anyone at the party serve alcohol to Brian Brewster?"

"I don't know," I said. "There were a lot of people there, and kids were helping themselves to whatever was on the table."

"Will you submit to a Breathalyzer test?" he asked me.

"Yes," I said.

They gave it to me. I passed. Then, at one fifteen, the awful phone call to Dad. When the officer hung up, he said, "Wait over there. Your father said he'd be here in about forty minutes."

When Dad got to the station, he didn't say a word. He hardly even looked at me. Just hugged me to him, so tight I could hardly breathe. On the way home I alternately cried and froze up, terrified of what might have happened to Liz or Pamela. Then Dad said he'd seen Liz come home, so I knew that at least she was okay, but I still worried about Pamela. I answered every question Dad asked me as to who, when, and where, but to all the whys, I had no answer. *Why* did I go someplace else when I'd only told him we'd be at the Steak House? *Why* would I go to a party at the home of someone I didn't even know? *Why* didn't I call him as soon as I saw they had alcohol and no adults were present?

I tried explaining, but there was no answer that satisfied him: I told him that when we left the restaurant, it was too early to go home; that we really thought it was Keeno's cousin; that we didn't know there wouldn't be adults in the house. . . .

I was exhausted and tight with tension when I finally walked inside the house.

"Oh, Alice," Sylvia said, her shoulders drooping with relief when she saw me. "You're okay!"

"Yes," I said.

"Was anyone else hurt, Alice? Are there other parents we should call?"

"I've been trying to find out about Pamela, but I don't even know what car she was in," I told her. "They said Brian was taken to a hospital. I don't know how bad he was hurt. . . . And I don't know who was in the other car, the one he hit. Somebody said he might have killed a kid."

"Oh my God!" said Dad.

I was numb with fatigue, and so was Dad. I curled up in one corner of the couch as he made calls to the police to see how badly Brian was hurt, but they wouldn't tell him anything and said all the parents had already been notified. It wasn't until we had called Pamela's house and found out she had been in another car and was safely home that we all went to bed, exhausted.

I slept until almost eleven the next morning, when the phone started to ring. While Dad and Sylvia were at church, I got all the news.

Brian had plowed into the side of another car at a rural junction only a quarter mile from where the party had been. The other car had gone through a stop sign. The air bags in Brian's car had protected him and his front-seat passenger, but Brian had two broken fingers and a dislocated shoulder, and the guy in the front seat with him had injured his knee. The three girls in the back were bruised and one had whiplash, but otherwise, they were all right. A little kid who had been asleep in the backseat of the other car was either seriously hurt or dead. That's all anyone knew.

Liz told me that my dad had called her house when he saw her come home, asking if I was there with her. She'd told him I was probably on my way home with someone else, that the car she got in was full.

At lunch the air was so thick with disappointment and disapproval that I felt smothered by it, even though Dad reached over once and patted my arm. Did they have any idea how scared I had been last night? I wondered. Did they think I had *wanted* this to happen?

"Well," I said finally, "what's the punishment? Am I grounded for the rest of the year?"

Dad looked at me helplessly. "How can I punish you when all I wanted last night was to hear that you were safe?" he asked. "I know you didn't plan it. But how many times have I asked you to call if . . . ?" He didn't finish.

"I know, I know," I said. "But if you'd been there, if you'd been in my place, you'd have been confused too. I thought I had a ride home. I didn't think . . ."

But that was it in a nutshell, of course. I didn't think.

It was the talk of the school on Monday. Brian wasn't there, and most of the kids at the party were from another school, so the rest of us were still guessing at what really happened. Pamela, Liz, and I just stood in the hall hugging each other. We didn't need words.

The construction workers were picking up for the day when I got home from school, putting away their tools, calling out to each other. Sylvia's car was out front. She rarely got home before four thirty or five, especially with all that pounding and clanking going on. I wondered if she'd taken the afternoon off.

I opened the door and started for the stairs, but she stopped me. "Alice," she said, "we need to talk."

I walked into the kitchen and dropped my backpack on the table. "What about?" I asked, knowing only too well.

"Sit down," she said, a teacher's tone in her voice.

I *almost* said, *I prefer to stand,* but something in her face told me I'd better sit. Sylvia remained standing in her pin-striped pants and rayon blouse, arms folded across her chest.

"I have something to say," she said, "and with Ben out of the house, it's a good time to say it."

I dreaded what was to come.

"I married your dad because I think he is one of the kindest, most intelligent, most wonderful men I've ever met," Sylvia said. "And when you love someone, you want to protect him from hurt. You want to be there for him when he's sick or worried or frightened. And in all the time I've known your father, Alice, I've never seen him as worried as he was Saturday night."

I swallowed. I wanted to look away, but there was something so intense in her face that I had to watch.

Sylvia went on: "I'd wanted to go to bed at eleven, but Ben said he'd wait up for you, so I decided to wait up with him. About eleven fifteen he said, 'If they just went to the Steak House, I'd think they'd be back by now.' I reminded him that you were allowed to stay out till midnight on weekends, that maybe you'd gone to a late show."

Sylvia didn't look away either. Our eyes were locked. Outside, I heard the construction guys driving away.

"He called Elizabeth's house when he saw her come home," Sylvia continued. "Liz told him you were getting a ride with someone else. He called Pamela's, but no one answered. She probably hadn't reached home yet. Then, about twelve thirty, someone called and asked if you were all right. Ben asked who it was—what they were talking about—but the person hung up."

Sylvia sighed and put her hands behind her, resting on the countertop. "Alice, it was like your father aged ten years after that last call. Every line in his face was deeper. He didn't want to use the phone in case you'd be calling, so I gave him my cell phone and he tried calling your cell several times, but there was no answer and he began calling police departments—in Gaithersburg, Silver Spring—to see if there had been any accidents. He called the Steak House, but it was closed, and I had to stop him from getting in his car and driving out there. I told him that if you *had* been in an accident, you could have been airlifted to a shock trauma unit in Bethesda or Baltimore—who knows where?—and that he should stay right here until someone called."

I felt an indescribable sadness rising up inside me.

"It was one fifteen when the phone rang and he heard someone say, 'Mr. McKinley, I'm calling about your daughter. . . .' His face went as gray as the ashes in the fireplace. All he could say was 'Is she all right?' and . . . the relief in that face when they said that you were . . . !"

A tear escaped from the rim of my eye and rolled down my cheek. I couldn't look at Sylvia anymore.

"I'm . . . I'm sorry," I wept. "I *told* him how sorry I was. I didn't realize . . ."

"I know you didn't know all of this, and your father would never tell you, so I am," Sylvia said. "I want you to know that last Saturday night was one of the worst nights ever for your dad. He was like a caged animal, wanting to get out and *do* something, and there was absolutely nothing to do, Alice, but wait."

She pulled a tissue out of her pants pocket and blew her nose.

I just went on sniffling. "The . . . the evening had started out so well," I said. "Just a bunch of us having dinner together. We've been to the Steak House a lot of times. And when Keeno said he just wanted us to stop by his cousin's house for a birthday party, it didn't seem so bad. It was only nine o'clock."

Sylvia handed me a tissue from the box on the counter, and I blew my nose too.

"But it took a long time to get there," I continued, "and it wasn't exactly a cousin's house. You're right. That's when I should have called."

Sylvia let out her breath and looked up at the ceiling a moment. I think we were both feeling exhausted. For probably a full minute we just remained there in silence, staring off into space.

"You know what?" she said finally. "Ben's working late tonight and I'm too tired to cook, but I'm hungry enough for popcorn. I'm going to make a big bowl of it. Let's kick off our shoes, go sit on the couch, and eat popcorn. And talk."

The last thing in this world I wanted just then was popcorn, but Sylvia opened the cupboard, pulled out a bag, and stuck it in the microwave. "Oh, heck," she said. "Let's put in two."

I sat silently at the table as Sylvia stuck in another bag, then stood watching the seconds go by on the clock, waiting for the popping to begin.

Strange, though, what just the aroma of popcorn will do for you. It reminds you of only good times in your life, because whoever heard of eating popcorn when you're sick or mad or grieving? Nobody eats popcorn at funerals.

As the corn began to pop, it sounded like an artillery range, and the expanding bags began taking up the whole space inside the microwave.

"Maybe you're not supposed to pop two bags at a time," Sylvia said. "You don't suppose they'll explode, do you?" We smiled.

"I'll get the bowls," I said, and took two large metal mixing bowls from the cabinet. When there had been no more pops for the recommended two seconds, Sylvia took the bags from the microwave, and we pulled at the tops to let the steam out, then poured the popcorn into the bowls. In the living room we kicked off our shoes and sat down on the sofa, bowls on our laps.

"Ah!" Sylvia said. "Supper!"

We chewed delicately, however. Politely. Finally Sylvia said, "I guess I was really, really angry at you Saturday night. I was furious, in fact, that you didn't call and tell us where you were or what had happened. Ben could only imagine the worst."

"I just . . . there was so much going on . . . I didn't think I could leave until I found out if Pamela or Liz were in that car. Then the police came and took my cell phone," I explained feebly.

Sylvia didn't say anything for a minute or two. Then she said, "I just wish that every teenager could have the experience of one night—just *one* night—of the anxiety you put your dad through."

"You talk as though I did it on purpose!" I said.

"No. It wasn't purposeful, it was thoughtless. But, I suppose, if I put myself in your place . . ."

"I just wish you'd try to understand me more," I said.

"I suppose you do," said Sylvia. Her hands were motionless now on the sides of her bowl. "I guess I've not done a very good job of that. It's not easy coming into an already-formed household. I've found myself getting annoyed at small things. . . ."

"I guess I've been pretty mad at you too," I said. "I mean, now and then. Off and on."

"Yeah?" said Sylvia. She propped her feet up on the

coffee table beside mine. "So . . . tell me about it."

"You're my analyst now?" I joked, and she laughed.

"The only thing I have to throw at you is popcorn, so you're safe," she said, and began to eat again.

I took a deep breath. "Well, like you said, it's hard for us, too—for me, anyway—to have someone come in and join the family. We just do some things differently from you, that's all. Sometimes you seem angry, and I can't figure out what I've done. Other times . . . other times you don't seem to be thinking of me at all. You just barrel on with your own plans—about the remodeling of the house, for example—like you . . . like you're taking over."

"Hmmmm," Sylvia said. "I guess I do get excited about things, and assume everyone else feels the same way. Ben's such a sweetheart that he doesn't usually object, and I just go sailing along." She looked over at me. "Anything else?"

"Yeah," I said. "Why haven't you ever yelled at me about riding that motorcycle?"

Sylvia looked startled for a moment. "Someone's been talking," she said.

"I wormed it out of Marilyn," I told her, "so I know you saw me that day. Why didn't you ever say anything?"

"Because later that day you told me that you had done something you wouldn't do again, and I guessed you were talking about that motorcycle ride. I wanted to give you the benefit of the doubt. And Ben's had so much on his mind lately, I didn't want to add that as well."

I told her then how it had happened.

"I guessed it was something like that," she said. "I think I know you *that* well. Anything else? Anything at all?"

"I can't think of anything at the moment," I answered. "But if I do, I'll let you know."

"Promise?" she asked.

"Promise."

She sighed contentedly and leaned her head back. "This is the best dinner I've had all week," she said. "I've got to remember this when I'm too tired to cook."

Our stocking feet were touching now, and Sylvia rubbed her toes against mine. "Let's think about dessert. What would taste good after eight cups of popcorn?"

"A caramel sundae?" I suggested. "With chocolate ice cream, of course."

"Of course," said Sylvia. "Whipped cream?"

"Naturally. And a maraschino cherry," I told her. "No nuts."

On Tuesday, I saw a small cluster of kids standing in front of the glassed-in bulletin board in the front hallway.

"Hey, Alice!" Sam called to me. "Come and look."

I walked over. He pointed to the story that had appeared in the *Washington Post* on Saturday, second page of the Metro section, with a picture of the demonstration outside the school. STUDENTS CHOOSE CONTROVERSY was the headline.

The reporter had written that fourteen students from Mrs. Cary's eleventh-grade speech class had demonstrated in support of her controversial assignment to examine both sides of an issue that affects them emotionally.

"An irresponsible and dangerous precedent," said the objecting parent, Marsha Shoates, who is considering removing her daughter from the Montgomery County Public School System and enrolling her in homeschooling instead. "It's unfair to ask students to reveal some of their most deeply held beliefs and then demand that they challenge them."

The article mentioned some of our signs, quotes from us, and then one from our principal:

"We're proud that our students take their assignments seriously," he said. "We're aware that it's difficult to examine an issue one feels strongly about, but the object here is not to change an opinion necessarily, but to help students learn to study a controversial subject from many viewpoints—the hallmark of an educated person."

Scott came up to me then and gave me a hug. "Hey! You did it! You made the *Post*!" he said. "This gives me some ideas about a story on censorship when we get back from winter break. Don got some great photos."

I probably clung to him a nanosecond longer than he clung to me, and then . . . I couldn't resist. It was either now or never. I reached up and kissed him on the cheek. He looked down at me, puzzled, but only smiled and turned to someone else. Embarrassed, I bleated, "We *all* did it! The power of the press, huh?"

I'd thought he at least liked me, and I suppose he did. But it wasn't the way I liked him. I thought of going up to him sometime in private and saying, *How do you get over someone you're crushing on? Someone who doesn't feel the same way about you?* just to let him know what I was going through. But I couldn't. If I'd been at his house instead of Tony's? If it had been Scott who had nudged me onto the bed? Would I have resisted? Maybe not.

We got our PSAT scores that same day, but I didn't open mine till I got home because I wasn't sure what to expect. Dad has never pressured me to get all A's or worry about whether a grade has a plus or minus beside it. "Just do the best you can, Al," he always said, and I tried. I get more B's than A's, but I don't get many C's, except in math, so I guess you could say I'm a B+ student. Still, the PSAT sounded so *official*. Like, whatever I might have thought of myself before, the PSAT was the real McCoy. The PSAT was *truth*; it was my *future*. Pass or fail, sink or swim, what would it be?

My heart was actually racing as I opened the envelope. I read that the test measures three things: critical reading skills; math problem-solving skills, and writing skills, on a scale of 20 to 80, with 80 being the highest score you could get. The halfway point between those two numbers would be 50. I turned the page to see my scores:

Critical reading skills:	74
Math skills:	48
Writing skills:	77

I guess I did better than what I'd expected in reading and writing and about what I'd feared in math. The total of my three scores was 199 out of a possible 240, and the report said that the average for high school juniors was 147. I *wasn't* so dumb, then, except in math. I *would* go to college!

I *wouldn't* have to clean public restrooms or Porta-Johns. I put my report on the little stand beside Dad's chair and treated myself to a handful of M&M's.

Brian came back to school on Thursday, one hand bandaged up, a bruise on the left side of his face. His court date was three weeks away, and he wasn't supposed to talk about the accident, but he did. We gathered around him in the cafeteria.

"Yeah, I had a few more beers than I should have, but the thing is, the other guy had been drinking too, we found out! They said I was speeding, but he's the one who ran the stop sign."

"Brian, what about the people in the other car?" I asked. "Was anyone killed?"

"No. The driver's mostly okay, and the older sister didn't get hurt much. It was only the kid in the backseat who got thrown, and if she'd had her seat belt on, she'd probably be okay," he said.

"But how *is* she?" I demanded.

"You think they'd tell us anything?" he complained. "Dad finally called the hospital and got someone to give us the story, but it wasn't too bad. Broken pelvis or something. I feel bad about that, but she's going to be okay."

Gwen and I looked at each other in disbelief, then at Pamela and Liz.

"Brian, it's possible that the little girl is going to have some physical problems for the rest of her life," Gwen said.

"Maybe, but you don't know that!" Brian protested hotly. "Bones can heal. But if they take away my license for a year, what am *I* supposed to do?"

We could only stare.

"What you're supposed to do is suck it up," I said. "*That's* what you're supposed to do." I wadded up my sandwich wrapper, picked up my tray, and left the cafeteria.

Gwen and Pamela and Liz followed me outside. I felt so hot, I literally had to cool off. I sat down on the stone wall, the same wall where I'd been watching Tony and his motorcycle friend when they'd called me over. I just felt . . . I don't know . . . like . . . like I was leaving something behind. But it was Liz who put it into words.

"The old gang just isn't the same anymore, is it?" she said.

I looked out over the street where cars were moving—the traffic pattern constantly changing. "Is that it?" I asked. "I'm feeling so . . . split! I'm just so furious at Brian and how he doesn't even seem to care! After all that, it's still all about him. *He's* changed."

"I don't know, has he really?" asked Pamela. "Or was he like this all along? Maybe we're the ones who have changed."

"It's not just Brian," I said. "I don't even like Jill and Karen anymore. They used to just puzzle me. Now . . . they don't like *me* either, and I'm not sure I care."

Gwen sat down on the wall and put her arm around me. "Hey, girlfriend," she said. "*We* still like you."

"You're one of the newer members of the group, Gwen. What do *you* think?" I asked. "How do we seem to you?"

She appeared to be thinking it over. "I guess I've never expected people to stay the same," she told me. "Sometimes we change for the worse, sometimes for the better. There were some things I liked about Brian, some things I didn't. But, hey! There were even things I didn't like about *you* after I got to know you."

"What?" I said, turning to face her. "Like what?"

I couldn't tell if she was laughing or frowning. "I don't quite know how to say this, Alice, but did anyone ever tell you that you can't sing worth a darn?"

We all broke into laughter. I bumped her with my elbow. "Hey, just because you sing in a church choir, you don't have to be so uppity about it," I said.

"Let's go," said Liz. "I'm freezing."

The bell sounded, and we went inside.

17

Lester's Goof

Snow. Beautiful snow. Our last day of school before the holidays, and I woke to a four-inch snowfall. Schools were opening two hours late, so I ate a leisurely breakfast in my pajamas beside the kitchen window.

The blanket of white covered the piles of lumber, the bricks and cement blocks of the construction crew. It frosted every branch, every twig of the azalea bushes and the maple. I felt as though it buried all the mistakes and quarrels of the past few months and gave us all a fresh start. If only.

Pamela called and suggested we put on boots and hike the mile and a half to school, just for the fun of it. I called Liz, and she said she'd do it. So forty minutes before school began, the three of us set out with wool caps pulled down over our ears, scarves whipping about in the wind. Other kids were doing the same, and we called to each other in the frosty air, the sun almost blinding as it reflected off the snow. It was intriguing to be the first to make an imprint in the soft white stuff, and yet, looking around, I felt guilty about mucking up the landscape. If only the mistakes we make could leave no imprints at all.

"What are you doing for Christmas, Alice?" Pamela asked.

"Not much," I told her. "Not with all this renovating going on."

"I suppose I'll spend Christmas with Mom and New Year's with Dad and Meredith. We'll probably go out to eat," Pamela said.

"Have they set a wedding date yet?" Liz asked, remembering that Pamela's dad and girlfriend had gotten engaged over the summer.

"No, I think maybe they get along better when they only see each other a couple of times a week," Pamela said. "It works, and that's fine with me. I hate quarreling. If I ever marry, we'll have to sign a prenup agreement saying that whichever one of us starts a fight has to apologize first."

"Yeah, right," I said.

"We're going to my aunt's house," said Liz. "She's got kidney disease and wants to have Christmas there while she can still do the cooking and decorating and stuff."

"I hate sickness and death and dying!" I said loudly. "I want it to *stop right now!*"

Liz laughed. "Me too. Throw in war and global warming while you're at it."

"I wonder what kind of Christmas Molly's going to have," I mused. "It'll probably be the worst Christmas of her life."

"Let's take her some snow!" said Liz.

"What?" I said.

"Snow. Let's go visit her tonight and fill a plastic container with snow, seeing as how she doesn't get out in it."

We laughed. "Deal!" I said.

It was a good day at school. The teachers were easy on us and didn't pile on a lot of work for the holidays. Most had given us long-term assignments in advance, and it was up to us whether we wanted to do them over Christmas.

The cafeteria was noisy—everyone talking about where they were going over the holidays. Tony and I were still politely avoiding each other, and that was fine with me. I was totally relieved that *that* was over. I heard from someone that Patrick had already left town with his parents for their usual skiing in Vermont and wouldn't be back until after New Year's. Gwen had a ton of relatives coming. Everyone had something fun to report except

Brian, who didn't want to talk about the holidays. He was furious because the insurance company wouldn't go along with his claim that his car was totaled. Not only were they not paying him all he thought he should get for repairs, but they had upped his rates as well.

I made a point of searching out Amy Sheldon as the others left the cafeteria, and I sat down with her as she was finishing her sandwich and a carton of milk, sucking noisily on her straw when she reached the bottom.

"You were mad at me the other day, weren't you?" she asked, staring right at me the way she does. It reminds me of a baby's stare—the way little kids stare at strangers with no self-consciousness at all.

"Not really," I said. "I was sort of mad at the world."

"How can you be mad at the whole world?" Amy asked.

"Easy," I told her. "I was just having a bad day. I'm sorry I was so rude."

"That's okay," Amy said. "I was just wondering why I haven't got my period yet, since I'm old enough and everything."

"You're small, Amy, that's probably it," I told her. "You just have a bit more developing to do, and your body will catch up. Everyone's different."

"Yeah, and some are more different than others," she said.

"Hey, Merry Christmas," I said.

"You too, Alice," she answered, and gave me a big smile.

We took the bucket of snow to Molly that evening. Gwen and Liz decided we should carol on her front porch, so Gwen drove us over in a brother's car. Liz, Gwen, and Pamela—all three—have good, strong singing voices, and I was sure my job would be to stand there holding the plastic container of snow with the big red ribbon on top. I was flabbergasted when Gwen handed me, instead, the metal triangle and stick from a kid's rhythm set and instructed me to make a loud *ping* after each phrase.

I stared at it. "How did you *know*?" I asked.

"Know what?"

"That this is what they gave me in grade school to make me shut up," I said.

The others stared at me, and Gwen looked conscience-stricken. I told them how the music teacher had made us sing a song a group at a time, then two at a time, to figure out who was singing so seriously off-key.

"I'm *sorry*!" Gwen said. "I only did it as a joke."

But suddenly all four of us burst out laughing.

"Hey, I'm over it now," I said. "I'll ping your little triangle. I'll even tap-dance if you want me to."

It was just growing dark as we gathered on the Brennans' porch. We had told Molly's mom we were coming so the TV wouldn't be on. Unless you've got a whole choir, it's hard to compete with a TV set.

"Silent night, holy night,
All is calm, all is bright . . ."

The girls sang, and I went *ping!*

We were halfway through the second verse when the porch light came on, and Molly's curious face appeared at the window. Then she broke into a smile and left to open the door.

"Oh, you guys! You're the best!" she said. "Come on in!"

Mr. and Mrs. Brennan were smiling in the background, and two of Molly's sisters were watching from the stairs.

We came in, laughing, and handed Molly the plastic tub.

"What's *this*?" she exclaimed, sitting down on a chair in her jeans and sweatshirt. "Ooh, it's cold!" She lifted off the lid and shrieked. "You nuts! You're absolutely crazy!"

"We thought you'd like a little taste of the great

outdoors," Liz said, and I went *ping* on the triangle.

The Brennans laughed as Molly playfully buried her face in the snow for a second and came up all frosted. "Put it in the downstairs freezer for me, Mom," she said.

"Yes, and when you're well, we'll have a snowball fight, no matter what month it is," said Pamela.

"I've been feeling a little better this week," Molly said. "My legs don't ache as much."

We had other small gifts to give her, and then we sat and talked for a while. She'd seen the story in the paper about the demonstration—about speech class and about Jennifer Shoates and all the different topics we'd discussed in class.

"I don't know, I sort of agree with Jennifer that it's a raw deal to tell you to choose something personal and then make you take the opposing point of view," Molly said.

"But if you knew at the beginning that you'd have to do that, you'd choose a subject you're only lukewarm about, and what would you learn from that?" I argued.

"Maybe you're right," said Molly. "But frankly, I think Jennifer was brave to stick it out. If my mom had come to school and made a scene, I'd have died of embarrassment."

"No, you wouldn't," said Pamela. "My mom

embarrassed me in New York last spring, and I'm still here, aren't I?"

"How's she doing, Pamela?" I asked, knowing her mom was still bitter about Pamela's dad's engagement to someone else, even though they were divorced, and that it was Pamela's mom who had run off with a boyfriend in the first place.

"Better. At least we've both learned to listen. We're talking about stuff we couldn't before," Pamela told us.

"That's what you guys do for me," Molly said. "You listen. I'm glad you came over."

As soon as I got home from the Melody Inn the next day, Sylvia and I set to work decorating the house. We were probably the last ones on the block to get a tree up and the lights on—a wreath on the door and vases of holly on the mantel. There's not a lot of motivation to decorate a house surrounded by piles of bricks and lumber, but we got in the spirit and even fashioned a wreath to put on the Porta-John.

The cat sniffed warily at the Christmas tree and brushed her back along the lower branches.

"Drink it all in, Annabelle," I told her. "This is as close as you're going to get to Mother Nature. Thank goodness you're not a dog, or you'd probably pee on it."

I went to the Christmas Eve service with Dad and Sylvia a few nights later and loved walking out through the little woods surrounding the church to the parking lot afterward, in the darkness of the midnight hour, silently, softly, all of us holding lighted candles. I could see these little dabs of color moving through the trees, then each one going out as people got into their cars.

George Palamas and his fiancée were treating Les and his other roommate, Paul, to dinner at a fancy restaurant on Christmas Eve, so Les didn't come over to our place till Christmas Day.

Sylvia had made a wonderful brunch, and we helped ourselves throughout the long and happy present-opening time. We'd stop for coffee now and then, or for another piece of quiche, or perhaps some chocolate or melon. The snow had melted down a little, but a white Christmas is such a rarity in Maryland—southern Maryland, anyway, where we live—that we kept looking out the window, remarking on a blue jay that alit on a fence post or a cardinal, gorgeous against the snow.

One by one the presents were opened and admired, slipped on to check the size, passed around to enjoy, or set aside for further inspection later on. If we work at it, we can stretch the opening of presents out for an hour or two, with potty breaks now and then or recess for a round of cheesecake.

Les usually tucks his gifts to us at the very back of the tree, and he did the same this year. There was a joint present to Dad and Sylvia and a separate box for me. Dad opened his gift from Lester, and both he and Sylvia exclaimed over the digital camera he had bought for them, with a promise of four hours of instruction on how to use it.

"I don't know that four hours will do it, Les, but this is a great gift," said Dad.

"Now you!" said Les, reaching for the last box, which he handed to me.

It was a beautifully decorated Nordstrom box, all silvery and shiny with a huge, sparkling silver ribbon and bow.

"Wow!" I said, and slipped the ribbon off one side. Nordstrom is a really upscale store—not quite Saks or Neiman Marcus, but it has very nice stuff. I opened the lid and found a card on top of the tissue paper.

"'To heat up those cold winter nights,'" I read, and folded back the tissue paper.

"What?" Lester yelped, jerking forward. I startled as he lunged for the box, but it was too late. I found myself holding a red bikini trimmed in white rabbit fur.

"Wow!" I said again.

Les tipped back his head and howled. We stared.

"You got the wrong box!" he bellowed. "No! No!"

My jaw dropped. This was absolutely fantastic! Now I knew what he was giving his new girlfriend, and I tried not to laugh. But Lester was devastated. Dad and Sylvia looked amused too, but they were trying to look sympathetic.

"What time is it?" Les cried, looking around for a clock. And then, "Quick, Alice! You've got to come with me. Put on your shoes and bring the box. We've got to get somewhere before three."

I grabbed my shoes, pulled on my jacket, and followed Lester out to his car with the box, the lid, the tissue paper, the card, the ribbon, the bow, and the fur-trimmed bikini.

"Merry Christmas!" Dad called cheerfully from the porch.

18

Keeping Warm on Winter Nights

I slid into the bucket seat next to Les, and he backed out of the drive.

"Darn!" I said, looking at the fur bikini again. "I would have been a hit at sleepovers!" I had to press my lips together to keep from laughing out loud.

"It's not funny," Les muttered. "She's got your present instead!"

"Yeah? So what's so awful about *my* gift?" I asked.

"Nothing, but it's not right for Claire," he answered.

"So what am I supposed to do? Go grab it out of her hands and give her this one instead?" I asked, neatly placing the fur bikini back in the box, folding the tissue over it, and putting it all back together.

"She's been at her sister's house and said she'd be getting back around three or four," Lester explained.

"I left her present—*your* present—outside her apartment door this morning. I'd *swear* the silver one was for you and the gold for Claire. The silver ribbon must have been for Claire and the gold for you. How could I have been so *stupid*?"

"What does she look like? Really?" I asked.

"She's got long brown hair. Straight. Sort of bangs. Medium height, weight. Maybe a little top-heavy."

"What's her apartment number?"

"Uh, 302."

"And you left the package at her door?"

"Right there on the mat, propped up against the doorframe. You can't miss it," Lester said.

Les was driving ten miles over the speed limit in a business area.

"Slow down, Lester! We don't need a ticket!" I said.

I just couldn't stop grinning, though. I kept thinking of that note—*To heat up those cold winter nights*—and it sent all kinds of images swirling through my head. I was beginning to think that Dad was right: that however mature Lester had seemed when he was dating Tracy, there was still a part of him that hadn't settled down yet, and that twenty-four for a man—well, for *some* men, maybe—was still a little young for marriage.

Les turned onto a street just over the D.C. line

where there were several blocks of four-story brick apartment buildings. I looked at my watch.

"What time?" asked Les.

"Three seventeen," I told him.

"Oh, jeez," he breathed out. "If she's home, I'm toast."

He passed her building and pointed out the door. "Go inside," he said, "walk up to the third floor, and trade the boxes. Then come down. I'm going to park a block away so she won't recognize my car."

This was better than a spy movie!

We rode a block farther, and Les parked, then sank down low in the seat in case Claire drove by. I got out with the present under my arm, turned up my jacket collar, and started off.

Patches of ice had formed on the sidewalk where snow at the sides had melted, trickled down onto the concrete, then frozen. I had to make my way carefully to keep from falling, and I didn't want to step in the shoveled snow.

When I got to the right building, I tried to open the outer door, but it was locked. *Now* what was I supposed to do? Lester hadn't said anything about how I was supposed to get inside the building itself. I looked around. No one was coming up the walk. No one looked as though they were heading for this address. *Lester, you imbecile!* I thought.

Something moved beyond the door, and I could just make out a man coming down the stairs. He came up to the door, opened it, and looked at me curiously, waiting there on the steps.

"Thanks!" I said, smiling, and put one finger to my lips. "It's a surprise!" Then I slipped past him and went inside.

Up the stairs I went to the second floor, with its two apartments, one on each side. Up another flight to a landing, then on up to the third and the two apartments there: 302 and 304.

There on the mat was the present, the one wrapped in gold ribbon and bow. I reached down and replaced that box with mine and headed back down the stairs. One flight to the landing, another flight to the second floor. . . . As I was going down the last flight of stairs to the ground floor, I saw a woman come inside carrying a small overnight bag in one hand, a shopping bag full of presents in the other. She had long straight brown hair, wispy bangs, medium height. . . .

I slipped the present I was holding behind me and stared straight ahead as we passed.

"Hi," she said.

"Hi," I answered, and didn't stop till I was outside.

"Did you do it?" Les asked as I slid in the passenger seat beside him.

"Yes, you idiot!" I said, showing him the package. "But how was I supposed to get in the building? The front entrance was locked!"

"Oh, man, I forgot!" he said. "How'd you do it?"

"A man was coming out, and I squeezed by him."

"Clever girl!" Les said. "You're a winner!"

"And you know who I met coming out?" I asked him.

Les reached for the key in the ignition, but his hand dropped. "Claire?"

"Yep."

"Did she *see* you?"

"Of course she saw me. She didn't see the box, though. I kept it out of sight," I said.

"Did she *say* anything?"

"She said 'hi.'"

"What did *you* say?"

"I said, 'Oh, you're the one with the big boobs that my brother's so crazy about.'" I sighed impatiently. "I said 'hi' and kept going, Lester! What do you think?"

"Did she recognize you?"

"How could she? Not unless you carry around a picture of me in your wallet and show it to everyone you meet," I said.

"Fat chance," said Lester.

"Anyway," I said as he started the engine, "let's

see what you bought for *me*. From Nordstrom too! And this better not be a mistake for *another* one of your girlfriends."

"I should be so lucky," said Lester.

It wasn't for a girlfriend, that's for sure. I took off the gold ribbon, folded back the tissue paper, and lifted out, not a fur-trimmed bikini, but a high-neck red flannel nightgown with a narrow white ruffle around the collar and cuffs.

To keep you warm on winter nights, the card read.

I could see why he wouldn't want to give this to a girlfriend, but I couldn't hide my disappointment, and Les could tell. He glanced over at me when I didn't react.

"You don't like it," he said.

"Last year, when I turned sixteen, you gave me a gorgeous silk robe," I said. "What am I doing? Regressing?"

"I just thought that with all the renovations going on, the house would probably be drafty and you'd be cold. A flannel gown would feel pretty nice then," said Lester.

"It would feel pretty nice if I were a virginal spinster living in Alaska with no prospects of marrying, ever," I told him.

"Hmmmm," said Les. "Now which of those descriptions doesn't fit? Let me guess—spinster, Alaskan. . . ."

I sure didn't want to have *that* discussion, so I said, "Would you mind very much if I exchanged it for something else?"

"Not at all," he said. "Get whatever you want."

"Thanks," I told him. "It'll be red, but it won't be a granny gown."

His cell phone rang just then. Les reached in his jacket pocket. "Don't you make a sound," he warned me. And then, into the phone, "Hello?" He immediately turned his head away from me. "Hi, baby," he said. "Merry Christmas."

I grinned and leaned back against the seat.

". . . Glad you like it," Les was saying. "Yeah . . . Yeah . . . Well, I can't wait to see you in it. Listen, my sister just came in, so let me call you back. . . . Sure thing. Bye."

"I don't know why whatever you had to say couldn't be said in front of your sister," I teased. "I mean, you'd think you were going to spend the night with her or something."

"Or something," said Les, and we laughed as he turned the car toward home.

I wondered if it was the same for Lester as it was for me—that sometimes you know you're just treading water, passing the time, and that your real self is just waiting for the right moment, the right person, the right you.

• • •

We got our usual call that afternoon from Uncle Howard and Uncle Harold down in Tennessee, wishing all us McKinleys here in "Silver Sprangs" a Merry Christmas. They told us how different it was not having Grandpa McKinley around any-more to supervise the decorating of the tree, as he always did from his La-Z-Boy recliner, and we talked to my three aunts, too, and wished them all a Merry Christmas and a Happy New Year.

Sylvia called her sister Nancy in Albuquerque and her brother in Seattle, and then we called Aunt Sally and Uncle Milt. It was Uncle Milt who answered the phone.

"Milt, so good to hear your voice!" Dad said. "How *are* you, and Merry Christmas!"

The rest of us couldn't hear Uncle Milt because his voice is soft compared to Aunt Sally's, but we could tell from Dad's end of the conversation that Uncle Milt was doing much better. Sylvia talked to him next, then Les, and after I told my uncle how glad I was to know he was feeling better, he handed the phone over to Aunt Sally.

Aunt Sally wished me a Merry Christmas, like she always does, but something was different. Something was wrong.

"Did *you* have a nice Christmas?" I asked her.

"Well, yes and no," she said. I heard Uncle Milt in the background saying, "Now, Sal, don't begin. . . ."

"What happened?" I asked.

"Well, Carol said she was having trouble with her telephone for a month now, which is why I couldn't reach her at her apartment, so I drove over there last week with some cookies and a mince pie, just so she'd have a little something to nibble on before Christmas, you know."

I knew what was coming even before she told me, and I realized I hadn't reported back to Aunt Sally after Thanksgiving as she would have liked.

"And I got the shock of my life, Alice," Aunt Sally said. "A woman came to the door whom I'd never seen before and told me that Carol doesn't live there anymore. My daughter has moved in with her boyfriend and didn't even tell her own mother! Why is the mother always the last to know?"

"Probably because she loves you the most and didn't want to hurt you," I said. Sometimes my answers positively amaze me.

"But . . . we were always so *close*!" Aunt Sally said, which wasn't exactly true, and now she was weeping a little.

"All the more reason not to hurt you," I said.

"You've met him, Alice," Aunt Sally went on. "They were there for Thanksgiving. What did you think of her boyfriend?"

"We liked him a lot," I said. "If Carol's happy, then you should be happy for her."

She sniffled. "Well, I'm going to try to do that. I'm going to try not to judge her."

"Good idea," I said.

"But you know what they say, dear," Aunt Sally said. "If you can get the milk for free, why buy the cow?"

"*What?*" I said.

"If a man can get sex for nothing, why should he bother to marry?" she explained.

"You're not suggesting she *charge*, are you?" I said, trying not to laugh.

Aunt Sally gasped. "No, no! I just think that if Carol has marriage in mind, she should hold out till then."

"You and Mrs. Shoates would get along great," I said.

"Who?" asked Aunt Sally.

"Never mind," I said. "It's not important. What's important, Aunt Sally, is that now you know, and now you and Carol can be close again."

"How did you get to be so wise, Alice?" Aunt Sally said. "My goodness, Marie would be so proud of you! She really would."

Maybe I'd make a good counselor after all, I thought. I pictured myself in my office at school. During Spirit Week. On Pajama Day during Spirit Week. In red. Red silk pajamas. And I knew what I was going to buy at Nordstrom when I took the granny gown back.

19

Call from a Friend

The construction crew didn't work between Christmas and New Year's. The bricks lay undisturbed, the equipment untouched, the Porta-John standing alone in the front yard.

"Oh, the blessed quiet!" Sylvia said. "I was beginning to hear their constant hammering in my sleep."

"Enjoy," said Dad, "because the real noise begins when the men get back and start tearing down the back walls."

"At least these few days will give us time to move everything out of our bedroom and into Lester's," Sylvia said. "I still don't know how we'll do it. We'll practically be living on top of each other for a couple of months. I hope we can all keep a sense of humor."

"What about the downstairs?" I asked.

"The back walls in the kitchen and dining room come down too," said Dad. "All the dining room furniture has to be squeezed into the living room. The refrigerator needs to go there too, and a plumber's going to set up a temporary sink."

"Wow," I said. I wasn't sure whether this sounded adventurous or awful. We'd gotten used to the huge sheet of opaque plastic hanging beyond the back door of the kitchen and the windows of the dining room, and for now, anyway, there were walls in front of it that kept out the noise and the cold.

Sylvia grabbed my hand. "Come on. Let's go snoop while the workmen are gone," she said.

I got my jacket and followed her outside. We made our way around to the backyard, stepping over stray boards and bricks. The frame rose up two stories, with waterproof sheeting tacked to the outside. We got to the makeshift steps leading to a back entrance and stepped inside. It felt strange to be standing inside the skeleton of our new addition.

It was like a huge tent. There was a roof but no floors yet, neither upstairs nor down, waiting for the old walls to be torn down before flooring could be seamlessly added. There were only a few planks to walk on leading from front to back and side to side. Gingerly, we walked along one of the bottom boards.

"I'll bet this is where the new fireplace will be," Sylvia said, pointing to a large cement base.

"And I can see the layout of the closets—those little sections there and there," I said, walking a little farther. "This part's the family room, isn't it?"

"Yes. And over there's the study," Sylvia said. We turned slowly around, looking in all directions. "I suppose it will take some getting used to—all these changes."

"Oh, I don't think so," I said. "Having the old bathroom all to myself won't take any getting used to at all!" I grinned.

"In the meantime," said Sylvia as we walked back to the front of the house, "we're going to be very crowded. We'll practically be eating off each other's laps and sitting with our knees up to our chins."

"I'll probably spend a lot of time in my room," I said.

"Good thinking," said Sylvia. "But it will all be over in a couple of months, and then we're going to love it! Hope so, anyway."

As though a white Christmas weren't enough, Mother Nature gave us an encore. Two days after Christmas, we found not four, not six, not eight, but eleven inches of snow blanketing the area, with more to come.

"The weatherman's predicting thirteen inches," said Dad. "A good day to stay inside, I think. I'm not even going to open the store. Marilyn's already called to say she can't get her car out, the side streets are unplowed, and David's still out of town visiting his parents."

I didn't mind at all holing up with a good book—*The Color Purple*—and a cup of mint chocolate cocoa. Annabelle waited for me to finish the cup, then delicately licked the inside of it, and after that, she helped herself to my lap.

By afternoon we could hear snowplows in all directions, and by the following morning, roads at least were plowed and lawns were heaped with the sparkling white stuff, like meringue topping. I was debating whether to finish my book or drive to the mall and look for bargains when there was a loud *thunk* as something hit the storm door.

"What in the world was *that*?" said Sylvia.

"UPS maybe?" I guessed. Before I could even get out of my chair, there it was again: *thunk*. I went to the door and opened it.

"Roz!" I shrieked delightedly at my wonderful friend from grade school, who used to live near us in Takoma Park. "What the heck are you doing over here?" I walked to the porch railing.

"Come on out!" she yelled, packing another snow-ball and hurling it toward me. It hit a post and exploded, showering me with snow crystals. I yelped.

"Come on! Let's build something!" Rosalind called.

"Yeah? Remember what happened the last time

we built something? Remember that snow cave that fell in on me when you kicked it?" I reminded her, laughing.

Another snowball hit my shoulder.

"Okay, okay, let me get some boots and stuff on," I said, and went back indoors.

I traded my flannel bottoms for heavy jeans, and by the time I got outside, Rosalind was already turning the Porta-John into an igloo.

It was one of the best ideas she'd ever had, and Roz was the original Idea Girl. We set to work rolling large orbs of snow up against the sides of the Porta-John, then medium-sized balls on top of them, and smaller balls on top of the medium. We filled all the spaces in between, packing it down well, until three sides of the blue metal structure were encased in snow. I got a stepladder, and we packed snow onto the roof. It was entirely covered now, all but the door, which still sported the wreath I had hung there at Christmas.

Neighbors driving by slowed and stared, then broke into smiles. Dad and Sylvia came out to admire it, and Sylvia even took a picture with the new digital camera Les had given them. Then Rosalind and I sat on the front steps, drinking hot tea, and I thought how wonderful it was that when everything else seemed to be changing, we had a friendship that went right on being the same.

• • •

I decided I wouldn't go out on New Year's Eve. Gwen's family was having a sort of open house, but it would be mostly family I didn't know, and Mark had planned to have a party, but it seems Brian was the only one who could come for sure, so Mark's parents scrapped the idea. Pamela had to help out at a party her dad was giving, and Liz was babysitting her brother. I could have invited myself to any one of their houses, but when I thought about what I really wanted to do, the answer was to stay home in my old scruffies and watch a movie on TV. I didn't really want to party. I didn't even want to watch the stupid silver ball descend at Times Square. Was I growing up, I wondered, when I could admit I was content being very un-New-Year's-Evish, and could even reply, if friends asked how I'd spent the evening, that I'd stayed home and watched a movie? Read a book?

That afternoon, however, something hugely embarrassing happened. The toilet stopped up, and though both Sylvia and I used the plunger, we couldn't get it unstuck. Dad was at work, so Sylvia had to call an emergency plumbing service to come out.

We stood by as the plumber tried his luck with the plunger. Then he went down in the basement with his machine and tools to shut off the water and open up the sewer pipe.

"Ma'am?" he called up to us later.

Sylvia went back downstairs, and I followed. We were afraid he'd tell us that he had to get a new part and that we'd have to go out in the yard in front of all the neighbors and use the Porta-John.

"Found the trouble," he said. "Now, I don't want to embarrass anyone, but I'm going to have to remind you that sanitary things can't go down your toilet. A little two-inch item like that can cause a big problem." For one hundredth of a second he held up a pink plastic tampon applicator before dropping it in a bucket at his feet.

I could have died on the spot. I knew that, and I'm not sure why I'd been so careless with my tampon, but before I could even think, I heard Sylvia saying, "I'll certainly be more careful from now on."

The plumber went on lecturing us about what should and should not be flushed down the toilet, but all the while I stood there staring at the back of Sylvia's head. If ever I felt she loved me, it was then.

When the man had gone, I said, "I'm so embarrassed! You didn't have to take the rap for me, Sylvia. I should have fessed up."

And Sylvia said, "Well, I wouldn't want him to think I was *past* menstruating, now, would I?" And we laughed.

• • •

Dad built a fire that evening—the last chance we'd have to enjoy our living room as it was, and I sat on the floor as close to it as I could, Annabelle on my lap. She sat facing the flames, her eyes closing. Every so often a log snapped or popped, and her cat eyes opened momentarily, her ears twitched, and then she drifted off to sleep again.

"Her fur's getting warm," I said to Sylvia. "You don't think she'd self-ignite, do you?"

"Better scoot away before your socks catch fire," Dad said. He and Sylvia were on the couch, his arm around her shoulders.

"When we get the new addition, we'll have two fireplaces," said Sylvia. "I tried to persuade Ben to let me have one in our bedroom, too, but he put his foot down."

Dad just jostled her shoulder and grinned.

I sat watching the flames dance along the top of the log. "I could probably fit the whole gang in that new family room when it's done," I said. "It'll be a great place for parties."

"You can use it as often as you like," Sylvia told me.

More pops and crackles from the fire. Annabelle startled momentarily, extending her claws to keep her balance, then closed her eyes once again.

"She's like a hot water bottle on the legs," I said.

"Too hot for me. Here." I handed her to Dad. "You wanted a cat on your legs in the winter, you got it."

"What more could a man ask?" said Dad, taking Annabelle. "A wife by his side, a daughter at his feet, and a cat on his lap. This is contentment."

New Year's Day was gray and cold and bleak. It was too cold to go outside and fool around, and there was school to get ready for the next day. The whole revolving wheel of life—school, supper, sleep . . . school, supper, sleep—would begin all over again.

But even the cycle seemed new somehow. Different, anyway. Like it was the new side of the old me. Like I was letting more of my real self show through.

I called Molly and wished her a happier new year; told her that when she felt up to it, I'd bring over a board game and beat the pants off her. I gathered all my papers and books and stuff for school and cleaned out my backpack. Did a load of wash so that my gym clothes and jeans would be fresh for a new semester.

The phone rang in the hall. Most of my friends call on my cell phone, so if the house phone rings, I let someone else answer. But Dad and Sylvia had gone next door to have drinks with a neighbor, so I padded out into the hall and picked up the phone.

"Hello?"

"Happy New Year," said Patrick.

"Hey! You're back!" I said. "Have a good time?"

"Yeah, we did. Snow was a little too soft, but I had some pretty good runs. How about you?"

"Well, I don't have the runs, if that's what you're asking," I joked, and he laughed.

"Anything exciting happen while I was away?" he wanted to know.

What I wanted to say was, *Patrick, a lot of things happen all the time that you never know about because you're always away. You're missing out on a lot of good times with the old gang.* But I didn't, because not all the stuff with the old gang is "good times." It's not even the same old gang anymore.

"Well," I said, "workmen are coming tomorrow to tear down the back walls of our house to build a new addition. And Rosalind came over a few days ago, and we turned the Porta-John into an igloo. I can't wait to see the men's faces when they come tomorrow."

He laughed. "Now, that sounds like it was fun."

"It was." I brought the phone into my bedroom, Annabelle jumping after the cord as it dragged on the floor. When I climbed up on my bed, she jumped up too and began kneading my legs, my thighs, looking for a place to burrow down.

"So what's up with you?" I asked.

"Well, I made a decision and applied for early

acceptance at the University of Chicago," he said.

"Hey! Good luck!" I told him. "What all did that involve?"

"For one thing, I did the Uncommon Application. It's online, and I had to answer the question 'If you could bridge a gap in the space-time continuum, what would you do?'"

"*What?*" I said. "I don't even understand the question."

He laughed. "It's just something to make you think. To get the creative juices flowing—give them a taste of how your mind works."

I knew right then I'd never apply to the University of Chicago. "Why did you choose that school?" I asked.

"Terrific political science program. Since I'm not sure of what I want to do later, I figured that might be better than international relations. Too much like my dad's field."

"Well, I hope you get in," I told him. "If you do, maybe I could see you sometime when I'm in Chicago visiting Aunt Sally and Uncle Milt."

"That'd be great!" said Patrick. "Actually, though, I'm calling to ask you to the prom."

I stared openmouthed at the wall. "The *prom*?" I said. "Patrick, that's six months away!"

"Five," he said. "It's in May. I figured I'd better ask before someone else snapped you up."

"I'd say five months is pretty early," I told him, still dazed. And then I realized I hadn't given him an answer. "I'd love to go with you, Patrick," I said. "I'll look forward to it all spring."

"I've been looking forward to it all year," he told me. "But I figured September might be a little too early to ask. I'll see you tomorrow, okay?"

"Tomorrow," I said, and gently, still smiling, put down the phone.

What's next for Alice and her friends? Here's a look at *Almost Alice*

It had to be in person, and they all had to be there.

Gwen was at a meeting over the lunch period, so I couldn't tell them then. I waited till we went to Starbucks after school before I made the announcement:

"Patrick asked me to the prom."

Two seconds of silence were followed by shrieks of disbelief and excitement:

"Five months in advance? Patrick?"

"You're kidding me!"

"When?"

"Yesterday." I was grinning uncontrollably and couldn't help myself. "He called. We talked."

"He called. You talked. What is this? Shorthand?" Gwen demanded. "Girl, we want details!"

"Wait! Hold it!" said Pamela. She jumped up, went to the counter, and bought a huge cup of whipped cream, then liberally doused each of our lattes to celebrate.

"Now dish!" she said.

"Well, I was just hanging out in my room, getting my stuff ready for school, when I heard the phone ring."

"He didn't call you on your cell?"

"I'm not sure he knows the number."

"I'd think he would have had it programmed in!"

"It's been two years," I told them, working hard to defend him. Defend whatever there was between us, though I didn't know myself.

Liz rested her chin in her hands. When she looks at you through half-closed eyes, you realize just how long and thick her eyelashes are—longer than any girl's lashes have a right to be. "Oh, Alice, you and Patrick!" She sighed. "I knew you'd get back together. It's in the stars."

Gwen, the scientist, rolled her eyes. She was looking especially attractive, her hair in a new style of cornrows that made a geometric pattern on top of her head. The gold rings on one brown finger matched the design of her earrings, and she was definitely the most sophisticated-looking of the four of us. She was also the only one who had visited three colleges so far and who had even picked up scholarship forms. "How long did you guys go together, anyway?" she asked.

"I guess it was about eighth grade that I really started liking him. The summer before eighth through the fall of ninth grade." I was embarrassed suddenly that I remembered this so precisely, as though it were always there at the front of my consciousness. "We actually met in sixth, but sixth-grade boyfriends aren't much to brag about."

"He did have his goofy side," Pamela agreed. "Remember that hot day at Mark's pool when you fell asleep on the picnic table? And Patrick placed two lemon halves on your breasts for a minute?"

"What?" Gwen shrieked.

"Yes, and when I woke up, everyone was grinning and no one would tell me what happened. And I couldn't figure out what those two little wet spots were on the front of my T-shirt. Like I was nursing or something!"

We yelped with laughter.

I continued. "And the year he gave me an heirloom bracelet for my birthday that turned out to be his mom's, because she didn't wear it anymore."

"I never heard that one," said Liz.

"And Mrs. Long had to call me and ask for it back," I said. We laughed some more. I wondered if I was being disloyal, telling all this. That was the old Patrick. The kid. That was then, and this was now.

"So what attracted you to him in the first place?" asked Gwen. "Besides the fact that he's a tall, smart, broad-shouldered redhead? I wasn't in on that early history."

"Well, he wasn't always as tall or broad-shouldered," I said. "I guess it's because he's the most motivated, focused, organized person I ever met. His dad's a diplomat, and they've lived in Japan, Germany, Spain. . . . In some ways, he's a man of the world."

"And then he falls for Penny, the jerk," said Pamela. "I'm glad that's over."

I saw three pair of eyes dart in my direction to see how I was taking that, then look away. Wondering if I'd cry myself sick again if things didn't work out this time with Patrick. I remembered Elizabeth's organizing a suicide watch when Patrick and I broke up, so that a friend called every quarter of an hour to see if I was okay. I tried not to smile.

"Well," I said flippantly, "a lot can happen in the next five months. You know how everything else comes before fun where Patrick is concerned. And I didn't say we were back together. I just said we were going to the prom."

"But this is his prom, and then you can invite him back for yours!" said Liz excitedly, since Patrick's in an accelerated program that gets him through high school in three years.

"Yeah, and with two prom nights to make out, you know what that means," said Pamela.

"Will you stop?" I said.

To some girls, a prom means you're a serious couple. To some, it's the main event of high school. To some, it's the biggest chance in your life, next to getting married, to show off. And to some girls, it means going all the way.

"Well, I'm glad for you," said Gwen. "But I hope we don't have to talk prom for the next five months."

"Promise," I said.

"Some couples were just meant to be," Pamela said. "Jill and Justin, for example. They've been going out forever."

"What about you and Tim?" I asked. Tim had taken her to the Snow Ball last fall. A really nice guy.

"Could be!" said Pamela.

"So are you going to ask him to the Sadie Hawkins Day dance?" asked Gwen.

"I already have," Pamela told us, and grinned. Then she turned serious again. "Patrick better come through this time, Alice. He owes you big time."

If my friends didn't quite know what to make of Patrick, neither did I. I'd always thought of him as special somehow, but . . . My first boyfriend? More than that. Patrick was someone with a future, and I didn't know if I was part of that or not. Or wanted to be.

But you can analyze a good thing to death, so I decided to take it at face value: He really, really liked me and couldn't think of anyone he'd rather take to the prom. Now enjoy it, I told myself.

Our house was a mess. Dad and Sylvia were having the place remodeled, with a new addition on the back. Their bedroom, the kitchen, and the dining room were sealed off with heavy vinyl sheets so that dust and cold w od against one wall in the upstairs hallway. The rest of their furniture was pushed into Lester's old bedroom, where they were sleeping, and their clothes were piled all over the place in my room. Downstairs, the dining-room furniture had been moved into the living room along with the refrigerator and microwave, and the construction crew had fashioned a sink with hot and cold running water next to the fridge. We ate our meals on paper plates, sitting in the only available chairs, knees touching.

"Maybe it wasn't such a good idea to stay in the house during remodeling," Dad said that weekend when we didn't think we could swallow one more bite of Healthy Choice or Lean Cuisine.

"But think of all the money we're saving by not living in a hotel!" said Sylvia. "The foreman said that if we can put up with painters and carpenters doing the finishing touches, we might be able to move into the new addition by the middle of March."

Fortunately for us, the construction company had another contract for an expensive project starting April 1, and had doubled the workforce at our place to finish by then.

Dad was at the Melody Inn seven days a week, Sylvia was teaching, and I was at school, so we didn't have to listen to all the pounding.

Lester came over one night and took us out to dinner.

"Hey," I said over my crab cake, "why don't we move in with Lester for the duration?"

He gave me a look. "Don't even think it," he said. "I'm surviving on five hours of sleep a night while I finish my thesis."

"Oh, Les!" Sylvia said sympathetically.

"You need to get some exercise," Dad told him.

"I run to Starbucks and back," Les said.

"But . . . you're not seeing anyone at all?" I asked.

"Not much," said Les.

It was hard to imagine, but somehow I believed him. Les had made up his mind to graduate, and he was hitting the books.

"What about that girl you were going out with at Christmas?" I asked him.

"It's over," said Les.

"Already?" exclaimed Dad.

"Too high maintenance," Les told us. "All she wanted to do was party, and I can't afford the time. So I've sworn off women till after I graduate."

That was even more difficult to imagine, but I felt real sympathy for my twenty-four-year-old brother right then. I decided that somehow, sometime around Valentine's Day, I . . . or Liz and I . . . or Liz and Pamela and I . . . or Liz and Pam and Gwen and I were going to plan a surprise for Lester. I just didn't know what.

Patrick has called me twice since he invited me to the prom on New Year's Day. He didn't call to chat, exactly. He either had something to tell me or a question to ask. You could say he's all business, but that wouldn't be true, because he has a good sense of humor and there's a gentleness that I like too. I just wish he were more accessible. He runs his life like a railroad—always busy, always going somewhere, getting somewhere.

But there was a lot more to think about during the second semester of my junior year. The SATs, for one. I decided that January would probably be my least hectic month, so I'd take the test on January 26, then take it again later if I bombed the first time. Getting my braces off was item number two. I also wanted to spend more time with our friend Molly Brennan, who's getting treated for leukemia, and to persuade Pamela, if possible, to audition for the spring musical, Guys and Dolls. I'd signed up for stage crew once again.

Tim Moss was doing a lot for Pamela's self-confidence. Pamela's pretty, she's got a good voice, and has a great body. But ever since her mom deserted the family a few years ago and ran off with a boyfriend, Pamela's self-esteem has been down in her socks. Lately, though, now that her mom's back and living in an apartment alone, Pamela's seemed a little more like her old self, and once she started going out with Tim, she really perked up.

Sylvia, my stepmom, said that one way to tell if a guy is right for you is if he wants what's best for you, encourages your talents, and—at the same time—has a good sense of self and where his life is going. She was speaking about my dad and her decision to marry him when she said that, but I think Tim Moss would just about get an A on all three.

"Go for it," Tim told Pamela when we were talking about the musical the other night.

"I'll think about it" was all she said, which is one step up from "No, I'd never make it," which is where she was last week.

And speaking of Sylvia, I'm getting along better with her. Even Annabelle, her cat. Our cat. The cat I'd said such awful things about last year. Sylvia and I are both trying to communicate more. If she wants my help with some big household project, for example, she doesn't descend on me some weekend when I have a ton of homework or something else planned. And if I want to use her or Dad's car, I try to remember to tell them in advance, not just spring it on them.

I guess you could say that for me and my friends, cars and driving are a big part of our lives. They were sure a big part of Brian Brewster's, whose license was just suspended last week in court because he hit another car in December and badly injured a seven-year-old girl. She was in the hospital for three weeks with a broken pelvis and other injuries, but I think Brian would have to break his own pelvis before he'd worry more about her than about the fact that he can't drive for a year.

I don't hang around much anymore with Brian and his crowd. Patrick seems able to move in and out of a crowd whenever the spirit moves him; if there's one thing Patrick Long is not, it's a label. But mostly I go places with Pamela, Liz, and Gwen.

The four of us have different interests much of the time, but we still tell each other a lot of personal stuff. Liz and I used to go running together on summer mornings and sometimes after school. But I wasn't fast enough for her, so she joined the girls' track team this semester. Pamela was taking voice lessons; Gwen got a job as a receptionist in a clinic twice a week after school; and I promised my friend Lori that I'd join the Gay/Straight Alliance at school to show my solidarity with her and her girlfriend, Leslie.

But there was one secret I hadn't told anyone: I had a crush on Scott Lynch, a senior, the editor in chief of The Edge. Last fall I'd done everything but beg him to take me to the Snow Ball, but he'd asked a girl from Holton-Arms. So when another senior, Tony Osler, asked me, I'd gone with him. And because Tony seemed more interested in getting into my pants than anything else, that didn't last very long. Now I was going to the prom in May with Patrick and was wildly excited about it, but Scott was still on my mind. Is life ever simple?

I have to say that Jacki Severn, features editor for The Edge, is not my favorite person. She's got an eye for copy layout and she's a good writer, but she isn't easy to work with. When I got to the staff meeting on Wednesday, she was on one of her rants.

"I think we ought to change the name!" she was saying. "It's historically inaccurate."

Now what? I wondered, exchanging glances with Don Spiro, one of our photographers. Hissy fit, he scribbled on a piece of paper and shoved it across the table.

"What's up?" I asked the others.

Scott was balancing a pencil between two fingers and offered an explanation: "Remember that last year the school decided to replace the Jack of Hearts dance in February with something more casual?"

I nodded. "Something fun and silly and utterly retro, like a Sadie Hawkins Day dance."

"Right. Well, the dance committee has scheduled it for February twenty-ninth, because the twenty-ninth happens only once every four years, sort of a nice kickoff for the first Sadie Hawkins Day dance. But Jacki wants to call it the 'Turnaround Dance.'"

I gave Jacki a puzzled look. "And if we call it

'Sadie Hawkins,' the world will end?" I asked, making Scott smile.

But Jacki sure didn't. "I've researched it, and Sadie Hawkins Day first appeared in a Li'l Abner comic strip in November 1937. If the whole rest of the country celebrates Sadie Hawkins Day in November, it's ludicrous to hold our dance in February unless we change the name."

"I doubt that the whole rest of the country even knows who Sadie Hawkins is," said Don.

"It doesn't matter!" said Jacki. "Besides, there's another SAT scheduled for March first, the day after."

"But not at our school," said Miss Ames, our sponsor. "And the newspaper has no authority to change the name of the dance. 'Sadie Hawkins' still lets people know that it's girls' choice."

"But—," Jacki began.

I was sitting at one of the computers and had Googled the term Sadie Hawkins Day. "Hey!" I interrupted. "Here's a West Virginia school that holds a Sadie Hawkins Day dance every February twenty-ninth."

Scott jokingly banged his notebook down on the tabletop. "Sold!" he said. "Next topic . . ."

Jacki gave me a long, hard look and angrily picked up her pen.

The topic may have been closed, but it sort of sealed the antagonism between Jacki and me. I guess I never quite forgave her for trying to do a story on Molly and her leukemia without any thought as to how Molly might feel about it. And Jacki probably never forgave me for being there with some of my friends, sitting on Molly's bed and eating a pizza with her—Molly in makeup, to be exact—when the photographer arrived to take a picture of a pale, limp girl in a lonely bed. Not exactly the story Jacki had in mind.

HAVE YOU READ ALL OF THE ALICE BOOKS?

PHYLL[...]OR

STARTING WITH ALICE
Atheneum Books for
  Young Readers
0-689-84395-X
Aladdin Paperbacks
0-689-84396-8

ALICE IN B[...]RLAN[...]
Atheneum [...] for
  Young Rea[...]s
0-689-84397-6
Aladdin Paperbacks
0-689-84398-4

LOVINGLY ALICE
Atheneum Books for
  Young Readers
0-689-84399-2
Aladdin Paperbacks
0-689-84400-X

THE AGONY OF ALICE
Atheneum Books for
  Young Readers
0-689-31143-5
Aladdin Paperbacks
0-689-81672-3

ALICE IN RAPTURE,
  SORT-OF
Atheneum Books for
  Young Readers
0-689-31466-3
Aladdin Paperbacks
0-689-81687-1

RELUCTANTLY ALICE
Atheneum Books for
  Young Readers
0-689-31681-X
Aladdin Paperbacks
0-689-81688-X

ALL BUT ALICE
Atheneum Books for
  Young Readers
0-689-31773-5
Aladdin Paperbacks
0-689-85044-1

0-689-31805-7
Aladdin Paperbacks
0-689-81686-3

Aladdin Paperbacks
0-689-81685-5

ALICE THE BRAVE
Atheneum Books for
  Young Readers
0-689-80095-9
Aladdin Paperbacks
0-689-80598-5

ALICE IN LACE
Atheneum Books for
  Young Readers
0-689-80358-3
Aladdin Paperbacks
0-689-80597-7

OUTRAGEOUSLY ALICE
Atheneum Books for
  Young Readers
0-689-80354-0
Aladdin Paperbacks
0-689-80596-9

ACHINGLY ALICE
Atheneum Books for
  Young Readers
0-689-80533-9
Aladdin Paperbacks
0-689-80595-0
Simon Pulse
  0-689-86396-9

ALICE ON THE OUTSIDE
Atheneum Books for
  Young Readers
0-689-80359-1
Simon Pulse
  0-689-80594-2

[...]OMING OF ALICE
[Athe]neum Books for
  [You]ng Readers
0-689-82633-8
Simon Pulse
  0-689-84618-5

ALICE AL[...]NE
[...]
Simon Pulse
  0-689-85189-8

SIMPLY ALICE
Atheneum Books for
  Young Readers
0-689-84751-3
Simon Pulse
  0-689-85965-1

PATIENTLY ALICE
Atheneum Books for
  Young Readers
0-689-82636-2
Simon Pulse
  0-689-87073-6

INCLUDING ALICE
Atheneum Books for
  Young Readers
0-689-82637-0
Simon Pulse
  0-689-87074-4

ALICE ON HER WAY
Atheneum Books for
  Young Readers
0-689-87090-6

ALICE IN THE KNOW
Atheneum Books for
  Young Readers
0-689-87092-7
Simon Pulse
  0-689-87093-0

DANGEROUSLY ALICE
Atheneum Books for
  Young Readers
0-689-87094-9
Simon Pulse
  0-689-87095-7